W9-CIG-577

SALEM COLLEGE
LIBRARY

The Burton Craige
Collection of
North Caroliniana

WITHDRAWN

Gramley Library
Salem Academy and College
Winston-Salem, N.C. 27108

Hatteras Light

HATTERAS
LIGHT

PHILIP GERARD

John F. Blair, Publisher   Winston-Salem, NC

Gramley Library
Salem Academy and College
Winston-Salem, N.C. 27108

This novel is a work of fiction. Any references to historical events; to real people, living or dead; or to real locales are intended only to give the fiction a setting in historical reality. Other names, characters, places, and incidents either are the product of the author's imagination or are used fictitiously, and their resemblance, if any, to real-life counterparts is entirely coincidental.

Copyright © 1986 by Philip Gerard
All rights reserved
Printed in the United States of America

First published as a Charles Scribner's Sons hardcover in 1986.
First paperback edition, 1997.

The paper in this book meets the guidelines for permanence
and durability of the Committee on Production Guidelines
for Book Longevity of the Council on Library Resources.

*Front cover photograph of Cape Hatteras Lighthouse: Al Spicer
Design: Liza Langrall*

Library of Congress Cataloging-in-Publication Data
Gerard, Philip.
    Hatteras Light / Philip Gerard.
        p.   cm.
    ISBN 0-89587-166-1 (trade pbk. : alk. paper)
    1. World War, 1914–1918—Fiction.   2. War stories. gsafd.
    I. Title.
PS3557.E635H3   1997
813'.54—DC21   97-13261

Contents

Prologue

Spring-1918

FIRST THERE is the island.

A barrier island, one of the Outer Banks. A thin shield of sand shaped like an arrowhead pointing out to sea over the Diamond Shoals. Forty miles long, nowhere wider than a sure rifle shot, the surface a mat of sand, sea oats, and pitch pine trees retreating toward the North Carolina shore at a rate of several inches every year.

The backside of the island, sheltered from the wind and currents that assault the ocean side, is built up by sand deposited in the salt marshes fronting Pamlico Sound, while the ocean side erodes, so that the island retains the same width year after year, storm after storm, exact to inches.

Hatteras.

The shape changes. Hurricanes scour out a harbor and next season fill it in, build up dunes and flatten them. It's only sand, and sand moves easily.

The coastline, from Nags Head in the north to Hatteras Village in the south, is guarded by a chain of stations operated by the United States Life-Saving Service. Each station shelters a surfboat, nine men, a boatcarriage, a horse to pull it down to water, a Lyle gun and breeches buoy, and other rescue equipment. The surfmen, though officially in the employ of the federal government, are islanders to a man and always have been. Each lives within sight of his station.

Cape Hatteras Station clusters at the foot of Hatteras Light. Like all the stations, it is whitewashed clapboard with black shutters and cedar-shake roof.

The lighthouse is a black-over-white candy-striped obelisk of granite, bricks, and iron rising 193 feet from its octagonal base to the bonnet sheltering a first-order Fresnel lens whose beam is visible for twenty-six miles in clear weather.

It is the highest structure of its kind on the continent of North America, the descendant of the light raised in 1790 by Alexander Hamilton to point the way onto the Diamond Shoals, the graveyard of the Atlantic, where Hamilton himself almost perished during a stormy passage. In the four hundred years since Amerigo Vespucci came ashore here, more than two thousand ships have foundered on the shoals, seeding a population of castaways, reformed pirates, fishermen.

Hatteras Light is stepped on a floating foundation of pine ties crisscrossed over sand. No concrete footings, no sunken steel shaft, just floating there on the sand. It is two miles down to bedrock. When the sea reaches the foot of the lighthouse, as it someday must, it will not be long before it leans toward Africa and topples into the surf.

But not yet.

Hatteras Light

CHAPTER 1

1

PETE PATCHETT was the first to see the U-boat. The two-day blow had ended, and Patchett walked under overcast skies on the damp sand, barefoot, as usual, looking for gifts. After a storm, the ocean always left some prize for weather endured, and Patchett wasn't one to overlook the hand of Providence when it offered.

A good part of the economy of the whole island, for that matter, derived from salvage. In his time Patchett had claimed everything from booze to choir robes, boathooks to sailcloth, even a crate of chickens, all by right of salvage. He hoped for some largesse now as he moved down the broad beach with a light step. He was small enough to be taken for a child from far away, as he stooped to turn sand dollars in his hand before pocketing them in his filthy clamdiggers, or poked at inverted horseshoe crabs with sticks to right them. He had no fear of the open. Truth to tell, he enjoyed his stature out here, where just now he was, except for the lighthouse, the tallest thing around.

When he lifted his eyes, there it was, riding easy offshore on the wide, slow swells, a gray hump. He thought at first it was a whale, for all the dolphins playing around it. He squinted toward it, a hand raised to his brow Indian-style. He noticed oil in the surf, painted timbers from some boat or ship, nothing so very extraordinary. There was a war on, after all. They'd all read about it in *The Coastland Times* and heard about it more immediately over the wireless in the middle of the night, listening to the distress calls of vessels far out in the Atlantic.

He stared at the whaleen vessel innocently, lacking the sense to be afraid of it. Suddenly a puff of smoke appeared just forward of the hump with a noise like a thunderclap, and the beach in front of him erupted in a great blast of sand and air, knocking him down. Someone was shooting at him with a goddamn cannon.

Pete Patchett scrambled to his feet and ran.

2

OLD HAM FETTERMAN was carving. He was a modeler, a naval architect of miniatures, shipwright of a large and distinguished toy fleet. One of his ships, a Baltimore Clipper, stood under glass at the Smithsonian Institution in Washington, D.C. They had offered him a thousand dollars for it, but in the end he had donated it, for he was old enough to understand that money like that could only be trouble. He didn't fear for his soul, exactly, only for his incentive.

He was installed in Littlejohn's store carving an odd, flat hull when Patchy brought the news. He carried on for several minutes, ending his recital with a simulation of the shell exploding at his feet, complete with spittle.

"Patchy, hold your water," Littlejohn said. He affected a meer-schaum and was descended from pirates, so they said. His name-sake, so they said, had survived Blackbeard's beheading party at Teach's Hole on Ocracoke Island, the next landfall south of Hatteras. But that was no news—everybody on the island could claim no-torious parentage, if it came to that. The Royals, you know, came down from Francis Drake, the Englishman.

"I tell you we're in for it, boys. I seen it. Tried to murder me, all right." A submarine vessel, he claimed, "one of them *unterseeboots* you read about in the papers."

Littlejohn puffed his pipe and Fetterman carved, nodding. "I don't doubt it, Patchy, but your noise ain't welcome here."

Littlejohn passed a bottle of bootleg beer to Patchett. He was a man who knew how to behave in a crisis. "Here," he said, "this'll help, or nothing will."

Pete Patchett drank down that beer and three more and lis-tened to the rowdy gulls and the wind, and half an hour later he ventured back over the dunes to look for the U-boat. Of course, it was gone.

3

CHIEF LORD held the door of the life-saving station for Virginia Royal, who carried supper for her husband, Jack Royal, number-two man at the station. She had enough chicken and grits in her basket for the whole nine-man crew: Hal MacRae, Cyrus Magillicutty, Joe Trent, Will Fetterman, and the Chief. Toby Ban-nister and Ian MacSween were on beach patrol, and Malcolm Royal, the Keeper, was on tower watch.

"I hear there's trouble," Virginia said.

"Never mind," Jack said. "You think them poor Germans want trouble with us?" He took some supper and shared the basket around, carefully ignoring Virginia. No one had ever witnessed them in public embrace, let alone in here.

"Nevertheless, keep a sharp eye."

Cy Magillicutty, a man nearly as broad as Jack's brother Malcolm, said, "She's quiet tonight, Virginia. We won't be going out." It was true, what he meant. It was only May, and the hurricanes wouldn't be starting for another dozen weeks or more. There would be occasional squalls, but that was just weather, nature tuning her strings for a symphony of winter blows. This was the lazy time, a time to eat in leisure, sleep the nights through, and get the boat ready—recaulk the lapstrake, scrape and paint the bottom, grease the oarlocks with clean grease. They were getting the boats ready at the eleven stations all up and down the coast from Kitty Hawk to Cedar Island. Every morning and evening the crews rushed their boats to the water and beat out over the breakers for a lark and to show they could do it. Anyway, between the tower watch, the beach patrols, and the wireless monitor, they'd hear about trouble fast enough.

"You worry too much." Jack smiled handsomely. "You can't believe a rummy like Patch. He ought to have been home with his woman at that hour, not out scavenging on the beach. He's got the soul of a castaway, that one. A landsman, like his old man."

Virginia didn't stay and eat with the men, though she would have welcomed the company. Not that they would have stopped her, but it was a dangerous thing to get started. As it was, Virginia was the only woman besides Mary Royal, Malcolm's wife, routinely allowed to enter the common room of the stationhouse, and then only briefly to deliver food and messages. It was a men's preserve. She left and promised to send her boy Kevin with coffee for the late shift.

She paused briefly in the doorway, wanting to tell Jack she missed him, but when she turned they were all looking at her and she said nothing.

"She's a fine female," Chief Lord said after she had gone. "I wouldn't be sitting here with the likes of you if I had that one at home." He laughed profoundly, his eyes slanting darkly.

"You don't know," Jack said and wiped his mouth. "You don't know."

4

MALCOLM ROYAL stood nearly seven feet tall, taller in his boots. His weight was an item of speculation. When he had joined the Life-Saving Service at eighteen, he had weighed in at two hundred sixty pounds, and was considered lean for his height. His stomach had thickened in the thirteen years since. One of his hands could easily cover his wife's fist. "Paper wraps rock," Mary would say, laughing at his monstrosity.

Telescope in hand, he climbed the spiral staircase inside the tower, his trunk almost too broad for the passage, and though it was a strenuous climb for heart and limbs, as he ascended, his breathing relaxed, deepened, and he drew the stone-cooled air into the very bottom of himself and tasted it. He did not hurry, he did not pause. With a heavier step he would have been marching.

He took care to walk softly. His biggest fear was that other men should fear him. He was forced while still very young to practice subtlety, tact, restraint, lest he seem a bully and an exhibitionist through no fault of character. His every action was an exercise in exaggeration. His size made him timid, as he grew into it. He could not have located a fair fight in a radius of two hundred miles anyhow.

As on most evenings, he craved the solitude of the tower. He climbed, letting his back straighten, letting himself be as tall as nature had intended.

But nature had betrayed him, he felt at times, by letting him grow virtually unchecked. Malcolm had given up duck hunting at fifteen, an age when most boys start it, because he simply could not comfortably fit his finger inside a trigger guard. He could have used a Chesapeake long gun, but they were illegal forty years by the time he needed one. Still, it had given him his moments of brute triumph. Playing on the Hatteras nine as a teenager, Malcolm had been a gargantuan first baseman. Once at a game in Manteo he swung the bat so hard it broke in half in his hands without ever touching the pitched ball. Another time in Ocracoke Village he whaled a ball so hard the cover shucked off in midflight like a candy wrapper and fluttered to earth with all the ceremony of a shotgunned wad, while the innards sailed out of sight in a steadily unraveling parabola until either it was long gone or used up, nobody ever did figure out which.

Nearing the top, Malcolm stretched his arms inside their sleeves and felt his muscles bunch and loosen like fists, the joints unbothered by arthritis or rheumatism. It was a rare winter's night when his body complained of the cold. He thought of his chest as a furnace, and he stoked it aplenty. For breakfast he routinely consumed a dozen buckwheat pancakes, seven eggs poached or fried, a slab of bacon the size of a shoe, a bowlful of whatever fruit was in season, and four to six cups of strong coffee syrupy with cream and sugar. On a bet some years ago, he had eaten seventy-five crabs and drunk sixteen pints of beer in three hours. He had never vomited in his life.

Malcolm reached the iron door to the catwalk that compassed the turret below the Light and stepped out under a sky just beginning to come up in stars. He stalked the catwalk, careful not to let his oversized boots make any sound on the wrought-iron deck, the Light casting his head in a brilliant and fleeting halo. To the north he could see the island stretched hard toward Oregon Inlet, pulled to a tight neck at Kinnakeet. Just south was the point, then the island bent westward in a beach broad enough to drill cavalry on. It was windy on the catwalk. He flared his nostrils like an elk and lifted his head into it, sniffing the nascent starlight for the scent of storm.

He could navigate by the stars and by intuition, but he could triangulate only with difficulty. He had learned to use the sextant and compass dutifully rather than enthusiastically, because all his life he had wanted to do just one thing: keep the Hatteras Light. He was a man fulfilled in his ambition, who had never felt lacking or discontented in his profession. In the old days, he knew, when the hundred-foot-tall Colossus of Apollo still straddled the anchorage at Rhodes, when Alexandria raised her three-tiered tower 450 feet above the sea with a beacon visible for twenty-nine miles, the keepers of the lights were all priests, schooled in Pharology, the magic science of seamanship, navigation, pilotage, hydrology, astronomy, and omens.

His father, Seamus, had kept the Light all during Malcolm's boyhood, so even then Malcolm knew his heritage as thoroughly as a seminarian on the eve of Holy Orders. He gleaned it from the books in his father's collection, from the Lighthouse Service Bulletins that came with illustrated texts about new navigational aids, new reflectors, lenses, buoys, chimes, sirens, filaments, fuels, the possibility of radio beacons.

As a grown man, his strength was his advantage: he could carry a pony across his shoulders, pull a boat to water single-handed, carry a grown man under each arm, drunk or sober, the way another man would carry children. He thought of his job as a calling, of his calling as an adventure, of adventure as a way of life. He saw nothing remarkable in his profession, for he had grown too used to it.

He reigned at the Light at the pleasure of the Bureau of Lighthouses and the Department of Commerce, and did double duty as head surfman at the steering oar of the lifeboat, which duty came under the jurisdiction of the United States Life-Saving Service and the Department of Treasury. His badge of office was a short-billed cap with the metal insignia of the Lighthouse Service in painted gold set above the bill. His tools were the brass compass fixed in the housing of the Light itself and a thirty-one-inch brass telescope with a magnification factor of thirty.

He peered into it now, sighting out over the shipping lanes, trying to spy the shape of a German U-boat, though he had never seen one and could only guess how hard it would be to make out a grey hull on a grey sea at dusk. Nothing but water, nothing to worry a man. Malcolm had gone down to water at hazard better than two hundred times, and his crew was credited with saving almost a thousand men, women, and children of catholic nationality and origin. He had never learned to swim.

Away to the southwest now he could see weather moving in, dim and unrealized as an old memory.

He collapsed the telescope and went back inside the tower to climb the last short stairs to the carousel room, his *sanctum sanctorum*. He opened the iron door and entered, his ears tuned to the clockwork gears that drove the carousel. The walls were glass on every side, and Malcolm was briefly blinded by the glare of the rotating beam against the windows, shooting out to sea. He felt at peace in this room. For him the machinery held all the power and invincibility of a natural force, and each time he emerged from the carousel room he was stronger, refreshed in spirit.

Out on the catwalk again, he watched Virginia enter the station with her supper basket and watched her leave emptyhanded a few minutes later with that dispirited walk that signalled a life of perpetual disappointment come to the very proud.

He turned away, embarrassed for her. What was it about Jack? As boys Malcolm and Jack had wrestled almost daily, their bouts long and vicious. A quick punch, an open-handed cuff, and the pair would be on the ground, rolling in the sand and spitting it through gritted teeth as they struggled, always silently, to mutual exhaustion.

But now Malcolm had outgrown even that, and he had not touched Jack in years.

5

MAX WIEN was a long way from home, and it felt like it. Not because he could readily gauge distance—he could not even tell night from day, closed up as they were. But time assured him that the distance was great. They had been on patrol now for more than two months, by the calendar he kept on the bulkhead beside his hammock, each of the passing days struck out with the stub of a pencil.

He had not seen Papenburg for a very long time.

Earlier they had surfaced off what the charts had declared to be an uninhabited island, Cape Lookout, nothing but sand dunes and a lighthouse. As usual whenever they surfaced in a safe zone, the crewmen were permitted, two by two, to go to the tower for five minutes of fresh air. The air in the submarine got overloaded with carbon dioxide when they ran submerged, and it made the men easily tired. Also it made them stink a damp, rotting stink.

Max stood his turn like all the others, and it took all the will-power he could muster to force himself back down the hatch to the stink of confinement. He thought himself a prisoner now, after seven patrols, and held no real hope of ever leaving this vessel. This captain, Stracken, whom he had met at a cabaret on leave from his last boat, had told Max he reminded him of his son. Captain Stracken had arranged a transfer for him to U-55, one of the largest class of *unterseeboot*, a transatlantic submarine cruiser with forward torpedo tubes and 9.5-inch deck cannons fore and aft. Before the war it had made experimental commercial voyages, carrying jewelry, gold, bonds, and scientific instruments between Germany and South America in the stormless undersea. It carried fuel enough for fifty days' sailing, and had lately rendezvoused with a supply convoy on a moonless night in an untrafficked latitude in the mid-Atlantic.

The captain had adopted Max as a kind of valet. Stracken was an old hand, master of a merchantman before the war, who had never really abandoned the notion of a cabin boy, though Max's official title was surgeon's assistant. He lanced boils, dispensed liniments and vitamin pills, but his real job was to keep Stracken company.

The captain had no son: Max had figured it all along.

While Max stood on the tower, dolphins played around the boat. He stared in wonder till his turn was up. When he went below he heard one of the deck cannons thumping overhead, but it was just Bergen testing the range against the sand. Someone said there was a man on the island, but that was impossible.

Max had heard they were losing the war, and the news made no impression on him. It had been going on so long—ever since

Gramley Library
Salem Academy and College
Winston-Salem, N.C. 27108

he had been a man—that it all ran together. He had no family anymore; that was why he had enlisted in the U-boat Service in the first place. He listened to the engines.

They steamed the surface all day, recharging their batteries, and Max was called to the tower as they overtook a lightship. It was the *Diamond Shoals*, recognizable by the black and white diamond pattern of its paint. The captain laughed when he discovered his mistake. "Hatteras," he said, stubbing a finger onto the waterproof map. They had had a stormy crossing and had made landfall farther north than they had intended. Like the Plymouth Pilgrims, he thought, for he knew his history. Captain Stracken took new bearings by the lightship, then U-55 steamed north toward the smoke of a cargo vessel.

At sundown, they took the freighter by hammering her with the deck guns at the waterline. Torpedoes were precious—they must conserve them. She didn't burn long, settled by the bow and sank in a matter of a few minutes. There wasn't much activity on deck, for most of the crew were caught in their hammocks. She never even got her boats off.

"We will hide in the shoals," Stracken said.

Behind him Hatteras Light burned, and the lightship *Diamond Shoals* rode at station somewhere in the gathering fog. Max Wien went below and felt the world closing in around him, stifling him, and he couldn't get his breath for a long time.

6

HAM FETTERMAN carved by lamplight in Littlejohn's store on the Kinnakeet Road long after it was closed up for the night. He was allowed. Sixteen of his ships lined the shelves in back of the counter. He was Littlejohn's pride, master of all the sailing ships of the imagination.

His hands worked all by themselves, shaping the soft wood by feel. He built like a shipbuilder, not a modeler: laid a keel and then proportioned all the rest. He could manufacture to flawless scale all the fittings and brightwork, all the shrouds, stays, halyards, canvas, capstans, binnacles, whaleboats, lifeboats, transoms, hatch covers, cannon, crowsnests, crosstrees, gangways, companionways, coamings, dodgers, cockpits, wheels, even the ship's bell.

He held this new one in his hand, stroking it like a cat with the other. It was ugly, all right, but even ugly things must be built well. It had the hump of a whale and the belly of a shark, and there was no complicated rigging.

He worked it some more with the ivory-handled rigging knife. Whalebone, scrimshawed with a tableau of men in boats after a right whale, souvenir from the *Charles W. Morgan*. Fetterman had watched Teddy Roosevelt's ship pass off the Light in 1898, twenty good years ago, carrying home the remnants of his fevered troops. Fetterman had been old even then. It had been night, and he had seen only the ship's lights, but there were Teddy Roosevelt and the Rough Riders steaming back from that other war.

Ham Fetterman reached for his fifth bottle of beer and wondered what was the use of getting old if nothing new was ever going to happen to you.

7

KEITH ROYAL, Malcolm's youngest brother, was living in the Keeper's house adjacent to the station with Malcolm and his wife Mary. Malcolm, ten years Keith's senior, had married late: he was slow getting around to things like that. His bride was closer in age to Keith.

Mary Royal was born a Dant and raised on the island. Half a dozen times she and her sister Virginia had been south to Morehead City to visit cousins, and twice Mary had gone alone to Savannah. She had thick raven hair and worried over her figure, as most of the island women did not, she knew. Malcolm was a man of moment on the island, and she carried herself accordingly.

In the kitchen, his back to her, Malcolm was packing a lunch pail and a vacuum bottle of coffee. His shirt fitted him like a sail at the back, and Mary always loved how big he was even though it scared her. It was like living at the foot of a mountain, and when he came to her in the night she often held her breath, as much from fear as from fascination.

"You're going?" she said. "You just came down from the tower."

"Seems like I ought to be over there, you know. Just in case." He had a way of wrinkling his eyes above his beard so that just a shard of blue showed out from under each brow. It made him look gentle.

"I wish you wouldn't. You don't have to." It was an old argument. The other members of the crew lived in enforced celibacy, permitted to spend one night at home after every nine-day tour, though of course there was plenty of day leave during the quiet times. Malcolm, who could go home whenever he pleased, had always felt self-conscious about his privilege, Mary knew, and was reluctant to take advantage of it.

He put a hand on her shoulder. She wasn't a small woman, but next to him she looked like a child. "If anything happens, I want to be there. It wouldn't do not to be there."

Keith came in from the beach, where he had been walking. "You want company?"

"I'll have plenty of that. You stay here and be company for Mary. I guess I can handle a few Germans, all right. If anything happens, I'll telephone." Malcolm never used the telephone.

"I'll sleep light, Malcolm," Keith said.

"You do that, boy."

Malcolm went out. It was beginning to drizzle. There would be no real storm, and in the fog the U-boat would be as harmless as a wet match. Still . . .

Overhead he could see the Light, circling through the thickening fog. He nodded to it, pulled down the brim of his cap. They would be sounding the fog signal all night.

8

"I'M GLAD YOU CAME BACK," Mary said. She and Keith were drinking coffee and playing cribbage, a game he had learned up north at college. All the young men played it at Harvard; it was the thing. He would teach her poker one of these nights when he knew her better.

"You don't mean you missed me," he said. "I was just a kid when I left." Even he laughed at that. He had been gone just about three years, one year short of a degree in history. He hadn't come back even once in all that time, and Malcolm had taken it hard.

Jack had confronted him when he got back. "What right?" he had demanded. "What right?" But that was Jack. Malcolm was the brother he loved. Jack was too hard on people, on everybody, on himself. That was why Malcolm was Keeper.

"Sure, we all missed you. Malcolm used to talk about you for hours on end," Mary said. "He would read your letters—he couldn't understand how you could write so much. You were all we talked about that first year."

She was still getting over the baby, Keith thought. She had miscarried in April, last month, and he had come down immediately upon receipt of Malcolm's first letter in three years. He couldn't say honestly that the letter had anything to do with his impetuous homecoming, but he knew well enough that Malcolm was a man who needed a child.

"Malcolm wants me to join the crew. He says they're short-handed." One of the Trent boys had gone off to Canada to be a flyer in the war. Keith just didn't know. Joining the crew would be a promise to stay. No one was sure if he would stay, least of all Keith, who had left school in midterm.

"He needs you, all right, but not like that."

"He says to take my time, think on it. That's what he said."

"Malcolm thinks everybody has time. Tell me, what made you come home all of a sudden? I know the obvious answer, but that can't be all there is to it."

"I don't know exactly. I guess it was time." That was the only honest explanation he had: it was like a bell had sounded in his brain signalling time was up.

"Malcolm should have written sooner then," she said, "or I should have. But I didn't really know you." Mary, knew him now, though, through his letters. He had made conversation possible in her house.

"It wasn't that," he said.

He moved her pin in the pegboard and sipped coffee, a luxury since the start of the war. Most of the islanders were back to drinking yeopon tea, a bitter, stimulating brew, but Malcolm, with typical providence, had laid in a stock when he saw the shortage coming. Outside, the drizzle went on. Keith looked past Mary, out the window. There are things out there, he thought.

9

AT DAWN, Malcolm Royal rubbed his eyes with the heels of his hands and made his entry into the life-saving station logbook in a coarse hand: "The sea, she hid from us all night."

10

PATRICIA PATCHETT, old Fetterman's granddaughter, was irked at her husband. "Peter, you should be doing useful work, man's work. The *Hermes* needs paint, this shack is falling down around our ears, your kids run around like ragamuffins, and you spend your time sucking up suds and conjuring submarines. I swear I don't know what to do with you."

Patchy meditated on Stede Bonnet, the gentleman pirate of the capes who had turned to plunder on the high seas to get away from a nagging wife. He wondered if he would ever have the gumption to go a-pirating.

She was right about the *Hermes*, a beamy Jonesport lobster boat that Patchy ran to and from the mainland, ferrying supplies by contract for Littlejohn and any others that required goods. He ran on his own schedule, an eccentric one heavily dependent on his mood. But it needed an engine more than it needed paint. Trust a woman, he thought, to worry over the appearance of a thing.

"I'll see about the boat today, don't you fret, woman," he said.

Just now, *Hermes* was berthed at Oman's Dock a dozen miles south in Hatteras Village. He understood from Oman that he could get replacement parts for overhauling the engine on credit, but he had not been down lately to check. This morning was as good a time as any. It would get him out of the house. He loved his wife as well as any man, he supposed, but sometimes she just made too much noise.

"Before you go running off to gossip with Oman, there's some loose boards on the shed. Practice on them."

I know what I'd like to practice on, he thought, gripping the hammer. He dug out a sack of nails and went to work on the shed at the back of the house. He had been meaning to do it for weeks, but he enjoyed the adventure of beachcombing so much he often talked himself out of his chores, especially in this fine weather. You never knew what you might find. It could change your life, all at once, just like that.

"When you get to the village, I'll be needing some things."

"Go to Littlejohn's."

"That man's a pirate. Besides, he doesn't have what I'm wanting."

She didn't want to run into old Fetterman, he thought, that was all.

Patchy hadn't had the nerve to go down to the beach since yesterday afternoon, but suddenly he wasn't in the mood for errands. He drove home the last nail and shook the side of the shed half-heartedly to test for stability, then left the hammer where it fell and trotted across the road and over the dunes.

11

PATCH PATCHETT was amazed at what the storm had left: piles of lumber, still cabled together in great bales. Enough to build a house, a mansion, enough for fences, sheds, porches, a new boat. He danced about in front of the great blond bales landing like barges on the beach of Buxton. He was a wealthy man now, he shouted and didn't care who heard. He hopped from foot to foot, clapping his hands jubilantly, hooting his thanks to the god of storms. When Cy Magillicutty came by on beach patrol, Patchy claimed all the lumber officially by right of salvage.

"Mine," he said, "all mine!" His head swam with the realization that he was the new economic power on the island.

Cyrus shook his head. "We'll see. You guard it while I report to Malcolm." And he went away in a hurry.

Then Patchy remembered: there had been no storm. The body of the first man he found washing in the surf was blackened, as if by fire.

CHAPTER 2

1

At Oman's Dock, Alvin Dant, Virginia and Mary Royal's uncle, smoked a long pipe and watched the fog. It was early, and in an hour or so the fog would blow clean away, he knew.

Alvin and his son Brian were ready to shove off. It was only twenty-five miles out into the Gulf Stream, and the fishing would be good in this weather. It was almost always good, except during the worst storms, though sailing into the stream could be a tricky business. Not so long ago Alvin's brother Dennis had disappeared with a good boat in fair weather not twelve miles off the Light, and nothing ever came ashore from the wreck. Alvin had the caution of a family man.

Alvin's daughter, Dorothy, would be twenty-one tomorrow, and they planned a celebration. He thought he had done well raising her to womanhood without a wife. She looked nothing like Brian: she was a petite brunette, like her mother had been, while the boy was tall, lanky, and blond. Dennis had looked that way in his youth.

Alvin had ordered a Singer sewing machine for Dorothy all the way from Norfolk, knowing it would be the last thing she would expect. It had cost him dear, but it was what she really wanted so she could make some decent clothes for herself, and he felt she was entitled to a few good things. He knew little enough about what a young woman needed.

He fixed his pipe and stepped aboard while Brian cast off the bow and stern lines. He turned her over. The engine sounded good this morning, strong.

Oman advanced down the catwalk. "Al, have you heard the news? There's dangerous water out there." He gave the details, which were sketchy, an elaboration of Patchy's minor adventure. "If I was you, I'd be staying with the fleet."

Alvin Dant nodded from the wheelhouse. "I hear you, Frank. But the fish are neutral, they tell me."

"Keep an eye skinned, all the same."

Alvin Dant waved, then steered his boat away from the dock and throttled for open water.

2

When he spotted Patch Patchett windmilling over the dunes and heading for the station with Cy Magillicutty's rocket flare marking a smoky roostertail in the sky behind him, Malcolm Royal knew he had been too quick in entering the log. The man runs with his hands flapping like wings, he thought.

Patchy burst through the door. "Malcolm!" he wheezed. "You have to come see—"

"A ship?"

Patchy nodded and gulped air. Cy Magillicutty came in. "Now how did you get here so fast?" he said to Patchy.

"Must be something special," Chief Lord said. Jack Royal was on his feet and throwing open the door of the carriage house while the others gripped the tongue of the boatcarriage at the handles and rolled it outside. Chief Lord brought the horse, Homer, from the corral and with MacSween's help harnessed him. In two minutes they were in the surf, pulling over the combers.

"Pull, boys, pull!" Malcolm said. There was lumber all over the surf now. He sat in the stern and handled the steering oar. Cy Magillicutty crouched in the bow with a boathook to ward off flotsam.

"Malcolm," Chief Lord said quietly, "we won't find them. If it happened that far out that we couldn't see it, we won't find them now."

"Pull," Malcolm said. Chief was right, of course, but they had to make sure. There was always the ghost of a chance.

"The bastards," Jack said, "the sneaking bastards."

"Pull," Malcolm yelled. "For the love of God, pull!"

3

OF A CREW OF THIRTY-SEVEN, they recovered only three, all of them on the beach. Littlejohn supervised the burials, as was customary, and Malcolm notified the authorities at Portsmouth by wireless.

Malcolm stared at the sheet a long time before he wrote anything down. He dipped the pen in the inkwell and, under the date, wrote in a painful and barely legible hand: *Put to sea at 0730 & searched five hours. Rescued not a soul. We shall be busy from now on.* And signed it, *M. Royal, Keeper, Cape Hatteras Station*, recalling an old line of his father's: And the sea gave up the dead which were in it.

4

DOROTHY DANT WAS alone in the house. She had been up before sunrise to fix breakfast for Brian and her father, then had gone back to bed. She slept late, and when she woke just lay in bed for a full, delicious half hour, savoring the fact of her impending birthday, stretching and squirming luxuriously, feeling sexy and vigorous and ripe. Her birthday was always a lucky time, and this time her luck had delivered Keith Royal home to her. Something would be decided tomorrow, she felt sure. She would see to it.

When she finally slid out of bed, the fog was gone and the day was bright. She splashed cold water on her face and let it dry in the steady salt breeze coming in at the kitchen window.

Then, outside, she mounted an old balloon-tired bicycle, and Rufus, a big mongrel retriever, bounded over.

"Come on, Rufe," she said, "we're going to the beach."

And she pedalled off, Rufus trotting gamely behind.

5

ALVIN DANT STEERED his Friendship sloop into the fog, listening. He had converted her to a powerboat himself, cutting away the deep keel, then uprooting the thick wooden mast and installing a gasoline engine and a wheelhouse forward of the cockpit, now a covered well for storing the catch.

He had heard of things happening to the north, off the Wimble Shoals at Kinnakeet, and wondered if he ought to turn south, out of harm's way. Stay with the fleet, so Oman had counseled, and that's where the fleet would surely be. He considered it. He packed his pipe and relit it behind the glass of the pilothouse.

He was a man who had lost a brother and a wife and whose children were now nearly grown. Dorothy, he was sure, would soon marry that youngest Royal boy, Keith, the college man. Anyway Alvin hoped so. He was a good boy from a respected family, a

Hatterasman. You had to be born here to be a Hatterasman. That would keep her here, if anything would. He owned his boat outright, as he had for years, and, for a change, he owed no one beyond the week.

He would head north, following the fish, never mind the Heinies. A fisherman had to go by his nose.

"Brian."

The boy appeared from the deck, where he had been folding nets.

"Take the wheel."

Alvin went belowdecks and uncased his shark rifle and an old double-barreled shotgun his grandfather had used against the Yankees when they had invaded the island. It was a birdgun and couldn't be counted on against a submarine, but it felt better to have something. Alvin broke it and loaded both barrels, then fed five shells into the magazine of the rifle. He took the weapons and a box of shells for each back to the pilothouse.

He would give the boy the rifle, if it came to that: he was the better shot. Brian was used to the rifle and had killed half a dozen sharks with it during the past two seasons. If it came to that, he guessed it wouldn't matter.

The sun glowed weakly through the thin fog. To the northwest, Hatteras Light was just a flash. It burned dusk to dawn, and during storms or fog the Light stayed on even in daylight, blowing a fog signal every half hour to help blind sailors find their way past the shoals.

Alvin stood over his son's shoulder, watching him hold to course. Brian stood well at the wheel. They were twelve miles off the Light now, he reckoned, just about the place where his brother's boat had foundered, another Friendship sloop, sister to his own. But watching Brian steer with sure, knowledgeable hands, it just didn't seem possible.

Alvin had always imagined sanctuary in sight of the Light, as though it were watching over him. The seas were flat now and there were fish out there, or something: he could smell it.

"Here you go, boy. I'll take her now," he said, and stood at the wheel, his back broadening against his shirt, feeling ready.

6

THE FUTILE SEARCH for survivors abandoned, Malcolm stayed on at the station to ready the Light, which had to be done each day before eleven A.M., according to Bureau of Lighthouse Regulations. That meant hauling two five-gallon pails of kerosene to the top of the tower. Then cleaning the Fresnel lens, inspecting the four concentric wicks of the incandescent oil-vapor lamp that would radiate 80,000 candlepower for twelve hours, dusk to dawn. Last, using a hand crank, he must rewind the carousel "clock"— the mechanism that would keep the Light rotating in precisely timed circles through the night. Usually, it was a two-hour job. This day, it took him almost four, but when the sun went down again, the Light was operational.

His hands were so blistered and swollen when he stood down and returned to quarters that Mary had to open the door for him. She wrapped his hands in grease and towels and put him to bed, then sat up with Keith, not talking.

Finally, she said, "It's worse when they don't save anybody, isn't it."

Keith pulled on a sweater and left her alone with her husband.

7

IN THE HOUSE he had lived in since boyhood and which stood on the only hill in Buxton Village, Seamus Royal, father of two of the best surfmen on the island, studied navigational charts by the light of a coal-oil lamp. He was seventy years old, and he knew these charts as well as he knew the birth records in the family Bible, but he thought he ought to be sure of his territory. If Patchett was right, if there really was some kind of submarine out there, somebody would have to find it, and he supposed he knew those shoals as well as any man. On a dusty shelf between sepia photographs of himself and his sons stood a plain teak frame that held the Gold Medal for Life-Saving, which he had won twenty-eight years before.

He smiled sadly. Two, not three. Only two boys, he thought, carrying on his life's work. Tomorrow he would call all his boys together and get drunk with them, all three now, and find if he couldn't do something about Keith. Give him an oar. And get him married to that Dant girl, if he could. She had spunk. When a man gets only three nights a month alone with his wife she had better be lively as a whore, and be able to fend for herself the rest of the time.

It would all come to pass, he was sure, it would all be arranged. There was never any escaping the right thing.

Seamus got up from the kitchen table and, from a locker at the back of the house, brought a long oilskin case. In his oarhardened hands he carried it to the table and unlaced it for the first time in ten years.

It was a Krag-Jorgenson, an old Army rifle he had bought at surplus from the Spanish War in '01. He cleaned the heavy grease out of the barrel and swabbed the bore with solvent and oil. Seamus took his time. He paused to light another pipe.

"There," he said, raising it and aiming out the window, down the hill, onto the beach. He sighted on the lightship *Diamond Shoals* until the fog covered her. He worked the bolt without injecting a cartridge. He had a box of them somewhere. He worked it again. "There," he said, reluctant to put away the rifle. He would just hold it awhile.

8

PATCH PATCHETT NESTED in a fold of sand dunes with a blanket pulled around him Indian-style, watching the thin moon over the ocean. The moon rode above a low fogbank, while the Hatteras Light pulsed out across the sea, casting fast shadows over Patchy's square bales of lumber. He watched and finally, restless, slept.

9

LIEUTENANT (JG) TIM HALSTEAD and his crew of six motored up the Core Sound into Pamlico Sound aboard *Sealion*, a converted smuggler, and put in at Hatteras Village, the only navigable harbor on the island except for Oregon Inlet at the far northern tip. *Sealion* was a high-powered rumrunner shaped like a cigar with a chopped-off tail and an armored cockpit, recently taken in a raid in the Florida Keys.

Halstead ducked behind the fairing and lit a maduro cigarette as the forty-two-foot speedboat roared between two anchored fishing boats, rocking them with a powerful wash. He cut his engines at the last minute—he wanted to make an entrance. He bloused his shirt and straightened his cap.

Since the *Hauppage*, headed for Fort Dix with lumber for troop cantonments, had been reported sunk by a mine yesterday, it would be necessary to guard the coast. *Sealion* could throw two torpedoes, and she had a very accurate two-inch gun mounted forward, besides a .30-calibre Browning machine gun at the cockpit.

The rumor in Beaufort was that a U-boat was hiding in the Diamond Shoals, the way U-boats had been showing up all over the coast lately, but he didn't really believe that. It was too far from home and they were losing the war, now that America was committed. The Marines were in Flanders and the Kaiser was washed up, all right; it was only a matter of time. Waiting in Beaufort, attached to a communications station, Halstead had figured the war would be won without his help, long before he ever got a combat assignment.

But I'm a submarine chaser now, he thought. He was an Academy man, commissioned for exactly three weeks, in the right place at the right time. His men stood at attention at their posts, ready to berth. The fishermen who had not gone out today were all looking at him, but he did not allow himself to smile. Their safety was in his hands, and he must not seem too arrogant about it. He spit his cigarette into the drink, felt the thrill of command.

He put in at Oman's Dock to top off his tanks. He left Blotner, the engineer, on deck watch, and led the rest of his men ashore to find a mess.

"The Marines have landed," Oman said to nobody in particular as Halstead's crew moved down the pier and into the village, thick with the smell of fish and salt. The Light Halstead must defend was farther north, near Buxton, but he must be prepared to defend the entire island, if things went that far, and a little reconnaissance wouldn't hurt. The Navy would be trucking fuel down from the north, but in the meantime he must secure temporary provisions and materials to build a mooring and a bivouac.

Halstead had no idea that wood, like almost every other commodity, had been an expensive import on Hatteras Island since the time of the Hattorask Indians, except for a few stands of gaunt pine milled locally and suitable for fencing, firewood, and not much else.

"You want wood, go up to Buxton beach," the storekeeper, one of Oman's cousins, said with no hint of irony. "They've got plenty of that article, U.S. Government issue."

It took him an awkward minute of reflection before he understood what the fellow meant. He said something appropriate and went out, and within the hour they were plying Hatteras Inlet on their way to the Light.

"They've got a strange sense of humor down here, sir," Ensign Cross said. "They ain't got any use for Yankees, neither."

"Never mind, we'll manage." Halstead vowed to be a little sharper when they landed next. What with all the preparations to get under way to his new station, he hadn't slept at all in some thirty hours. But he was prepared, that was the main thing. He had four years of the best military training in the world, good people were counting on him, and he would acquit himself with honor. He was now in the kind of situation that made a man a hero or a fool, and he had no wish to be the latter.

10

THEY SURFACED IN FOG, and the captain swept all the horizons with a field glass, nodding, as if in approval. Max Wien stood at his elbow, watching the Light arc through the thick air. They heard the distant horn, each blast resounding like the hoarse lament of some great cave-bound creature.

Captain Stracken nodded again. "And tell me this, young man: why have we seen no cutters?"

Max looked blank. He had nothing to offer in the way of strategic advice, but the captain didn't seem to mind.

Stracken continued, quietly, "This is their highway, the big boats. With that Light, we can come and go as we please, and we will always know exactly where our quarry will pass. *Wir werden den Weg nie verfehlen.* We will never lose our way. We will hide when we please and strike as we will, and never miss. *Gott sei Dank für das Licht.*"

They were in the heart of the Allied shipping lanes. Fuel from the Louisiana Gulf coast, grain from the Mississippi Delta, lumber from South America, munitions and troops from the southern posts, all passed off the Light, riding the current of the Gulf Stream close to the Diamond Shoals, the Graveyard of the Atlantic, with only the Light to guide them on their way.

"From now on," Stracken said, "the Light will betray them."

Max said nothing.

With the Light, Max thought, the captain was right: now they could not miss. Even the blackest night they would know exactly how close they could go without running aground. They would destroy much for their country. They were *der Haifisch*—the shark.

"Tonight we take the lightship," Stracken said. "It is of no use to us, and it can report our position on the wireless." The lightship stood farther out, a beacon to the deep draught vessels, an extra precaution against the shoals. Kraft, the first officer, looked for a moment as if he were going to protest. It didn't matter now anyway, Max knew. They had already gone too far to be forgiven by men who still believed in anything.

They cruised the surface for another hour, riding the slow swells and listening to the dull crash of far-off breakers. I could swim to there, Max thought. But he had never learned to swim. Papenburg had no warm ocean, only icy creeks running into an icy lake from the mountains. He felt the sun grow stronger on his filthy uniform shirt and wished he could feel it full on his naked back and shoulders.

When they lost the fog, the captain took them down, and Max held his breath against the bad air, but he could not hold it for long.

11

DOROTHY DANT, Alvin's girl, had her mind on Keith Royal. Why had he come back? She was pretty sure she was in love with him. Having him home again had been her ardent wish, but it was disturbing all the same to have him so close now. She had come down to the beach with Rufus again today to be alone outdoors and to prepare herself to see Keith later.

This afternoon she would decide how to receive him when he came. He had been back almost a week now, and she imagined him working up his courage to call on her, though the times she'd gone north to steal a weekend with him while her father and Brian were gone with the fleet Keith had received her with little ceremony. It was hard to think about things with him around.

From the beach, she watched a motor launch pass northward. A man in a white uniform saluted from the cockpit. She dove into the water running and swam a dozen long strokes from the beach.

Gramley Library
Salem Academy and College
Winston-Salem, N.C. 27108

Out past the launch, now disappearing up the coast, was her father's boat. And up where the Navy launch was headed, Keith's brothers stood by a lifeboat. His brothers were men of courage, and their courage was so taken for granted it was hardly spoken of. She did not know if Keith had that kind of courage. She hoped not.

Dorothy treaded water easily and looked toward the island. From out here it looked like desert. She would marry Keith, and he would take her away, that was that. The two of them could go back to New England, to Harvard if that's what he wanted. Or anyplace else that lasted. She lingered in the deep water, and Rufus swam in little circles around her.

12

LITTLEJOHN PLAYED with the wireless and got details about the lumber ship.

Old Fetterman carved.

He could not get the shape exactly right, but it would come, it always did. His hands would understand the thing long before his head. Sometimes he built with miniature planking, so that the inside of the hull was hollow, ribbed for stiffness, but this hull he carved. This hull was a creature; he could not yet fathom what was inside.

"You're making progress," Littlejohn said. "Though I can't say I admire it. You should make a schooner. You can never have enough schooners."

"I've built all the schooners I'm going to for now."

"Have it your own way. Still, a man can't have too many schooners."

The knife slipped into the meat of his knuckle, and Ham Fetterman didn't flinch. He watched the blood come up dark in the sickle-shaped cut, let a single big drop fall to the floor and covered it with his boot. "Littlejohn, come here," he said, almost amused. "I'm bleeding."

13

LITTLEJOHN'S WIFE APPLIED the bandage on Fetterman. She had hair the color of old tin, parted exactly in the middle and kempt as a powdered wig, and a complexion dark as an Indian's. No one knew her as anything but Mrs. Littlejohn, name enough for anybody.

"A little drawing of the blood is good for you, especially at your age," she said. "It goes all sour if you keep it bottled up." She passed Littlejohn a knowing look. "But it's a bad omen to do it by accident. Be on your lookout."

Littlejohn swore and went back behind the counter where he kept the beer, listening to his wife mutter as she went out: "The beast that ascendeth out of the bottomless pit shall make war against them, and shall overcome them, and shall kill them."

CHAPTER 3

1

JACK ROYAL was the kind of man who usually turns to soldiering: steady, physically competent, unyielding and resourceful in confrontation, unburdened by imagination. He stood six-feet two-inches tall and had jet, oily-looking hair combed straight back from a low beak. His beard was thick and short-cropped, his moustache heavy and combed to a rakish oxbow. His eyes were dark and sullen, though he thought of himself as untroubled and easygoing. It confused him that others seemed to find him a brooding, unhappy character.

He sat on a whitewashed bench in the common room and

whipped the frayed ends of a spare coil of line for the Lyle gun. He took longer to do it than Chief Lord would, and his product was not so stylish, but the ends were wrapped to last, and the line would part before the whipping unraveled. He worked with his feet planted like jacks, parrying the marlin-spike with his sailmaker's palm as if he were dueling with himself. He judged his own integrity, as he judged other men's, by the work of his hands, not his head.

Chief Lord sat opposite Jack in a chair made of rope woven over a wooden frame. The Chief was playing his guitar, the music syncopated and bluesy, his head nodding time. He never took his eyes off Jack.

Without missing a note, he said: "I know what you're thinking, I know what you're always thinking."

Jack didn't bother to look up. "Oh, I forgot. You're a mind reader. I've heard all that crap before."

"You're thinking, the only reason he's in charge and not you is that's he's so big."

It was true. Jack had always believed that size alone caused Malcolm to command. "Am I supposed to argue with you, Chief?"

Chief continued his music, slipping into a seventh chord, pleased by the sound of it. "You don't have to get defensive with me, Jackie. I'm old enough to know what's between you and him."

Everyone on the island had heard of Jack's last fight with Malcolm, outside the schoolhouse. That time Jack didn't get up, and the encircling crowd saw that never again would he be a match for Malcolm. Standing over Jack, his back to the sun, even Malcolm seemed surprised.

What Jack wanted now was to escape the shadow, to command his own boat, to be a link in the great chain that held history in thrall.

"I have seen your story a hundred times before. I have heard it told in far places, in the glottal tongue of pygmies and the nasal pout of viceroys. With and without vowels, in words you could not sound—"

"And now it's story time."

"No, Jackie," Chief laughed, "I haven't got any stories today. Try me tomorrow." He put up the guitar.

Jack finally raised his eyes. "Don't stop playing. Not yet."

Chief went back to it, plucking the strings with his coffee-colored fingers, closing his eyes to hear the music better.

"I'm glad you like it, Jackie. Music has charms, they tell me."

Jack finished whipping the ends and just listened to the music, something he rarely did, but Chief's playing was hypnotic, his fingers spiderlike, weaving their intricate tunes. His hands were smallish and articulate, what the islanders called talking hands. He could turn a card or chord a guitar like no man.

"These are strange times," Chief said. "You can hear it on the night wind, in the way the cows talk to one another at the milking. Malcolm will need your strength."

Jack understood weakness, but he had no use for it, especially in himself. Somehow, he could never quite shake the conviction that it was his own fault for not growing as big as Malcolm. As a very little boy, he had wanted nothing so much as to be just like Malcolm. As a man, he had not changed so very much.

"You just keep playing," Jack said.

2

CHIEF LORD'S HERITAGE was almost as much a mystery as his standing with the Life-Saving Service. As late as the War of the Rebellion, the keeper of the Hatteras Light had been dismissed for employing Negro assistants—slaves—whom he could trust to maintain the station while he went about the loftier duties of lighting the lamp each night and keeping the log.

But Chief Lord's parents had not been slaves, that much was certain. He hailed from San Salvador. His accent was refined, his wit celebrated, his stories full of bawdy, outrageous lies that even Patch Patchett recognized as such but never objected to.

He told a yarn, for example, of his mother the queen and her timely exile under guard of scarlet-suited soldiers to a mountain retreat, where the lizards grew as big as dogs and tiny men roasted and ate one another when game was scarce. He boasted of sailing swift, rake-masted schooners through American blockades to Cuba and the Philippines, delivering whiskey, guns, and women; of whoring on remote Alaskan islands with white women who cursed in Russian; of making and squandering several fortunes in opium, gambling, and ivory.

Once, on a wager, he showed the men on station how to fight with a sword, what he called fencing. Only he didn't call it a sword, but an *épée*. His legs bowed as if spring-loaded, his arms whipped like willow wands, his mouth maintained a wide showman's smile as he dodged and ducked, parried and thrust, shaved candlesticks and parted lines.

He claimed familiarity with the language of animals, and it was true that dogs and cats, horses and goats were always showing up in his vicinity, making bold, uncharacteristic noises. His skin was so black he claimed to have been reared in hell, where he was done to a turn before being loosed full-grown upon a world of pirates, smugglers, and soldiers of fortune. He had been all of those and more, a man of many rough lives.

Yet he could tell the age of cognac by its bouquet, the quality of a cigar by the rustling sound it made rolling between thumb and forefinger. His waist was narrow, his shoulders broad but not heavy, his face lean and handsome and beardless, though on his upper lip he wore the fashionable, thin moustache of a gentleman. His wife was a mulatto, though it was rumored she was not his wife at all but a captive taken in a raid on another shore. Either identity suited the islanders. She rarely spoke and almost never accompanied him in public. She kept his house on the Sound side, away from neighbors.

Malcolm found him reliable and smart, tempered by a kind of racially-honed tact that kept him from seeming arrogant, most of the time. Malcolm, if he could have gotten away with it, would have elevated Chief Lord to First Assistant, but he knew in a dull way that it was possible the Bureau of Lighthouses and the Life-Saving Service didn't even know Chief was a Negro, and to call attention to his service might bring a supervisor from Portsmouth and dismissal for them both. It was possible.

Anyhow, Chief Lord lived in comparative comfort. Some said he was a bootlegger, others claimed he had cached a treasure of jewels and gold notes in that private house of his, still others that he had independent means available to him in the form of monthly bank draughts—blackmail? ransom? inheritance? It was well known that his woman made regular sorties into Hyde County on his business.

He was a man, at any rate, who had made some kind of fortune from his adventures, and who traded on that fortune for a modest house on a quiet island and the company of men like Malcolm Royal.

3

THEY SURFACED with the lightship silhouetted between them and the island. Max Wien guessed the lightship was not armed. The big light on the beach swiveled like a searchlight, but it was too far off to discover the submarine. With a loudhailer, the captain raised the watch of the lightship. He handed it to Max.

"You have three minutes to abandon ship," he shouted. His English, though limited, was flawless, and he had practiced that line. It was one advantage of the travel he had done before the war, when he had studied briefly at Oxford and met a girl and learned to drink buckets of ale without losing his composure. "Three minutes," he shouted again. The bosun mimicked him in Morse with the signal lamp, just to make sure there was no misunderstanding.

He watched the lightship's crew scramble into a boat and lower in a hurry, then make for shore, one of them shaking his fist. That would be the captain, Max thought. Max's part in this was over.

"We will not use a torpedo," Stracken said with some pride, it seemed to Max. He winced as the deck gun boomed sharply. The radio mast on the lightship popped and fell, and the light quivered on its tree but did not extinguish. The next round went into the bridge, but there was no fire. Max thought the lightship crew were still awfully close to be shooting like this.

The captain suddenly ordered, "Cease firing." They had other prey. The wireless operator had picked up a schooner beating away fast to the west. Stracken chased her for half an hour on the surface but couldn't get within sight of her. "She must be using her engines to help her make wind," the captain said. "That's what I would do. Let this be a lesson to you, Max: finish what you start." They headed back to finish the lightship.

A dozen men were halfway to shore in their lifeboat when U-55 returned for the kill.

Bergen put two more rounds into her and she exploded and heeled over on her beam ends. The thick mast that held the light pendulated in a slow arc until it slapped into the water. Max imagined it hissed as it went out under the dark waves.

Captain Stracken looked well pleased. The small boat bearing the ousted lightship crew was all but invisible now. The *Diamond Shoals* stayed afloat momentarily, then was gone. Max stood at the rail and stared, feeling his stomach turn over. He couldn't help but think there was something dreadfully wrong about putting out even a tenuous light on such a treacherous shore.

The captain said in German: "We have blinded the cyclops, now we hide with the goats." They went to ground in the Wimble Shoals, on the map the northern facet of the diamond.

4

DOROTHY DANT WAITED at Oman's Dock with Rufus.

"Maybe they're onto a good school," Oman said, bringing out

tea. "Maybe they're onto a really big run. God knows, their luck hasn't been much lately. Could be it's changing. It's about time."

"Could be," she agreed. That's the way it would go sometimes, if her father didn't want to lose the fish. He would stay out all night and through the next day, all week sometimes, and run the Inlet with the old fat-waisted fisher ballasted with blues and mackerel.

But he would not miss her birthday, he had promised. "Not if we net the whale that ate Jonah," he had said.

Oman had known Dorothy since she was a baby, had known her father all his life, and he had been her uncle Dennis Dant's best friend. "Don't fret, girl," he said. "Your dad's a man that don't need looking after."

But the other boats were already in, all the ones that were coming in. She hailed some of the fishermen, but nobody had seen her father's boat all day. One of them thought he had headed north, where the trouble was. The others had all shied away south, to the Ocracoke banks.

Oman followed her to the end of the dock. "He can take care of himself, girl, he always has," he said with a hand on her shoulder. She nodded, remembering her Uncle Dennis. He could handle himself, too. He always had.

5

Alvin Dant saw the flash far to the east of where his boat rode heavily on the swells, stalled. Just at the moment, he could have used spars and a sail. Brian was working on it now, but he held out little hope. It sounded to him like something was really wrong this time, like a piston had snapped or the block had cracked. He was not an optimist.

He knew what the flash was and he could guess what it meant. He had seen a boat explode once from an unvented bilge. And he expected when he looked back that way after the flash the lightship would be gone, and it was.

"Brian," he said, reaching the rifle out of its case. "Come here, we have to get ready."

6

"HERE COMES A LITTLE BOY in a sailor suit," Cy Magillicutty said, and they all got a good laugh out of that. Lieutenant Halstead entered Cape Hatteras Station and introduced himself. He had run his cigar boat into the fishing pier above the Light and left his crew on board.

"I've come to assume command," he told them.

"We're surfmen," Jack Royal said. "We don't need no fancy pants telling us where to hang our oars."

Halstead reddened but recovered himself. "You're Coast Guard, and in time of war the Coast Guard answers to the Navy, and that's me. We are at war, gentlemen. You don't have to like it."

"Where's the news in that," Malcolm said. Still, he had a sinking feeling this Halstead was right. "Plan One, Acknowledge"—the prearranged signal to establish a chain of command—had been broadcast to all the life-saving stations in April a year ago, but it had not meant anything until now.

"Which one of you is John Royal?"

"It's Jack around here." He stepped forward.

"All right, Jack it is. Congratulations. You're going to be my second officer. I'll need a man who knows this coast."

Jack looked at Malcolm. "I can't leave the station."

"Yes, you can," Malcolm said. He knew orders when he heard them.

Chief Lord was so quiet he seemed to be saying something.

Jack set his shoulders and forced himself to take three deep breaths. At the third breath they all heard it except Halstead, booming out faintly above the sound of the breakers: cannon fire.

They rushed to the crest of the dunes, from where the second boom and the muzzle flash were unmistakable even to Halstead.

"Off by the lightship," Malcolm said.

"I'll fetch Homer," Chief said quietly. The other men were already beating it back to the boathouse for gear.

"Wait a minute—I didn't tell you to go out," Halstead said to Malcolm.

"We have to go out, whether you say so or not." Malcolm strode back to the boathouse so fast that Halstead ran to keep up. He advanced on the crew as they trundled out the boat and slipped in the hitch. "Jack Royal!" he shouted, and Jack, after a moment of wondering whether to hit him, rubbed his hands together as if to warm them, and followed him. Keith, who had seen the whole thing, marveled that Halstead looked no older than the boys he knew at school. Malcolm's crew heaved the boat into the foam, and Malcolm wondered how they would ever be able to rely on a man who couldn't even hear cannon fire above the sound of the sea.

7

CAPTAIN WALTER BARNETT, late master of the lightship *Diamond Shoals*, brought his crew safely over the combers and then capsized them at the foot of the lighthouse, hard by the jetty. Losing the lightship left a bilious taste in his mouth, and when the lifeboat came for him he ignored it and rode his oar in. He had to: he didn't know how to swim.

8

HAM FETTERMAN CLOSED his eyes and ran his hands over what he had created so far. Rough. He fished a piece of emery paper from his toolbox. He did not often use emery paper, but this one was just too rough, and he had a feeling this hull should be smooth and cold as stone.

The hull shaped under his hand, and his fingers resisted the bulge of the tower. He set it on the windowsill and sat down again in his straight-backed spool chair. From his flannel shirt pocket he drew a burl pipe. This one had lasted years and had a thick cake that made for a cool, sweet smoke. He regarded the hull, such as it was. He stared at it and puffed, his eyes a fury of concentration, his old body rigid. He stared, trying to imagine it metal, not the soft island pine it really was. He tried to imagine it hollow, full of men, tried to imagine himself inside, and could not. It was just too big a leap. He could go no further till he did that.

To Littlejohn's surprise, Ham rose from the chair and left without a word, still smoking, the burl pipe clamped between his few good teeth. Littlejohn stood at the store window and watched Ham Fetterman cross the road and wander through the gap in the dunes toward the beach, where the old man had not walked in years.

9

VIRGINIA AND MARY ROYAL JOINED Dorothy at her house on the Hatteras Road. Virginia's seven-year-old boy Kevin was there, along with Ham Fetterman, the Littlejohns, and old Seamus Royal. The young men were missing.

Seamus had left his Krag wrapped in oilskin outside, so as not to alarm the ladies. The world was going crazy—he had seen it happen before. Like when the Yankees came and picked the island clean of food back in '62.

But this was worse, because there was no way of telling just what the threat was or how long it would last. When General Burnside's army of twenty thousand had blundered ashore at the Bight of Hatteras and marched up and down the length of the island and the Union fleet had shelled the unimposing sand forts on the Inlet, you could see what you were up against. Seamus had been just a boy then, but he remembered those long columns of bullying, ravenous soldiers, and how his cousins had ferried him across the Sound in a bugeye in the dead of night to wait out the war in the Hyde County tidewater. That was the only time Seamus had left the island. When he returned, he saw how the Yankees had stripped it like ants: the freshwater cisterns were dry, and homes and buildings had been demolished for wood to fuel the Yankee steamer fleet.

Fetterman, older by far, remembered the face of the only islander the Yankees had managed to kill with all their shelling and charging: a slow-witted deaf boy, shot in the back for failing to answer a sentry's challenge.

And now the government that had invaded them without cause or provocation during that old war had sent a puffed-up snippet in a toy boat. A Yankee. And once the Government came in, it generally took a lot of getting rid of.

At first there wasn't much talk. They ate from baskets the Royal wives had brought: chicken, pork, fresh-baked goods, cider and beer. Fetterman kept Rufus in scraps.

"There's a lot of fish out there," Littlejohn ventured.

"It's the right time of year, all right," Fetterman said. "It surely is the right time of year. The blues will be running any day now. Oman will make a bundle out of salt fish, what with the war on."

Kevin brooded through supper and then said: "I'd like to blow that Heinie submarine out of the water, kaboom!" And Dorothy finally cried, as she had been wanting to do ever since coming back from Oman's. She knew her father's luck as well as anyone.

"He probably broke a net or something," Mary said. "You mustn't let your imagination carry you away."

Virginia poured tea. She thought it bad luck even to talk about it while the man was at sea, worse luck when their own men were going out so much. Better leave it to Providence and hope for the best.

"I know how to stop it," Fetterman said. The conviction had been growing in him since this afternoon when he'd walked the beach.

"Don't you dare say it," Littlejohn warned. "Not yet." Littlejohn limped over to Fetterman to back up his words with proximity. In

'89 Littlejohn had come ashore to Hatteras from the shipwrecked East India schooner *John Shay*. He had jumped from the aft rail onto the oaken bottom of a lifeboat which capsized anyway, thirty feet of free fall, and broke his leg for good.

"Stand fast, Littlejohn," Fetterman said. "I've lived through the War of the Rebellion and the Spanish War and the assassination of three presidents and the return of Halley's Comet. I guess I can live through this."

Mary wanted to give Dorothy a diversion from this kind of talk. She knew about the sewing machine Alvin had bought for Dorothy, since Mary had helped pick it out of the catalogue, and now she brought it out of its hiding place in the closet. But the unveiling of it only brought on fresh tears from Dorothy, and pretty soon Mary and Virginia were sobbing right along with her. Mrs. Littlejohn did not cry, but her eyes were bright with remembered grief.

Littlejohn and Fetterman escaped to the porch, arm in arm, where they smoked and talked of old wars.

10

MINUTES AFTER THE SURFBOAT had gone out, Lieutenant Halstead had his cigar boat under way with Jack Royal beside him at the helm.

"We're going after him in this?" Jack was incredulous. The *Sealion* had none of the beamy balance of a surfboat—she was too long and narrow to be stable in rough water. Jack laced on a cork lifevest, knowing that if they ran into weather this boat would go down in one quick swamping.

"Why don't you call in a cutter? You don't even have depth bombs. Aren't you supposed to have depth bombs to chase a submarine?"

"There are no cutters," Halstead said. "Use your head. If we had cutters, do you think I'd be here? I'd still be in Beaufort listening to the radio." And in the same breath: "Stand by torpedoes, stand by guns." They ran without lights and made for the place the lightship was supposed to be, even though they already knew she wasn't there. Halstead concentrated on what he would do in the next few minutes if they overtook the U-boat, and summoned all the confidence of his training. He assumed a martial bearing and offhandedly gave the helm over to Mr. Cross. He must make this all seem very routine to the men, else their fear get the best of them. Everything seemed very loud to Halstead just now. He tried to think about strategy, the tricks of maneuver, and drew a blank.

"You're out of your goddamned mind," Jack said.

"Four thousand yards and closing, Mister Halstead."

"Let's hope the rotten thing is gone when we get there," Jack said. "Otherwise we're cooked."

"Don't let's get squeamish," Halstead said above the noise of the engines, wondering why. He had never talked that way before, though he had heard somebody say exactly that in a London pub he'd visited once on a school trip. A man with no hands had bellied up to the bar and demanded a drink. At sight of his uncovered stumps, the barman, new on the job, had blanched. The man had smiled wickedly and said, "Lend a hand, then. Don't let's get squeamish," and the pub had erupted in hoots and laughter. A favorite joke among the regulars.

Jack ignored Halstead. If he ever really got started on this boy, he knew, he'd finish in a Portsmouth brig for good.

Halstead glassed the sea with binoculars, scared to death he would spot something that required action. He saw only a lifeboat with a dozen men in it making for shore off the Light, too far away to help. He watched the flimsy boat ride a high wave and then broach to and dump its occupants into the surf near the jetty. His instinct was to avert his eyes, but he watched anyway, sure that in the next instant he'd see the men dashed to pulp against the rocks. But Malcolm's surfboat played the jetty and plucked them out one by one, and the last rode an oar onto the beach. Halstead thought it a remarkable piece of seamanship.

"We missed him, Captain," Jack said.

"Not Captain, just plain Mister." At Halstead's order, Cross throttled back, and the roar of the engines quieted a bit.

"We still missed him."

"We'll get him next time he shows his face."

"He's probably watching us right now."

Halstead grinned stupidly, for something had just occurred to him. "He'll have to come up to get us, Mister Royal. We draw too shallow to take a torpedo."

Jack realized he was right, the Heinie would have to come up to fight, and it irked him that Halstead had figured it out first.

"Let's head in, Horatio. We're not doing any good out here—"

Halstead turned on him in a fury. "Stop that! Just stop that! Do you hear, Mister Royal? You will please observe correct military protocol aboard my vessel, is that clear?"

Jack Royal nodded, his face crimson to the neck. The crew were all watching, and he knew this was some kind of test for Halstead. Men like Halstead, he believed, were the reason the chain of history was straining to come undone all over the world. He read the papers enough to know that. But he said, "Yes sir." And bit his lip to keep from saying more.

By the time Halstead put in at the fishing pier again, it had begun to drizzle. Tomorrow he would start the men building a slip for the boat over by Buxton Woods, nearer the Light.

Jack listened to the snap of whitecaps and heard a storm gathering power in the south, down in Bermuda maybe.

This was not going to be as easy as Halstead had hoped. His uniform was drenched by the time he got to his tent, and he felt miserable. His mission here had gotten off to a bad start, the one thing he had promised himself he would prevent at all costs. He wanted to do this right, he believed in that. Writing reports by lantern light, he suddenly stopped, realizing his silhouette, feeling like a target.

11

MALCOLM HAD to put something in the log. Sometimes he figured the worst part of this whole submarine menace was the amount of writing it was causing him. He splayed his fingers as if stretching on gloves and gingerly took up his pen: *Lightship* Diamond Shoals *lost to Gmn. gunfire today. Crew got off in lifeboat with no loss of life & we put to sea in time to assist in landing them. Our Light still burns.*

12

MARY AND VIRGINIA ROYAL STAYED the night with Dorothy Dant. They did not expect their men home tonight anyway.

CHAPTER 4

1

AT LITTLEJOHN'S STORE Patch Patchett pilfered a bottle of beer. "Put it on my tab," he said.

"The only tab you got is in your head," Littlejohn said. Cy Magillicutty and Chief Lord laughed. Chief's laughter was rolling, melodious, thorough. The beer was not for sale anyway. This was a dry county, and Littlejohn's supply was bootleg that Patchy brought across from Hyde County on his erratic trips.

Cy and Chief were in for tobacco, tea, and sundries for the station.

"Peter and Pat Patchett," Cy said, including Patchy's wife.

"Sounds like a little outboard that's missing on one cylinder, don't it?"

They laughed some more and checked off provisions on the counter.

"How's that old bugeye coming along?" Chief Lord asked him. "Maybe you'll be needing it some of these days."

"I ain't needing it yet."

"You never know," Cy said. "We had ourselves a lightship until about twenty-four hours ago. You just never know."

Patchy drank and swiped a sleeve across his mouth. "That lumber were mine. The Navy had no right to it, none at all."

"It belonged to the Government," Littlejohn said.

"Like hell."

"And the Government just took it back, that's all."

"It was salvage. We got laws in this state."

"It weren't ordinary salvage," Cy said. "Don't be acting like it was."

"All the same, it were mine. Didn't I find it? Didn't I guard it? Didn't I report it? Didn't I spend half a damn day hauling and stacking it? And for what? Government. Huh."

Chief Lord let loose with a raucous laugh. "Guarding it from whom, Patchy? It's too enormous to carry off without a dray team and six or eight hired hands."

Patchy swigged his beer, morose. He didn't mind this, though. It gave him something to talk about. People were listening to him now. He had spotted the U-boat, sent out the alarm about the freighter, found the lumber. He swigged his beer, feeling pretty good about himself. He wasn't a bad sort. He was capable of things. He would have to get that across to his wife somehow.

Anyway, he had salted away enough stray planks to put a new wing on his house, if he felt like it. Or get Fetterman to help him build a new boat, something real and worthwhile for a change instead of another toy for Littlejohn's shelf. He might just hold on to that lumber awhile, though. Every piece was stamped U.S. Government, like somebody would steal it. That little nonesuch Halstead would probably want every stick of it back, if he knew, never mind that he couldn't use all the lumber he already had. It was piled up around his little encampment in ramparts.

Cyrus and Chief lingered awhile to play checkers, and Patchy spent the morning watching them play, his fingers twitching with their moves, his brain one step behind their decisions.

At eleven, Seamus Royal came in carrying his rifle and the game stopped. There were half a dozen men around.

"And what's all this? Don't be bringing that howitzer in here, Seamus," Littlejohn said.

Seamus ignored him, as was his wont. He was seventy years old and could do as he damn well pleased. "I'll just be needing some things," he said.

But that wasn't why he had come, and Littlejohn knew it. He was after news.

Fetterman had been lounging against the counter, keeping track of the checker game. Now he resumed his place in his carving chair, a tall, straight-backed spool chair of scarred oak. He had spent years in that chair, and no one else ever sat in it, whether Fetterman was present or not. Sometimes he tested his knives on the wood of the chair, leaving scars that would darken like old wounds. The arms were rubbed shiny from his sleeves. The floor at his feet was stippled with match burns and tobacco stains.

"Alvin Dant is two days gone," Patchett said. "Doesn't that bother anybody? Poor Dorothy—"

"You've got God's own eyes, but your brain is a potato," Fetterman said. Dorothy Dant had just come in, Rufus at her heels.

Fetterman settled deeper into his throne. Patchy produced an old filthy pipe with a cracked bowl and fussed with it.

Dorothy didn't appear to want anything special. She came in looking self-conscious and pretended to inspect some shirts.

Leaning on his cane, Littlejohn went over to her. "I have some tea brewing in the back, if you're interested."

"Yes. I could use a cup of tea."

"Pick out a breakfast roll to go with it, Dot."

MacSween arrived to fetch Chief and Cyrus. The place was filling up, as for a meeting. Outside were half a dozen horses and democrat wagons. Rufus took up his post by the door to look after them.

Dorothy sipped the yeopon tea and took delicate bites from the roll. Nobody spoke. Littlejohn drank coffee. MacSween stared at Seamus's rifle, but did not touch it. Patchett smoked, and his pipe kept going out. Cy Magillicutty and Chief Lord leaned on the counter. Mrs. Littlejohn appeared like a ghost and started to say something, then thought the better of it. Whatever she left unsaid hung in the air along with the recurrent snap of Patchett's matches.

Finally Dorothy said, almost whispering, "Mister Littlejohn, is there anything you can do?"

And yes, they all had their ideas about that.

2

MARY ROYAL HAD long ago dreamed of being an artist.

As a girl, she discovered watercolors and, though she could hardly afford the materials, set about learning how to paint. She built an easel from scrapwood and collected all sorts of paper. She never painted seascapes, and that's how Keith Royal knew she was an artist. Away at college he had remembered her often and, to his own shame, pitied her for marrying his brother. It seemed to him a fatal compromise.

Malcolm was over at the station now, and Mary said, "Virginia and Kevin will be along soon."

Keith was trying out one of Malcolm's well-smoked pipes. He had tried a pipe at college, but hadn't had the patience for it. Here there seemed to be more time for such things.

He couldn't keep it lit, though, and opted for a cigarette.

Mary was drinking tea, feeling guilty about having done nothing all day but laze about. She and Malcolm did not keep cows or goats or pigs, as many of the islanders did, nor did she have a garden to tend. His double duty as Keeper and surfman gave them a comfortable living. Even with a crisis on, she was at a loss as to what to do.

Keith was pacing. "Malcolm wants me to join up. Jack, too, I guess. Now they're shorthanded."

"Never mind what they want. We have enough professional saviors in the family already, don't you think?"

"I wish Dad would lose that damn gun."

"That's two of us. Sorry you came back?"

Keith shrugged. Maybe the reason he had come back had nothing to do with Mary or Malcolm or any of them. In the city, at college, he had grown tired of debating, tired of issues. There were no good answers now, not even history offered any good answers. Men all over the world were shrugging off a thousand years of civilization and culture. The killing had become so much its own excuse it was scarcely remarkable anymore.

Dozens of his college chums had enlisted in the first flush of patriotism after the declaration of war, and plenty of them would never be heard from again.

He had hoped that on this island, of all places, he would be free of decision. He would abdicate the responsibility he had already felt for being a student of history.

Mary said, "They'll come back, won't they? Uncle Alvin and Brian?"

"There's no reason to suppose they won't. It's just . . ."

"What?"

"I don't know exactly."

Mary looked at his pale, boyish face with its downy moustache, so unlike Malcolm's sunburned, bearded, rugged face. Without meaning to, she took his hand in her own and petted it.

3

DOROTHY DANT WENT to the Navy.

"I have my orders," Lieutenant Halstead said. "We are after a submarine. Rescuing people doesn't enter into it." Halstead stood on the dune as on the poop deck of a sailing ship, sidearm at his belt, directing his men as they worked. They were building a slip for the boat in the bight, in the back eddies from the offshore meeting of the Gulf Stream and the Labrador Current. And they were close to the Light now, as well. This was much better than the fishing pier, with the advantage of protection from the waves if not from weather.

"You must try to understand, Captain."

"Please, I'm only a lieutenant, ma'am."

"My father's been out there three days. Someone has to go out after him."

"Fishermen have been lost before. They always find their way home."

Dorothy was impatient, but she knew this boy was lost on the island. If she could offer friendship, he might come around.

"Look, you have to go out on patrol. All I'm saying is to keep an eye out for them. What would it hurt?"

The word hit Halstead square in the eye. Of course they would have to patrol. There was no real precedent for this sort of detail, but it made sense to be out on the water once in a while. They couldn't just wait around for the German to show his face.

Halstead looked at Dorothy Dant for a moment, trying to figure out how old she was, then decided it didn't matter how old she was. She was in trouble, and he could help.

"I'll think it over," he said. "But I'll need some information about the boat, his course, you know, that stuff. Would you have supper with me later and sort of brief me?"

Lieutenant Halstead was a man who could find her father and brother. Of course she would. "I'm not in the habit of dining in a tent, Lieutenant. I suggest you meet me at my home. It's not far."

Later, while Dorothy waited for Halstead, Rufus sat inside the screen door, raising his muzzle to sniff the air. From time to time he whined, but she didn't hear him above the rattle of the sewing machine.

4

THEY SURFACED before sundown, which Max Wien thought fairly risky. But he was glad for the air. He accompanied the captain to the tower, and Bergen scurried out to his place behind the deck gun.

It was a glorious time of day. Orange clouds swept in over the sea. The sky was all movement and deep color, churning toward darkness.

Max tried to remember what Germany was like. He had been wondering all day whether Papenburg had been invaded. Probably it had been. They had had no news for weeks now, and that was bad.

He could imagine the mud and wreckage of the war in the cobbled streets of his hometown. Some last-ditch street-fighting, men dodging about in the rubble of houses broken by artillery, bodies here and there—old men and boys, the last ones left—and dead horses still hitched in teams to their wagons. The winding street up the arbored hill where his father's house had stood now barricaded by the foreign army, the birches stripped and splintered by shellfire.

He didn't know if any of that were true, but it felt like it.

They were close to the island and running parallel to shore. There was the lighthouse, the life-saving station, cottages, a village of sorts. Poor, Max thought, not much at all. They were near enough to see the white horse stabled in a corral adjoining the boathouse. Max couldn't imagine what a horse was doing there. He marveled as the beast reared up on two legs and pawed the air.

Captain Stracken spotted the telephone lines almost at once on this pass. He had assumed that a place this remote would be without communication. He cursed and stared through the glasses.

Bergen fired on command, and a few seconds later a pole cracked in half, dragging down tangled lines. A mast shot. Below, the crew heard the news and cheered. Bergen fired three times more, one shot landing dangerously close to the life-saving station. God help us if we hit that, Max thought. He was not a faithful Catholic, but he crossed himself anyway.

Stracken and the first officer counted it a successful action. They cruised the surface and fired at telephone lines as far south as they dared to go. Then they turned north to the hunting.

5

ALVIN DANT KNEW they must be very far out by now. The Gulf Stream had pushed him north into the Labrador Current, and that had started him east, toward Europe. It was an awesome thought, to cross the ocean on a fishing boat.

At least the weather was fair, and they had plenty of provisions, barring accident.

The two of them had the engine stripped. It lay in disorder about the deck. Alvin's premonition about his luck had proved accurate: the engine had thrown a piston and cracked the head. The boat was too large to row, and they had no means of raising a sail. Alvin had checked the engine only yesterday, up to his elbows in grease.

"We had better stow this and secure for weather," he told his son. Fear balled in his stomach. But Brian seemed calm, even complacent, bored with the adventure.

Brian, a naturally hard worker, methodically cleared the deck of engine parts and stowed them below. He covered the engine bay and made an inspection of the deck before joining his father in the wheelhouse.

"I wish we could be fishing, Dad."

"That's two of us." It was hard to ignore the weapons so close at hand.

"Dad—did you ever know a German?"

"Well, there's a family lives on Ocracoke that's real German, Schaeffer. Oysterman and his wife. And then there's Fetterman and his people. But they're not real German, not that way. They're mixed up with everybody else by now. Why?"

Brian stood at the wheel as if steering, though they were at the mercy of currents and wind just now. "Just wondering, that's all. This U-boat. I was just wondering what kind of people could do that."

Alvin shook his head and put a hand on his son's shoulder. "Beats me, boy. God knows who they are. God knows who any of us are . . ." He regretted now his bravado in heading north when common sense and safety dictated the opposite course. He should have considered the boy. He realized all at once that he had never considered the boy, and turned away in shame.

"You worry so much," Brian said. "You act like we'll never make it home."

"And you? You don't worry?"

Brian shook his head slowly. "Why should I? You've always brought us home before."

Alvin Dant reached for the binoculars. He rubbed his eyes, and considered what a troublesome thing is faith.

6

WHEN THE FIRST SHELL SNAPPED the telephone pole, Malcolm and Chief Lord bounded to the door of the station almost in stride. Cy Magillicutty tried the phone and found it dead. The rest of them rushed to the windows or followed Malcolm.

Malcolm had a wild moment of panic when he ran around to the side of the station and looked toward his house, fearful for Mary. He wanted to run to her, and he took two strides in that direction as other shells fell, and then reined himself in. He had to stay at the station. He was Keeper. He cast an anxious eye toward the striped tower. He stood and watched the shells land, until the one that came near the station knocked him down. And except for Jack, he had never been knocked down by anything or anyone in his life.

Homer was plunging and rearing in the corral. Chief Lord handled him, calmed him when at last the shelling stopped.

Malcolm's ears rang in the abrupt silence. He stood uncertainly for a long, swimmy moment until his head cleared. Then he saw it: the flat, gray hull cutting the water offshore, barely visible between horizon and sea. It was smaller than he had imagined. He could make out three men on the tower and two more standing by the forward cannon. He had never seen anything like it. He wondered: how did Fetterman know? He ran inside for his glass and then stood in front of the open doors of the boathouse, staring after the U-boat.

They were two officers, by their hats, smallish men. And beside them an even slighter figure, blond, hatless, blue shirtsleeves rolled to the elbows.

"Can you see them?" Chief Lord asked. "Can you see the Hun devils?"

Malcolm shook his head. "He's only a boy," he said, and stared through the glass until the U-boat was well gone down the coast. He watched it fire again, the flash coming long before the crack of the gun, like lightning.

INSIDE THE STATIONHOUSE, Malcolm Royal lowered his body into a hard-backed chair and clasped his hands on the table in a two-handed fist. Chief Lord leaned against the wall nearby. MacSween came over. Cy Magillicutty sat down opposite Malcolm, and the rest followed suit, finding places around the table.

"This is getting serious," Cyrus said. "How much longer can we let this go on?"

There was a general murmuring.

"How long will the telephone be down?" MacSween wanted to know.

"Count on a couple of days anyway," Malcolm said. "Never mind. We'll use runners and signal lamps, the way our grandfathers did."

The men nodded and mumbled agreement, their collective voice steady as surf.

Toby Bannister, whose great-grandfather had been shipwrecked on the island and whose people now imported lumber, looked thoughtful. "You should know, Malcolm, there's an oiler headed our way. My brother's on it."

"When?"

"Tonight, tomorrow. Three days, maybe. You know how they are, what with the war on. You can't count on schedules. He always sends word, though. Thinks it's good luck for me to wave to him off the Light, no matter how far out he is."

"Then we'll be going out before long, I'm afraid. Chief—"

"Yo."

"Send a runner down to the Inlet. Have them pass it on."

"How about north?"

"Cyrus?"

"Yo."

"Waste no time."

"I'll be pulling my oar when the time comes."

"I know."

The two men left on their errands, but the others stayed in place. It was an unofficial meeting. They wanted Malcolm to tell them what would happen.

"I can't tell you what it's going to be, boys," he said. "But I can tell you we'll go out as often as we have to, U-boat or no. Anybody who feels he can't take that kind of risk . . ."

He had said all he was going to. There was bad weather reported coming up from the Keys, and a warship patrolling their waters.

"I was thinking," MacSween said. "Suppose it's more than one. Suppose there's a whole wolfpack—I've read about them. Maybe there's going to be an invasion—"

"That's enough," Malcolm said. "Visit your families during the days. Nights, I want every hand on station."

Later, he faced the austerity of the logbook's blank, smooth pages. He chewed on the end of his pen awhile, got up twice, finally sat himself down with the same effort of will it had required to keep the logbook day after day, year after year. After the date and time, he wrote: *Shelled today by Gmn. U-boat. Same sunk lightship, sure. All overnight liberty cancelled for duration of threat.*

And signed it, as always, stared at his own signature wonderingly, aware of the power and the magic: Malcolm Royal, Keeper.

God willing, he would keep them.

7

MARY ROYAL FOUND Keith's arms as soon as the first shell burst. Aware of how ridiculous it seemed, Keith sat down hard in a stuffed chair with Mary on his lap, shielding her with his arms, stroking her head and pushing it into his chest. Without her he would have panicked. Through the curtained window he could see the shape of his brother's station, shouting distance away, and at that moment he shut his eyes and kissed Mary's hair in a way he had dreamed of doing.

He held her, and the noise of the shells seemed to quiet. The concussions no longer felt as if they were in his own chest. He did not know if she even felt his kisses, but they sat together for a long time after the shelling had stopped.

CHAPTER 5

1

Lieutenant Halstead stood hesitating on Dorothy Dant's doorstep when the shelling started. It was not close enough to be dangerous, but he recognized a moment of destiny when it showed itself.

He pushed her inside and steadied himself on the doorjamb. "We're under attack. I've got to get the boat out."

Before Dorothy could answer, he was sprinting up the road toward the slip. He had picked a hell of a time to go courting, and he cursed himself as his arms pumped and his feet kicked high in his spring. It took four minutes to cover the distance to the cut in the dunes, another minute to reach his crew. They were good boys, already prepared to get under way.

He took his helmet from Cross. "Shove off, Mister Cross."

"Aye, aye, sir."

He relayed the order. The gunners shucked the rainproof sleeves off their gun barrels. The engineer revved the engines and they started headlong into their first wartime engagement. Halstead, who had not seen the inside of a church since his days at Sacred Heart High School in Philadelphia, made the sign of the cross.

It was no trick to find the U-boat. She was knifing along at flank speed, but the motor torpedo boat was faster in the short sprint. All Halstead had to do was steer toward the sound of the cannon. He ordered the guns loaded and was struck by how calm and authoritative his voice sounded. He stood beside Cross at the wheel in a manner he hoped was heroic.

"Is there a reason you're not zigzagging?" Jack Royal shouted at him. "He's had all day to find the range."

Royal was right, he thought. He must not be too daring his first time out. "Left fifteen degrees, Mister Cross. We'll come in from the sea. He won't be looking for us that way."

The cigar boat answered the wheel like a racing plane. The sheer speed of the thing unnerved him a little. He had seen plenty of ones like it capsized during training. It was not a forgiving boat. He was more at home on a sailboat. Before the war, he used to take his father's sloop out on the Delaware Bay. That was a boat that could take the weather. Royal was right about that, too: if *Sealion* ran into weather, they'd have all they could handle and more.

Jack Royal said: "You're using your head now, Halstead. I mean, Lieutenant. Can these guys shoot?"

Halstead glanced back at the machine gunner and then forward to the cannoneer. He honestly didn't know how they would do. They were steady shots when it came to raking target barges, but target barges didn't fire back. They might go to pieces, all of them.

"They'll be all right, Mister Royal."

"Just wondering."

"What can you tell me about these waters?"

"We're close in to the shoals now, but it won't matter. You draw so shallow. If he comes in, this Heinie will have more trouble than you. He can't go under very deep here. If he does, I'd throw your torpedoes at him."

"That's unorthodox."

Jack Royal sighed. He was trying to encourage this upstart, give him sensible advice. God knows, someone better. Jack knew these waters, he knew that was how to do it, common sense told him that much. Any other way would just be a shoot-out. "Have it your own way, Horatio. I'm just saying."

Halstead started to reprimand him, but caught himself. Royal might be right. There was nothing in the articles of engagement about this kind of encounter, so he would just have to chance it. He would loose one, and keep one. That would cover him. That's what he told Royal. The spray was flying but good now, the wind coming head on. He had always imagined it this way: salt spray stinging his cheeks, the rush in his ears from wind and engines, the boat slapping across the gray waves into harm's way, the men at his side trusting their lives to him.

The U-boat had not spotted them yet.

"I would not save anything," Jack Royal said. "I would take my best shot with all my fish and get the hell out. He can't chase you very close in or he'll beach on the shoals and break up with the tide—"

"We'll fire one torpedo, Mister Royal. We can't take unnecessary risks."

"You'll capsize us if you fire only one!"

Halstead gave the order to ready the starboard tube.

He was in an interesting position now, with the U-boat silhouetted between him and the island in the pale gold of a dying sun. He had the bastard broadside, and he raced the throttle and made his run at the enemy at full speed and no turning back. A classic maneuver. Binoculars were of no use now, they were closing too fast. He could read the surprise on their faces.

2

KRAFT, the first mate, spotted the American subchaser and raised the alarm. Captain Stracken swiveled his glasses and his face twitched. The American was crazy, coming at him headlong. He decided there must be another boat, a trap, a setup. Bergen had the forward deck gun on him and was fast finding the range, walking his shots across the water toward his bows. The American was running right into his pattern. Bergen was a scientific gunner, *ein Techniker.*

The aft gunner set up a crossfire.

Max Wien thought they had hit the American amidships, but he couldn't tell, because just at that moment the captain shoved him out of the way toward the hatch and the first rounds from the American speedster whistled close over their heads.

The captain ordered all hands below, and the gunners scrambled down the hatch like foxes going to ground.

"He has fired a torpedo, *Kapitän*," Kraft said.

"Does he have *Wasserbombe*?"

"I don't think so."

The captain gave an order and the helmsman wheeled the rudder to place his vessel head-on with the American. Already they were diving, Max's shipmates vaulting through the companionway like football players and piling in a heap in the forward torpedo room as the nose of the boat settled fast under their ballast. Max Wien listened to the hull for the sound of a propeller and smelled rank humanity all around him. He lay there, he could do nothing else. He wondered if he would hear the explosion. They were running right into the torpedo. Madness, unless it saved them, then it would be genius. The sweat popped out of his pores like beads of oil.

3

JACK ROYAL HAD THE WHEEL. Mister Cross was down, and so was the engineer. There was a hole in the filmsy starboard armor, and the metal was scorched. The mate sat between his feet, rubbing his head from the concussion.

Jack was shaking, but he kept his eye on the U-boat as it began to slip under the waves barely fifty yards ahead.

The machine gunner had not fired yet for fear of hitting their own cockpit, since the action so far had been head-on. But now with one torpedo gone, Jack veered hard left, crossing the U-boat's bow. The machine gunner raked the conning tower just before it disappeared. Jack saw the torpedo had gone wide, and he cursed. There was nothing to do now. If the Hun came back up, he'd have them easy. Darkness was coming on and the seas were building.

He held the wheel against the mate's protests and turned full throttle back toward the Bight of Hatteras. It was all he could do to hold her steady with only one screw turning and a heavy port list, but he wasn't shaking anymore. The machine gun had calmed him.

4

THE MOTORCAR AND TRUCK, bearing the insignia of the United States Navy, debarked the ferry at the head of the island, Oregon Inlet, and proceeded south along the only road worth the name through Chicamacomico and Kinnakeet toward Cape Hatteras. It took them three hours.

An ensign and a chief petty officer rode in the car. They had come all the way from Portsmouth. The truck, manned by two sailors in rumpled work blues, was carrying torpedoes, ammunition, and provisions for Halstead's command. They stopped at Littlejohn's to ask directions to the naval base, and Fetterman watched them with a dull eye.

"Government business," the ensign said curtly. Out the window

Littlejohn saw the others in the truck and shook his head.

"You don't say. I thought there'd be more of you along some of these days," he said. "I had hoped I was mistaken, but I should have known better."

He told them which cut to take in the dunes, but he didn't mention the earlier bombardment, or the fact that Halstead had taken his boat out to engage the enemy, or that Jack Royal was aboard. Nor did he explain why a dozen men and women loitered in the store, waiting for news. He didn't explain any of that to them, because they didn't ask.

Littlejohn decided he wasn't liking the way things were turning out at all.

5

DOROTHY DANT FOUND Keith sitting on the couch with Mary, holding her hand. She thought it odd for a moment, but she had other things on her mind.

"The Navy's gone out," she said. "Tim's taken his boat to get the German."

"*Tim*? Halstead?" Keith stood up. He thought he ought to go over to the station and see about his brother. He felt as guilty as a thief in church, and was convinced it showed on his face. He had the excuse of circumstance, but he didn't want it.

"The shelling was pretty close here, wasn't it," Dorothy said.

"Too close, if you ask me." Mary's voice sounded stiff and unnatural. "Can I get you a cup of tea?"

"Hey, what's going on here?" Dorothy was kidding at first, until neither one of them answered. Then she turned and left. Keith went after her. He shouted to her, but the wind carried off his words. She didn't turn. The breeze had turned into a wind now, and Keith leaned into it, following Dorothy through the dunes onto the beach. They had courted on this beach, had slept together cupped in the folds of the dunes.

He kept her in sight all the way up the beach and finally caught her on the point, where he held to her in the wind, trying to know just what he had done wrong, or what to do next.

6

MALCOLM WATCHED the torpedoboat come over the swells from the south, and from the way she was riding he could tell she was in trouble. The seas had risen to four feet, and the boat was damaged, listing hard to port.

"Chief, it's time," Malcolm said.

Chief Lord put Homer in his traces, and the men marched behind the boatcarriage down the beach toward the slip. In weather the slip was not a good anchorage, but it had one advantage: the currents off the point, where the Labrador met the Gulf Stream, would naturally eddy a small boat inshore.

"He'll bring her in," Cyrus said. "It's a rough landing, but he'll manage."

MacSween wasn't so sure. "He's not had much experience at this sort of thing, has he. You'd think they'd have sent an older hand."

They stood a hundred feet from the slip now watching the slow progress of the little motor torpedoboat. From the trouble the helmsman was having, Malcolm guessed one of the propellers was damaged.

"Jack's with him, ain't he," Chief Lord said.

Malcolm nodded, squinting into the wind, never taking his eyes off the boat. He would have to recognize the exact second when the odds shifted, and get his boat away in short order. His crewmen were filed along both sides of the boatcarriage, ready to launch her and man oars before he could finish giving the command.

"They're coming in," Chief said. "That boy is bringing her in."

Then she was close enough for Malcolm to recognize the helmsman. He nodded. "Good boy, Jack," he said to the wind.

"Good for him," Chief said, laying a hand on Malcolm's shoulder.

"They're going to make it!" Cyrus said. "That pipsqueak is going to bring her home."

Now they were all waving and yelling encouragement as the narrow hull knifed through the first of the big waves breaking over the shoals. The shallower the water, the higher the waves, and the greater the chance of her being caught in the curl instead of being able to simply ride the swell. This was pretty shallow water, Malcolm knew, even with the tide in.

"If she doesn't broach to, she'll make it," Malcolm said. Chief nodded. If she got broadside to a wave, the boat would founder before he could even get his lifeboat down to the waterline.

"She won't," Chief said. "Have a little faith. That's Jack out there."

Sealion crested one last high wave. Both bow and stern were out of the water now, the single prop revving in thin air, the whole boat levered like a seesaw on the peak, and for an instant it looked like Malcolm's worst fears would come true. The boat turned, ever so slightly, in the wind and current, then she slapped the trough hard and righted her course, and glided into the slip like a knife into an oiled sheath.

The slip was a curving finger of the séa some dozen yards across in which the boat could be moored parallel to shore behind a low sandbank that was flat or humped, depending on the day's wind.

Chief Lord stroked Homer's muzzle, and the surfmen watched Halstead's crew tie up without a word.

Halstead had lost his helmet. Jack stood at the helm in his surfman's uniform, his face shiny with spray and sweat. He unbuckled his cork life vest with some difficulty. Malcolm tried to lend a hand, but Jack shrugged him off.

"What happened out there?" MacSween wanted to know. Nobody said anything. Jack helped Halstead off the deck. They sat on the sand together, Halstead's eyes a glaze of concentration. The torpedoman and machine gunner removed the mutilated body of the engineer, wrapped in a tarp. The deck was slick with grease and blood. Chief Lord opened the tarp and the others looked at the armless man and turned away. They just wanted to confirm what was true.

The starboard hull of the boat was battered where the shell had hit, and the torpedo mount was wrecked. They would need another engineer, and a machinist besides, but Halstead would minimize the damage in his report. He didn't care to be sent into drydock and relieved of his command. This was his business now, and he would finish it. He had lost his first man in combat. He stared out to sea and knew it was not over, not by a long sight.

It took Malcolm a few moments to get Halstead's attention. Finally he shook him, and Halstead looked up. "Mister Halstead, we are in for weather. Your tents may or may not stand it. Come up to the station and have some supper."

Halstead nodded. The sun was almost down now, and the beach was strangely tranquil. He wondered what fearful things the submarine would do tonight, what more he would be responsible for.

And still he had not done Dorothy Dant any good, nor did he expect to, though just at that moment he would have given up his commission to have her arms around his neck.

Chief Lord was already driving Homer back to the station when the Navy car labored through the cut in the dunes and made for them, followed by a loud, ungainly truck.

"For you, I expect," Malcolm said.

"Mister Cross," Halstead said, "tell them not to unload. We'll billet at the Cape Station tonight."

"Aye aye, sir."

Halstead's crew climbed aboard the truck and squatted among torpedoes and ammunition crates. They rode up the dark beach toward the Light, the dead engineer laid across the tailgate like a trophy.

7

JACK ROYAL WALKED beside Malcolm and the surfmen and said nothing.

"It must have been bad," Malcolm said.

"We're lucky to be here. There's no other excuse but luck."

"You brought her in just fine."

"Like you didn't expect me to."

"Of course—"

"Don't say anything. You were standing by. You didn't expect us to make it."

"We didn't know who—"

"It doesn't matter, Malcolm. Not even you can save everybody." He stopped and faced Malcolm, as if daring an argument. "Not even you."

Then Jack strode on ahead of his brother. He despised Malcolm for his gentleness, his protectiveness, but he guessed now that he had fought Malcolm all his life just because he was his brother.

He let it go at that.

He wanted to see Virginia, but that was impossible. No one would leave the station tonight.

And anyway, what could he say to Virginia?

8

PETE PATCHETT SPENT the afternoon at Oman's Dock, working on the *Hermes'* engine. He had scavenged parts from a dozen sources, some of them willing, and was up to his elbows in grease, valves, and gaskets. He worked methodically and with purpose. He was not a good mechanic, but a dogged one.

Oman drew on a meerschaum and watched him in wonder. "You haven't done anything this industrious in years, Patchy," he said. "What's the occasion?"

Patchy ignored him and went on working. When the squalls started blowing in, he packed his tools. Tomorrow he would fix the bilgepump and replace the head on the motor. The paint could wait. The sails were serviceable, but might not stand weather. Nothing he could do about that.

In a couple of days, with luck, the *Hermes* would be well-found, seaworthy. He would have done that much.

9

DOROTHY DANT and Keith Royal walked hand in hand over the dunes, the wind pushing at their backs. They were cresting the cut when they heard the commotion behind them and turned to see the life-saving crew hurrying down the beach to the bight, where Halstead's boat was kept. They watched, still holding hands, as the boat harbored safely and the men accumulated at the slip.

Keith started to lead her down.

"No. Let's walk back."

"Don't you want to know what's going on?"

"I know what's going on. My father and Brian are out there somewhere, and no one will go out and find them."

"They'll be all right. Maybe we ought to go down and talk to the Navy right now."

"They can't go out again tonight. I don't think they care, either."

In the failing light, she looked very young. She trembled a little, and he pulled her close. The wind stung their eyes.

"It's been too long," she said, "and I don't expect them to come back now, if you want the truth."

"Shh. That's no way to talk." He was afraid she would start crying.

"Why did you come back? Not for me."

"It seemed right. It seemed like the time."

"Didn't you enjoy being a college man? Didn't you like it?"

"Of course."

"Then why did you? Who made you? Who?" She looked at him accusingly. "I thought I wanted you to come back here more than anything . . . I dreamed you would come home and take me away. That's what I dreamed. We could live anywhere you liked, I didn't care. You could teach or study, or whatever it is historians do these days. I didn't care—"

"Take you away?"

"Yes! It's not natural, the way we live. Nothing ever lasts. Do I want my children to grow up to be what your brothers are?"

"There's nothing wrong with that! They're good—"

"Do I want to go through what their wives go through every time they go out?"

"It doesn't—"

"No! I still want to get away, somewhere. Somewhere safe. You can have your beautiful sunsets and your goddamned lighthouse. I don't want them for my children."

They were walking fast now, into the setting sun.

"You always loved it here."

"Did I? Is that what you think? Listen. My mother died in childbirth because there isn't even a hospital here. It wasn't necessary! Don't you see? This is all so backward, so primitive. And Uncle Dennis drowned because he had to make his living on a goddamned fishing boat. There's nothing else here for men like that—"

"Don't get hysterical."

"I want to go. I hoped for you to come back and take me away. Did you? Is that why you came back? Tell me, and don't lie to me. I won't have you lying to me like they do to their wives, telling them everything is all right."

"Stop it. You're upset about your father. You have a right to be."

"Oh, I'm upset about more than that. I'm upset because I waited for you all this time, and now I don't know what to do with you. I used to sit on the beach and watch the ocean, and think that up in New England you might be watching the waves, too. Or at night, I'd watch the stars, picking out the constellations, and I'd imagine you were looking at them, too, out of the window of your dormitory room. Did you? Did you think the same thing, or was I wasting my time? Was I wasting my heart pining for a college boy with other things on his mind?"

He tried to remember. He had thought of her, and often. But he had been afraid of coming back to her. Plenty of times he had deliberately put her out of his mind. Still, he had thought of her. He kissed her now.

10

LITTLEJOHN'S STORE remained crowded long after closing time. Fetterman had resumed his throne and was carving with a purpose, as if the afternoon encounter with the U-boat had clarified his design. The tower was taking on detail, and his hands worked slowly, careful not to cut too deep at once. He bored a socket in which to step the radio mast, nodding as if he were beginning to understand something.

"They say that an armistice is coming any day," one of the men observed.

"Tell that to our Heinie friend."

"They say in the papers that the Kaiser is in the doghouse with the mucky-mucks in the army."

"The papers didn't do the boy wonder any good this afternoon," Seamus Royal said. "He'll kill them all before he's through."

"Aw, don't be so hard on the boy. He's only trying to help," Littlejohn said.

"He don't know these waters, that's plain."

"Jack's with him."

"Jack brought her in."

"That's so."

"It ain't lucky to ship with a pissant like that. Who sent him here anyway, I'd like to know. He's an outsider. He don't belong on our boats. Now I hear he's courting the Dant girl, with all the hardship she's going through, and him not even a Hatterasman."

Fetterman listened awhile and said: "You fools. Don't you know he's not the problem? You don't know anything, that's all."

"Well speak, man," Seamus said, "if you've got something to say. There are those of us who'd like to hear it before the beach is swarming with godless Huns."

Fetterman put down his work. "I don't know if you're ready to listen."

The murmuring stopped, and the place assumed a respectful silence. Ham Fetterman scraped his chair around to face them better.

"He's only trying to help, as Littlejohn pointed out. He's a good boy, in his way. Not one of ours, but a good boy." They waited for him to say more. "But it's our problem, see. Not his. Not the Navy's. Not the Government's."

"*We're* not at war, Ham." It was one of the elder Bannisters. "The Government's at war. It don't concern us."

Fetterman stuck his knife in the arm of the chair. "That's where you're wrong. We are the only souls it does concern."

They didn't know what to make of that.

"We are alone out here. We are an island, or have you forgotten? There's nobody to help us. When have they ever helped us? Can you name one time?" He swept the room with his eyes. "When they inoculated our cattle and killed half of them? When they dipped our sheep and did the same? When they taxed us for ferrying in our own supplies? When they bombarded our villages and sacked our homes because we wasn't Yankees? Think about it. That's all the help you'll get from the Government. Any man who thinks different is a fool. Now they're even bossing around the life-saving crews! And you expect them to take care of us?"

Nobody said anything. They knew he was right, but they didn't know what to do about it.

"We can't just evacuate, like in sixty-two," Fetterman went on. "There's just too many of us. We have too much to lose. We can't do that now."

"You're leading up to something," Littlejohn said. "Stop pussyfooting around it and get to the point."

"You don't have to listen to an old man half out of his mind if you don't want to." Fetterman turned from them again and stared out the window. It was dark now, except for the beacon of the lighthouse scything the sky, harvesting stars.

Fetterman was reluctant to put it into words, but the moment had come. He pointed out the window and timed it just right. When the light flashed across the windowpane, he said: "We can turn it off."

Then, Littlejohn's voice was thin and small, even in the silence, "And God help us."

CHAPTER 6

1

AFTER SUPPER, the men settled in to smoke and talk about the U-boat, but neither Malcolm Royal nor Lieutenant Halstead joined in. Halstead was discussing how to repair the boat with the mechanic who had come on the truck.

"She needs to be lifted out, Mister Halstead," the mechanic said. "I don't think I can fix damage like that."

"We'll fix her, all right. Tomorrow at daylight we start."

The mechanic shook his head. "But we've got to bolt that torpedo jacket to something that can stand the weight and the stress, that's all. Otherwise, when you fire it, brother, you're in for one rude surprise."

But Halstead thought he could do it. After all, he had been trained as an engineer at Annapolis, and if he couldn't handle a little challenge like this, then he might as well get into another line of work. He made some preliminary diagrams and, satisfied they could be executed, turned to the logbook.

He pondered the right words for half an hour before he made an entry, for this was the record that would stand about what had happened today, should anyone care to second-guess him. And if tomorrow he went out and didn't come back, it might well serve as his epitaph. Halstead was already beginning to admire the native jealousy of the written word. He had examined the station log, whose last four years covered barely fifty pages.

He wrote: *Put to sea in pursuit of German U-boat, as it was shelling the Cape. Approached from SE, loosed one torpedo, a miss. Raked conning tower with machinegun at point blank range, effect unknown. Quarry submerged and eluded further attack. One casualty, Blotner, M., engineer, killed by direct hit from deck gun. Damage to starboard torpedo mount and armor hull. Will handle on station.*

Will handle on station, he thought. Let's hope so.

Cyrus Magillicutty saw him writing in the corner of the bunkroom for what seemed a long time. Certainly Malcolm never had that much to say. "A bit long-winded, eh?" He meant no harm, but Halstead's stare arrested him: the lieutenant's eyes caught the lamplight and seemed to burn in their sockets.

Blotner's body was installed in Littlejohn's deepfreeze until the Navy could ship it to Portsmouth. Halstead would have to write that letter, too, but not right now. Tomorrow maybe, or the day after, when his head was clear and he himself knew what had really happened out there. In retrospect the action was much neater, a matter of triangulation, of geometry, of intersecting lines, mistaken trajectories, vectors, angles, planes, physics. Tomorrow he would calculate better.

He knew this much already: Jack Royal, not Tim Halstead, had saved the day, and that rankled like a bad hazing. He still couldn't bring himself to like or trust the man—he was just too offensive, showing no respect. It was difficult to inspire his own men to gallantry with one like that around. He wondered if they laughed at him behind his back, then thought of Blotner, locked away for good in Littlejohn's deepfreeze, and he felt ashamed of himself.

He closed the log and went downstairs.

"They say you're a 'Napolis man," Chief Lord said, handing him a cup of tea.

"That's right." But by now he hardly remembered what Annapolis looked like. He only had hazy visions of a fortress rising dark into mist, a hallowed place where consecrated men in white chanted military cadence and conjured dreams of glory.

"My folks are up that way, some of them, that is. Up on the Eastern Shore of the Chesapeake. I been there many times. It is a beauteous place."

"I used to sail the Delaware Bay. We'd come all way down from Philadelphia and make a weekend of it." He tried to remember who had been with him on those trips, but he couldn't now. A girl, someone, a Cathy, perhaps, a Susan. That part of his life was unavailable to him now.

"I hear you," Chief said. "I can handle a sail myself when the mood is upon me. We run across the Sound to Hyde County now and again, and it's a pretty trip. That's where we get our spirits, don't you know."

Halstead nodded. He was only half listening, his ears as full of surf as conchs, his eyes sore with the effort of focus, so that the surfmen, the room, his own crewmen, Chief Lord, all melded in a soft nebula of motion swimming in dense light, like iridescent fish schooling underwater.

He had another thought: Chief Lord was a giant. There were lots of giants in these parts, he decided, starting with Malcolm Royal, who was sort of head giant. They must be a separate race almost. Even their horses grew to epic stature. And they acted with a kind of fated arrogance, every bit like creatures from a fairy tale out of some grim, preliterate past.

"This submarine is the new beast in the forest," Chief Lord

said. "We've never had anything like her around here. It's the novelty that's frightening." He hooked an arm around Halstead's shoulders. "I have seen white men throw their mates overboard at sight of a right whale breaching under a full moon, his great black head horned with barnacles big as rain barrels, white as bone, sharp as obsidian. *Jonah*, they said, pitching each man over the rail in his turn, terrified to their bottom of a harmless whale."

Other men were listening now, quietly forming a circle around Chief Lord, gathering as men will at the edge of light.

"The Norse marauders carved their prows to resemble sea serpents, to paralyze their enemies with fear at sight of them advancing over the waves, silhouetted against the strange, bellied moon of their sails, shields raised like scales along the flanks of the monster, tiller poised like a tailfin. And their enemies scattered, overwhelmed, even those who did not believe in sea monsters." His eyes swept the perimeter of faces, and men looked away. The grandiose arc of his hands included them all. For once, Halstead, seated at his side, felt at the very center of things, included, somehow, in the irreducible core of truth.

"I have seen sea monsters," Halstead said, unaware he had even spoken.

Chief Lord nodded solemnly. "So have we all. That's the trouble, you see." He rubbed his hands together slowly, as if smoothing a thought between his dark palms. "I have heard cynical men, civilized men, scoff at the talismans of voodoo princes, and then watched those same men murder witches with holy instruments, daggers blessed at the altar of the Saviour. There is no kenning it. One must steer a careful course between sky and sea."

"What are you saying?" Cyrus asked. "Are you inviting us to be superstitious? There's no voodoo here, nothing like it."

"I am only wondering what to do about the submarine, Cyrus. That's all. It is something all our experience hasn't prepared us for."

Halstead imagined those sleek Viking craft, the rattle of flint arrows on iron shields, the horned heads of those godless warriors as they spilled from the belly of the serpent onto strange and backward continents, hacking and hewing through flimsy squadrons of natives, like nothing they'd ever seen before.

Then he thought of voodoo. He said: "Chief of what, Chief Lord? That's what I'd like to know."

Chief Lord turned his palms up and smiled. "I am the charmer, the consultor with familiar spirits, the wizard, the necromancer. Chief fencer. Chief horse-coper. Chief tergiversator. Chief liar."

The men's laughter broke in Halstead's ears and cleared them to silence.

Malcolm Royal came over and sat smoking awhile before he said anything. He had the suitor's respect for courtesies. "You took it on the chin today, Mister Halstead, but at least you were in there punching. Tomorrow your luck may change." Halstead nodded. "Any news on Mister Dant?"

Halstead had all but forgotten him. "Nothing from the Navy. He'll come in, by and by. Don't they all? I can't imagine the German being much interested in him."

"Littlejohn says none of the other fishermen have seen him. That's a bad sign."

"What can I do?" He couldn't be responsible for everything. Some men were not meant to be found, and some boats belonged to the sea the day their keels were laid.

"Not a bad question, at that." Malcolm tasted more smoke and exhaled it in quivering rings. "And I've got another one for you: Is it possible, I mean to say, could it be, that there's more than one?"

Halstead started. "I—I hadn't considered that. It never crossed my mind, but . . ."

"Well, you might consider it from now on. Have you ever seen just one shark in the water?"

2

THE CURRENTS WERE playing tricks with Alvin Dant's boat. It

was a clear night, and he swore once he could see the Light, way off to the southwest. Thirty miles, maybe forty—who could say? You could see it a long way off on a night like this one, the sky a glass vault and the air itself luminescent with remembered light. It twinkled like a landstar because of the extreme distance; still, it emanated hope.

He woke Brian. "Do you see it, son?"

Brian watched hard in the direction his father pointed. "See what?" he asked. "There's nothing out there."

"Out there, out there!" he said, but Brian's eyes never left his own. And indeed, when Alvin looked again, the Light was gone.

3

THEY DIDN'T GO up this time. The captain managed it all from the periscope bridge, for he was taking no chances. She was an oil tanker, and he didn't believe a country at war would let her steam up the coast unprotected. Somewhere out in the blackness, he was sure, lurked a destroyer escort.

His plan was to get in really close and fire one torpedo. He was running out of them, and from now on he wanted one ship for every torpedo. It was unheard of. Nevertheless . . .

"No destroyers in sight. I don't understand it." He scanned all points of the compass. The oiler was low in the water and making about eight knots. There was no chance of missing her: he had her broadside at a thousand yards. "We'll take her from seaward. We can't risk a warning. There's an escort out there, and if we show ourselves . . ."

Max Wien started to protest. They always gave a warning to an unarmed ship, especially a lone one with no chance for rescue from a convoy. But he kept quiet. He had been trained not to backtalk his captain. And maybe Stracken was right, maybe there was a destroyer out there, and then they would be the ones in need of compassion. But Max really didn't think so.

"It's been too easy so far," the captain said.

"Yes," Kraft said, "maybe it's the Americans who are desperate."

The captain turned. "I don't think desperate is the word."

It was quiet in the belly of the shark. Max listened to the sound of men breathing all around him, like the sound of one giant, many-headed beast sweating its moment of action. It was strangely serene.

"We should give them a chance to get off," he told Bergen. "Do you know what it's going to be like?"

Bergen cleaned his fingernails. He was always doing that. He shook his head. "And where would they go? Tell me that."

Max thought of the island again, impossibly far away. So this was going to be plain murder.

He thought perhaps he should pray. He recalled the young priest in Papenburg who had christened his sister's child before the war brought the plague to the town and death to the child. The priest had put the child into the water and held him there. Max had not believed in a priest so young, just as now he did not believe that his prayers could penetrate the submerged steel hull and escape to heaven, any more than radio waves could. So he didn't pray. Instead he clasped his hands very close together and listened to the succession of orders that would accomplish the destruction of the oiler.

The concussion rocked the bulkheads.

The captain pivoted the periscope for ten minutes, then ordered them to surface.

Curiosity, Max thought, that's all it is: we want to see the damage.

The night air was refreshing. He had the habit now of following the captain. If the captain fancied him an orderly, Max did not deny the arrangement. He stood between Stracken and Kraft watching the great ball of fire that had been a ship a few minutes ago. It was hard to tell just where the torpedo had struck, the inferno was so general. Max guessed amidships.

"She burns well," the captain said, and Max wondered how he felt. The man just stared, his eyes aglow with the reflection of the flaming hull. The explosions kept going on, and the water all around the ship was on fire. The black shapes of boats dodged about in the burning oil, some of them on fire. There were men in the water everywhere, and Max knew the U-boat couldn't and wouldn't rescue any of them—where was there room to put them?

The captain said to Kraft: "How is one to know, Gunther?"

Bergen was standing at the ready. "Shall I finish her quickly, Captain?"

The captain turned. It was brighter than daylight on the tower bridge just now. The flames rose hundreds of feet, stirring the air into a great sucking wind. Max felt it on his neck. And now, against the wind, the sound of men screaming, shouting, cursing.

"What for?" the captain said. "We can't hurt them anymore."

They watched the vessel burn for a few more minutes. Through the glass, the mate was trying to discover her name and registry by the bow markings, not an easy task with all the smoke and distraction. But as she burned brighter he had it.

"*Abilene City.*" He pronounced it badly. "American."

"There's nothing more to see. *Nun lassen wir uns mal in dem seichten Wasser nieder.*" Now let us make our bed in the shallows.

4

CHIEF LORD HAD the tower watch. He had hardly climbed up onto the iron catwalk that circled just under the light when he saw it, far out to sea: a pillar of fire. In fourteen years as a surfman, he had never seen anything like it.

His feet moved under him, carried him to the hatchway and down the long spiral staircase, his feet beating the iron steps like drums. He emerged from the tower shouting to the others, and ran to go hitch Homer.

Joe Trent and Ian MacSween, a mile apart on beach patrol, were halted by a burst of light out on the horizon. Each man sent up a signal rocket, and the two rockets flared in the sky at almost the same moment.

5

"WHAT A WONDERFUL EVENING," Mary Royal said. She and Keith were walking over the dunes. The night was breezy, full of the moon. The stars were muted. High, fast clouds scudded across the sky, throwing shadows like waves. She had asked him to take her for a walk.

"You two were out here a long time today."

"What of it." But he was smiling, and now they were through the cut in the high dunes and facing the ocean. The wind carried the rumble of surf.

"She's a sweet girl. Are you going to marry her?"

"Do you think that would solve the problem?"

"She's not herself. She's having an awful time."

"I think I'm just confusing her."

"And yourself?"

"Yes, I guess so."

"Nothing like this has ever happened before. Nobody knows how to act."

"Sometimes I go to bed at night, and I wonder if the world will still be there in the morning," Keith said. "And in the morning I wake up sweating, like I've just survived something."

The breeze was blowing out to sea. Mary gathered her hair into a ponytail to keep it from blowing around her face. She put her arm around Keith. "You know, it has always seemed hard here for men and women to speak. Does it seem strange?"

He walked forward a little ways, so that her hand slid off his windbreaker. "Strange? I grew up here, remember. I know how it is. Our father wasn't home more than a couple of days a month for as long as I can remember. I used to go down to the station to visit him. He would let me take my nap in the lifecar, and they made a swing for me out of the breeches buoy. My mother never saw him."

"I think Malcolm knew you were going away before anybody."

Keith thought that over a minute. He hadn't told Malcolm he

was leaving until the very last minute. He himself hadn't known for sure until then. The scholarship had been a quiet arrangement from the beginning, and now whenever Keith lay alone at night with nothing else on his mind, the thought of his leaving came to him with a feeling of sorrow and shame.

He hadn't spoken at any length with Malcolm since he had been back, but then Malcolm hardly ever spoke much with anyone. Keith recalled vividly, though, all those fights Malcolm and Jack used to have, how terrified they made him, how they never seemed to solve anything.

"Do you remember how I used to watch you paint?" Keith said. "I think watching you paint like that made me more determined than ever to see what else was out there. I think you did that for me."

"I sent you away."

"No, no, I didn't mean it like that."

"Then you'll stay awhile now?"

"Well, I'm not going anywhere right away. I'm out of the university."

"What?"

"I left without taking my final examinations. I had to come back." Three and a half years had passed in New England, and then he had felt an urgency to return right away, not to wait even the two weeks it would have taken to finish the term.

"They'd take you back, I know they would. You're brilliant. Why, I'd write a letter—"

"Oh, Mary, look!"

They saw a ball of fire out to sea and stood enthralled for a moment. "Lord," she said. Keith squeezed her hand, then started running up the beach toward the Light. "Where are you going?" she shouted after him.

He turned, still jogging backward. "Malcolm will be going out shorthanded. He'll need me."

Mary Royal watched him flee up the beach away from her, at terrific speed, it seemed to her. She felt the same rush of heartsickness she always felt when Malcolm's boat went out, but it was worse this time. Keith would be with him, pulling toward the flames on the water.

6

WHEN CHIEF LORD CAME bellowing across the short quadrant of grass between the lighthouse door and the life-saving station, the whole crew emptied onto the porch like dice spilled from a cup, Halstead's men among them. At that moment they marked the two orange flares the beachwalkers had launched. Malcolm ran to the corral behind Chief and helped him harness Homer, who was skittish and hard to manage.

"The tanker," Malcolm said, pipe still clenched in his teeth.

Chief Lord nodded, winded. The crew was hauling out the boat on its carriage. Chief climbed into the bow with the reins while Malcolm finished buckling the harness, and in two minutes from the time Chief had first appeared at the foot of the lighthouse, they were underway, cutting through the dunes on the corduroy road, their eyes fixed on the blaze at the horizon.

Halstead's men watched, unsure what to do. He was agonizing over what duty required of him when Malcolm shouted:

"Don't be trying this with that cigar boat of yours, or we'll be hauling you out, too."

"Let me handle an oar, then—"

Just then Keith appeared, arms pumping. All the surfmen had on their high boots, oilskins and bonnets, and life-vests. Keith had just his windbreaker, khaki pants, and canvas shoes.

"Can I help, Malcolm? Can I take an oar for you?"

Malcolm waved him along. He caught up when they were almost at waterline. Malcolm clapped him on the back, and shoved a life-vest at him.

"Starboard aft oar," was all Malcolm said. Jack resumed his old position at the waist, shaking his head. They rushed the boat into the breakers and vaulted inside, all but Malcolm, who shoved them just a little farther before he scrambled in over the stern and took up the sweep oar.

Keith pulled hard while his brother counted stroke. The first big breaker they hit lifted the bow almost vertical and slammed them hard into a trough. There were two more like that, and then the oars bit all at once and they shot forward over the combers. Already the Light seemed far away to Keith, and Malcolm's presence at the helm, haloed by the sweeping light, was all that kept his panic down.

Keith leaned into his oar with purpose now. They pulled for almost an hour to get within reach of the tanker, and it seemed a miracle she had stayed afloat so long. But the torpedo had not broken her back, only punched a hole in her and toplit her cargo, so that she was settling slowly by the bow.

"We're burning!" Cyrus Magillicutty shouted above the rush of the flames. They were into the oil now, and the gunwales of the surfboat were on fire. Chief Lord beat out the flames with his bonnet, and Malcolm steered them out of the oil.

"We've got to get in closer," Chief Lord said.

They were parallel to the oiler now, and Keith could make out the silhouettes of men huddled at the aft railing. As he watched, one by one they leapt into the flaming seas and made for the surfboat.

"Come on!" Keith heard himself shouting. "Get in closer! Can't you see them?" Malcolm nodded and steered into the oil again. Jack cursed. The men from the tanker were diving under the flames and coming up a little closer each time.

Finally the first of them reached the surfboat. The burning tanker lit the sky. There was no trouble seeing men in the water.

Wordlessly, Cyrus and Joe Trent started pulling men aboard, while the rest kept the boat from broaching to in the swells.

The sailors' faces were blackened and their clothes were all but burned off them. When Keith helped one of them crawl toward the stern, a pad of flesh came away in his hand. He wiped it on his jacket, and felt a knot behind his tongue.

"Lie on your backs across the thwarts between oarsmen," Malcolm commanded in a voice Keith had never heard, at once soothing in its control but threatening too. The sailors were hysterical at being saved, and Malcolm had to be sure they wouldn't capsize the boat: "Tuck your feet into the next man's armpits."

They took ten men aboard this way.

"That's it," Malcolm said. "Pull for the beach."

Just then, Chief spotted a lifeboat struggling around the stern of the tanker, in it a group of men with only two manning oars.

"Pull for the boat," Malcolm commanded. They pulled like drayhorses, and the hot blast of the fire watered their eyes and choked them and blistered their naked hands.

They came alongside and saw that the lifeboat had taken on a lot of water, and most of the men it held were badly injured.

"Chief, Jack—take her in." The two surfmen clambered into the lifeboat and Toby Bannister threw them a hawser, which Chief made fast to the bow. The two surfmen took up oars, and Malcolm's boat proceeded to tow them in, a slow and dangerous business. If either boat swamped, it could sink the other.

Keith had never worked so hard. By the time they were halfway to the beach, his hands were raw and his chest heaved for breath. His back was sore, and he was lightheaded and suddenly very cold, now they were away from the blaze with the stiff following wind in their faces.

"Pull, boys!" Malcolm urged, and they did. Keith felt inferior, out of his class, not a hero. His rowing on the Harvard crew had been a lark compared to this, his hands protected in their calfskin gloves, the course laid out for safety, the labor timed to allow rest, their craft light as a wing compared to this broad-beamed ark.

The wind gusted suddenly on their starboard beam, and it was all Malcolm could do to control the sweep oar with both hands. His eyes narrowed under his oilskin bonnet, and the Light seemed to get no closer. Malcolm fought the wind to a draw.

They left the lifeboat beyond the breakers and made the run to the beach alone. On Malcolm's signal, all hands shipped oars. They surfed the crest of the last big wave and were overboard all at once, waist deep in the foam, hauling in the boat the rest of the way by hand.

Keith was buffeted in the shoulder by the boat and sprawled on his face in the surf, swallowing salt water. Malcolm lifted him out with one rough hand.

"Steady, boy," he said.

A crowd had gathered on the beach, including Littlejohn and Fetterman and all their wives and families. Someone had sent to Kinnakeet for the doctor, and meanwhile Halstead's men organized litter details to carry the injured to the station.

"Good boy," Malcolm said to Keith. "Let's get under way."

Keith had almost forgotten: They had to go back for the others.

They rushed the boat into the surf, but this time it was more difficult. They were tired, and the seas had been building for the past two hours. Now the wind was blowing almost head-on. On the first try, the wall of foam tossed them back to the beach, and then twice more the sea rebuffed them.

On the fourth attempt, they stood on the curl of a breaker for one heart-stopping moment, then ducked into the trough and were under way. "I must be slipping," Malcolm said. It had taken three-quarters of an hour to go fifty yards.

With Chief Lord gone, Malcolm had put Keith on the Chief's oar, and now he pulled through a wall of pain the like of which he had never known in all the hundreds of miles he had rowed at Harvard.

In half an hour, they had gained the lifeboat, which had drifted south in the wind. Chief Lord hailed them, and they set about transferring first the injured and then the able-bodied to the surf-boat to run the beach again.

Chief and Jack climbed aboard last of all. When Keith moved to relinquish the stroke oar, Chief Lord laid a hand on his shoulder. "Stay put, boy. You got her here all right."

It was a fast run this time, with the wind on their quarter. The waves were faster. And when they had crested the last line of breakers,

and the surfmen were in the water, the boat broached to and flattened Joe Trent with a nasty clip to the head. Chief Lord yanked
him out of the water, and Joe staggered to the beach. When the
rescued sailors were unloaded, a Navy man wound cloth bandages
around Joe's head.

"Stay in," Malcolm told him.

"I'm going out." And he did.

This time it took nearly two hours to reach the tanker. Incred-
ibly, she was still burning, but had settled by half, and they saw she
could not stay afloat much longer. They pulled five men out of
the water and recovered two more bodies, floating on a hatch cover.

"She's going down!" MacSween shouted. They could hear the
violent wrenching and creaking of the last metal bulkheads caving
in under the weight of water, the sound carrying in ragged pieces
across the air, like shrapnel. They pulled so hard the oars warped
in their locks; they were frantic to outrun the vortex that would
claim the tanker and everything in half a mile of her.

When it was safe, they watched the flaming hulk settle the final
few fathoms and the fire extinguish in an acrid black smoke. In a
minute, she was gone.

"I hope we got them all," Malcolm said. But he had seen no
trace of the ship's master, nor did he expect to now.

The last run out and back took five hours. When they landed,
it was almost daylight. The waves ran fast and short. The crew
pulled the boat onto the beach and lay down in the sand as
Halstead's men pulled the rest of the survivors out of the boat. But
Malcolm stood erect, holding Homer's neck, for fully half-an-hour
until his men could find the strength to load the boat onto its
carriage and walk the three hundred yards to the station.

"Twenty-five," Littlejohn said. "You brought in twenty-five,
Malcolm."

"Twenty-seven," Malcolm said.

"Of course." Littlejohn hadn't counted the two bodies. "Only
two didn't get off at all. It's goddamn amazing."

"Don't be cursing, Littlejohn. Not on a night like this."

They plodded back to the station, put the boat away, and slept in their oilskins, and it was two days before Malcolm could unclench his fingers enough to hold a pen to the logbook. But it could wait, he thought, nothing would change.

7

THE NIGHT HAD TURNED NASTY, with a stiff onshore wind. Mary Royal reached the waterline just after the life-saving crew put out, and Littlejohn, who had picked up the Mayday on his wireless, brought the gang from the store. Jack's wife Virginia arrived by and by, leading little Kevin by the hand, all wrapped up in a miniature sou'wester.

More than a dozen people were gathered just back of the high-water mark by the time Malcolm's crew was halfway to the tanker, and they did not speak at all while they waited and watched and measured the lifeboat's progress on the moon-silvered sea.

The Navy men were unpacking medical supplies, and Halstead had his glasses out. He gave orders for a man to take the light-house watch in the event that (God help us, he said) there were any more ships in distress out there tonight.

Virginia heard him, and noticed that Dorothy stayed close to him.

Littlejohn said, "Don't you be worrying, Mary. That one knows how to handle a boat. For him, this ain't even weather."

"That's right," Kevin said, letting go his mother's hand. "Daddy and Uncle Malcolm can row a hundred miles a day!"

"Kevin, please . . ."

"Mister Littlejohn, why is it burning like that?" Mary asked. They still could not get over the fact of the tremendous fire, the like of which they had never seen before.

"Oil, Mary. Gasoline. She'll burn for weeks, if she stays afloat."

"Then the danger . . ."

"Oh, she'll go down tonight, mark me. She's been punctured to the heart, sure as we're standing here. She's got a hole in her, but it's in the wrong place, thank heaven."

Virginia gasped. "Will they come back?"

"To finish her, you mean." It was Fetterman, come limping up, arthritis grating in his knees, a bottle of beer in one hand, the other leaning hard on a crutch that he had carved himself.

Virginia stared at him. "Will they come back?"

Fetterman lodged the crutch under his arm and stuffed his beer bottle into his belt to free his hands and fussed with his pipe. He shook his head slowly. "There's no telling what that fellow will do. He's a different kind of critter altogether. But I expect even a Hun will have some decency in him."

"And if he doesn't?" Mary asked.

"Oh, I doubt he'll waste another torpedo. He only has so many, you know." But Fetterman didn't remind her about the deck cannons he had lately fitted to his model.

Mary was relieved, though she knew they should all wish the German would use up his warheads on a ship that was already lost. She looked out to the sea and tried to imagine Keith pulling an oar among Malcolm's crew, and couldn't. She wished he had taken his gloves.

"That son of a bitch," Virginia said. "That son of a bitch."

"Ginny—"

"I don't care." She yanked hold of Kevin's hand. "Take a good look, Kevin. Remember it. Remember what that son of a bitch is. He's trying to kill your father, to kill all of us. You don't forget that when you grow up—"

"That's enough, Ginny." Mary said. "Everybody's upset about this."

Kevin only looked frightened. Fetterman turned away, showing no emotion. All he felt, really, was a small sadness, the disappointment of things being repeated over and over again to no purpose, like repeating a grade in school all your life. He was not at all convinced Malcolm's crew could find their way back to the beach tonight; too much was already wrong.

8

ALVIN DANT COULD not have said what woke him. He'd been dreaming about old Fetterman. In the dream, he was standing over Fetterman's shoulder, watching him carve. It was Littlejohn's store, and a tremendous blow was going on outside, and all the men who would normally be out fishing or running the trading packets were sitting around the big coal stove and smoking, but their voices were a confused, foreign-sounding murmur.

The blow lashed against the windows, but the men inside didn't notice. Fetterman finished model after model in the dream, then deliberately smashed each one onto the floor at his feet, so that after a while there was a heap of broken toy ships covering the floor. Fetterman went about his work religiously, while the pile grew and the voices continued to make no sense, and the rest of the men ignored Alvin Dant.

Fetterman's eyes were narrowed and his jaw was set, as if the work were a duty, not a diversion.

Then, Dennis, Alvin's brother, was outside, waiting to be let in. A man was with him. Alvin couldn't see his face, but he was wearing a tall hat in the style affected by gentlemen. The door was locked. Dennis did not try to force it—he had never been a violent man. Meanwhile, the rain drenched him and the wind whipped the tails of his sou'wester around his hips and flattened the bill of his bonnet. He stood there with the Light behind him in its regular sweep, while inside, the coal-oil lanterns flickered on old Fetterman's hands as they went on and on building and destroying, now a frigate, now a schooner, now a seagoing tug.

In the dream, Alvin was trying to get past Fetterman's chair to go unlock the door, moving so slowly it could hardly be called movement, his limbs struggling against a paralyzing inertia. Just when he had his hand on the latch, his brother's patient face only inches away beyond the rain-tracked glass, the dream went black, and he woke to a brilliant light off on the western horizon.

"Littlejohn never locked his doors in twenty years," he said out loud.

"What?" Brian was already up, standing at the wheel again and watching the glow increase. The night was silent except for the lapping of water against the freeboard and the creak of rigging.

"She's pretty far off," Brian said.

"Not so very far."

"Out of our reach."

"Aye. Look at the poor thing burn."

Alvin remembered he had brandy on board, and now seemed like the time to break it out. He might as well have a drink with his son, if they had to watch that kind of destruction.

"Who is it, Dad?" Alvin listened for the edge of fear in his son's voice, but did not catch it.

"I don't know. Must be a tanker."

"I never knew a ship could burn like that."

"Here, have some of this." He took his own swig without waiting, then handed the bottle to Brian, who had never drunk with his father before. "Must be a tanker, that's all I can figure. I don't know what in God's name else."

"They don't care about that, do they."

"What?" He hit the bottle again.

"The men in the submarine. They don't care about the ones they burn."

Alvin snorted. "I can't tell you what a man cares about, boy. Let alone those pirates."

"You think we're very far out?"

"Who knows where we are. By all rights, we should be halfway to Scotland by now. But nobody has ever figured these currents out. Maybe we'll get lucky."

Brian moved from the wheel and found a seat from where he could still watch out the wheelhouse window. His hands were turning in his lap.

"Here—it's about time you tried one of these." Alvin dug a pipe out of his pocket and proffered his tobacco pouch. "Fill it loose, tamp a little, then fill it again. Top-light it first, then tamp it again. Then light it for good."

Brian was clumsy at first, but very soon his hands were steady, and he was puffing from the pipe. Alvin fixed his own.

"She'll burn all night."

"Like as not."

"We're not going to get back, are we, Dad."

Alvin reflected for a moment on his dream. He could not interpret it, but he was strangely comforted by it.

"I don't know, boy. I didn't think so at first, but now I don't know. I thought we'd drift off the charts, but if that tanker was caught in the coastal shipping lanes—I mean, he was steering by the Light, wasn't he—then maybe the sea doesn't want this old boat. Maybe we'll get back."

It was the longest speech he had ever made to his son. He often spoke for hours with Dorothy, and that was odd, he knew. A man was supposed to have difficulty talking to a daughter. A son was supposed to be a soul mate, the one who understood why year after year you did the same damned things for no better reason than that they were yours to do. But Dorothy had turned out different than he'd counted on. Maybe losing her mother like that had made her gravitate naturally to him. But no, that should have made the children turn to each other, and they never quite did that. Dorothy confided in him, and in Mary Royal, never in Brian.

And while he knew his daughter's love was a marvelous rare thing, it also scared him because he didn't quite understand it.

In whom did Brian confide?

Tonight, after that odd dream, and stemming from no connection with it that he could fathom, Alvin knew all at once why Brian had never come to him: simple fear. Brian was the child of his mother's deathbed, and Alvin Dant didn't know how, but he was very sure now that he had cowed Brian. He had made Brian responsible, not for making him a widower, but for taking away Dorothy's mother. It was all very clear now, and he took another drink. Brian drank, too, and smiled, as they watched the tanker burn.

Alvin recalled something else from his dream: the blood on

Fetterman's hands. Fetterman carved deep gashes in the meat of his hand with each stroke of the knife, so that the floor was littered with broken ships dappled with blood. Yet, he kept carving.

"Pray for a storm to wash us in, boy," he said, pausing to take a slug of brandy. "A storm will either sink us or save us."

CHAPTER 7

1

PATCH PATCHETT ARRIVED home very late and was surprised to find his wife and children gone. There was not even a note. His buttocks were sore from riding the mule all the way back from Hatteras Village, for he was not used to the trip. The *Hermes* had ridden at mooring for so long that not even he could remember the last time he'd taken her out.

He wasn't a sailor; he knew that. He was a beachcomber.

Once he had found a box of four dozen hats at the waterline. For weeks after he had worn a different hat every day—one day a bowler, next day a derby, a slouch hat for roaming the beach, and a touring cap of genuine pigskin for riding his bicycle. He had sold about half the hats to Littlejohn and given the ones he had no use for to his wife's relatives. People on the island still wore those hats, though lately his wife's uncle complained that the brim on his Panama was fraying and could he please get another? As if Patchy hoarded a salesman's stock in his shed.

His bounty was always short-lived, but he always shared it.

"So she's finally gone and left me," he muttered, not at all surprised, lighting a lamp in the dark house.

He was confused for a moment, though, because it didn't seem right that she would leave him on the very day he had begun to show some ambition about the boat. And she knew him well enough to know that when he set his mind to a thing he generally finished it, no matter how rare and silly the thing he set it to. He had, for example, spent the better part of a summer drilling a well that came up salt water and would always come up salt water, as anyone on the island could have told him, and did. But he had it in his mind that only having a well would save him the trouble of cleaning and repairing the cistern every spring.

Now he sat down to think, and once he had stopped scraping around on the floorboards with his brogans (a clumsy innovation for him, as he usually went shoeless), he heard the commotion out on the beach.

He listened over the wind and then curiosity got the better of him. He kicked out of his shoes and gained the crest of the dunes lickety-split and beheld an enormous crowd assembled on the beach by the Light. He spied a boat—it must be Malcolm's crew—land and nearly capsize, and only then did he register the fire on the horizon.

He knew his U-boat was out there.

"What's happened?" he asked Littlejohn.

"An oiler. Malcolm's brought some of them off, that's all I can tell you."

"He's going back out, then."

"Sure. What do you think."

"Hello, Patchy," Fetterman said. "Your wife's here."

"I don't mind. You got a smoke?"

Fetterman turned away, shaking his head. Littlejohn obliged him with his tobacco pouch, and Patchy had a time getting his pipe to go in the wind. He shielded the small flame with his hands till they were pink and hot.

"It's a good night to go out."

"Not so bad," Littlejohn agreed.

"Except it ain't the weather that's making that tanker burn."

"No, it ain't."

They walked among the crowd. "What you been up to, Patchy? I figured you'd be the first one out here."

"Had some work to be doing on the boat."

"You had it to be doing last February."

"You didn't happen to bring a bottle of beer or three, did you?"

Littlejohn laughed. "I don't know why I put up with you, Patchy. I don't know what you're good for."

Patchy reflected on that. It was an interesting question, one that had framed itself in his own thinking as he jounced along on the mule and cleaned the grease from under his fingernails with handfuls of sand on his way home. "You sold a lot of hats on account of me."

"And I bought a load of junk, too. Ah, well."

"Hey, Patchy."

"Mrs. Royal. Mrs. Royal. Dorothy." Out of the corner of his eye he spied Pat gaining on him with little Penny and Parvis in tow. Parvis was named for a great-uncle of his wife's who was sabered to death serving under Stonewall Jackson at Bull Run.

"Lordy, I thought you were dead and drowned," Pat Patchett said. "I thought the sharks had eaten your meager brains and spit out the gristle. Where've you been?"

"Working, what do you think?" He cast a smug sidelong glance at Littlejohn, who just then had a severe fit of coughing.

"You ought to do something about them lungs, Mister Littlejohn. You see there, Patchy? This night air ain't good for the kiddies.

I've got to get them home." Penny and Parvis slouched beside her like orphans.

"I was working," Patchy said. "On the boat."

"I'll be taking the children home. I don't want them coming down with the croup from being out on a night like tonight on account of you."

"He was working," Littlejohn said, between coughs.

"I heard him the first time. But I always like to give him a chance to take back a falsehood before it sets."

"I was fixing the damned engine, woman—"

"Hush! Don't be cursing in front of the kiddies. This ain't Littlejohn's back room. Shame on you. You'd think a grown man would know better, you'd think. I'm going home, Patchy, and I'm taking the kids. You can't stop me. And don't be bending Mister Littlejohn's ear till all hours, you hear?"

And to Littlejohn: "He only does it for the beer. You ought to make him pay cash or nothing. It was always good enough for my people. But he's a big man, likes to have credit. I'll give him credit. I don't know why I put up with it."

Parvis and Penny hadn't said a word. Mrs. Patchett yanked them off over the dunes.

"Patchy, it ain't even the season for hurricanes."

"Lord, you don't know," he said, shaking his head.

"Nothing wrong with my lungs."

"It's the cold air of the grave, is what it is."

"My wife says that, too."

Malcolm's boat was coming in now. They had smoked two bowls apiece. They went down to the waterline, and saw that the gunwales were all blackened. You could hardly make out the initials painted on the bows: U.S.L.S.S. for United States Life-Saving Service.

The Light roved the sky over their heads.

Littlejohn said, "I can tell you what this beach is going to look like by morning."

Patchy had already worked that out. Even now the swells were filmy with oil. By this time tomorrow, the waterline would be black from Kinnakeet to the inlet.

"There ain't any excuse for it," Patchy said.

Offshore the tanker still blazed. Malcolm's crew went out for the third time, and Patchy felt a pang that he could not go with them. But he had his own things to do.

2

WHEN MALCOLM ROYAL FINALLY ENTERED the events connected with the rescue of the *Abilene City* in the station log, he contrived to be alone for a long time to get it down just right. He thought he would have a lot of trouble getting it down the way it had happened. He wished it weren't necessary—surely nobody on the island ever forgot what happened. Or put another way: everyone on the island, together, remembered everything.

As far south as Ocracoke, as far north as Kitty Hawk, anyone could tell you, for instance, how Captain Benjamin Dailey rescued six crewmen from the *Ephraim Williams* on December 19, 1884. They could tell you that the seas were cresting at seven and eight feet with weather, and that Dailey's No. 1 man begged off to go to the bedside of his dying wife, and that his name was crossed off the logbook in heavy ink, as if that would eradicate memory of him.

But they all knew who he was—he was Patch Patchett's father, though the fact was never mentioned out loud on the island. Patchy's annual application to the Coast Guard was never acted upon or acknowledged, and there were those who said it never even got into the mail pouch for Portsmouth.

If you relied on what was written down, Malcolm thought, nobody would ever remember anything. On the island there was plenty of time for remembering, and your people told you what you had to know about all that had gone before. If you read about it at all, you read about it in the creases of their brows, or the knotty joints of their hands, or the pursed silence of salt-blistered lips.

Nevertheless, he drew a great breath, let it go, and commenced to write, slowly, because his hands were still raw: *Tower watch rptd. ship in distress just south of the Light. Put out in moderate seas at 2130 for tanker* Abilene City *which was burning badly. Took off 25 crewmen in three trips, secured boat at 0600.* Abilene City *sank in deep water, torpedoed in sight of land by Gmn. U-boat. Keith Royal volunteered to man an oar, acquitted himself well at risk. Ship's master and engineer's mate Geo. Bannister, of the island Bannisters, went down with the vessel. God grant them rest.*

He wondered if he should have put it in about Keith and Toby's brother. Well, it was an official document, and if Keith finally made up his mind to join the Service, he would already have a record in his favor.

Was it too personal about George, though? Maybe he should have mentioned the other dead men by name. Malcolm tried to imagine what it must have been like belowdecks where George would have been caught when the torpedo lanced the bulkhead. Almost all the men were burned, and he knew some would probably die of their burns by the time Halstead's convoy got them safely to the hospital in Portsmouth. But what was it like down there, inside, trapped, welded into your own coffin by fire that burned so hot it had no color?

Malcolm closed the log when the ink was dry. He laid a hand flat on the canvas cover and held it there. He felt, once again, he hadn't got it down exactly right.

He had rescued a lot of men in all kinds of circumstances—a millionaire who dismasted his yacht carrying too much sail in a blow, a smuggler running too close inshore at night in a fog, a Greek freighter that ran aground on the shoals in broad daylight with the captain so drunk he had to be carried off, and once even a Baltimore clipper in the worst gale Malcolm had ever put to sea in, certain he would never come back and risking only his brother Jack and two volunteers in the attempt—but he had never seen anything like the men who came off the *Abilene City*, their flesh peeling in strips, their faces boiling with welts, their eyes and noses sealed with pus and charred tissue. And most of them had swum through salt water in that condition.

He had no honest idea how so many had survived, and he took no credit for it, but two weeks later they gave him the Gold Life-Saving Medal anyway.

3

MALCOLM SAT on the porch thinking, his hands clasped, his body bent, not even smoking.

Toby Bannister sat down next to him and dragged on a cigarette, one of Halstead's maduros.

"Have you had any rest?' Malcolm asked.

Toby nodded but didn't answer. He was lean for a surfman, with a long torso and short thick legs that lent power to his stroke. His right shoulder humped with muscles from handling a portside oar for years. He had been one of the volunteers in the clipper ship outing, along with Chief Lord.

"They may find him yet," Malcolm said, knowing it was a lie. There had been enough of a miracle already. He was sorry he had said it.

"He was my twin," Toby said through teeth closed on the cigarette just enough to hold it.

"I didn't know that."

"Ah, well. We didn't look much alike. He had the best of looks, you know."

Malcolm was silent. For something to do, he pulled his pipe out of his pocket and wiped the rim of the bowl thoroughly with a handkerchief dampened with spittle, then filled and tamped it. Toby offered a box of matches, and Malcolm lit one and held it between his hands over the bowl, breathing in the smoke slowly.

"What I wanted to ask, why I bothered you . . ." Toby hesitated.

"What is it, Toby?"

"I want to take the tower watch tonight."

"You're on from eight to midnight, or am I wrong?"

"All night, Malcolm. That's what I want."

Malcolm watched the lighthouse. As he watched, the Light went on, all at once, like an idea. That would be Chief.

"Are you sure, Toby?" Malcolm looked to see what was in the man's eyes. "Maybe you should go home tonight. We can call you."

"You know better than that. I've never left my duty yet."

"I know, I know." He was wondering if that was as important now as it had been. The world was changing, things were getting more dangerous every day. Who knew where it would all lead? No, he decided—Toby was right: it was not the time to start making exceptions. "Do you want somebody to bring up coffee once in a while?"

"Well, I've had enough of tea." He flicked his cigarette into the sand and went inside, leaving Malcolm to sit for a while yet.

4

DOROTHY DANT BELIEVED her father and brother were dead. She did not see the point of Halstead's going out after them now, and she said so.

"We have to go out anyway."

"I know," she said. "You men always use that line when it's something you can't wait to do."

Halstead's boat was almost ready. With help from the crew, the new mechanic-turned-engineer had repaired the armor plate, trued the bent propeller shaft, and remounted the torpedo sleeve by bolting it through the deck onto a sheet of boiler plate under the deck planking. It stabilized the boat as ballast and slowed her down. She lost three inches of freeboard.

They had also mounted two Y-guns on the stern, each capable of throwing a depth charge packed with TNT. And now two powerful searchlights braced the cockpit, for night patrols. To Halstead, the lights seemed more dangerous than anything else.

"The weather's been pretty foul," he said. "I went over the charts last night with Seamus Royal—you know him?"

"Uncle Seamus? He's the grand old man of the island."

"Is he really your uncle?"

"They're all my uncles."

"Well, he may be a balmy old character, as the British say, but he knows this coast, all right. From what he tells me, your dad's boat would have been well away from the German each of the times he was sighted."

"Please don't be promising me anything."

"It may not be like your Uncle Dennis."

"All of them, every day, they all said he would come in, just wait and see."

"I know." He liked being in her house all alone with her, but he couldn't help thinking it was improper, that he was taking advantage of her misfortune. He never would have met her, she would never have come to him, except for her father.

"Did you ever think that he didn't drown? That his boat didn't founder out there?"

"That's a bad joke."

"It's not a joke."

"Then I don't know what you mean."

"I mean, suppose he'd just had enough. Suppose he had a woman someplace, or a yen to travel, to get off this sandbar. Suppose he was just fed up with the whole damned place and anxious to get shet of it."

"Don't you dare talk like that to me! My Uncle Dennis was an honorable man."

"I never said—"

"Then say what you mean."

"I mean, suppose he just wanted to leave?"

"Nobody leaves that way."

"His wife had run off—"

"She was a goddamn shrew, Mister Halstead."

He smiled in spite of her outburst. "*Mister?* I thought it was *Tim?*"

"Not if you're talking like this. That damned hussy ran off with a fireman in Norfolk. She used to tell my mother she was visiting family up there, but we knew better."

"You couldn't have known for sure."

"Her family was from Morehead City. That woman didn't know a soul in Norfolk except that man."

"Oh."

"Satisfied?"

"All I meant was, it would be a way a man could get a fresh start without having to explain himself and answer a lot of questions."

She thought about that, and couldn't decide whether to be shocked and hurt or glad, accepting the chance that her Uncle Dennis had just slipped his cable and gone off to voyage in his private worlds. Or maybe grief and shame had driven him off. He had left soon after his brother's wife, Dorothy's own mother, had died birthing Brian. And Dennis's affection for her had been out-right, if honorable. He had probably loved her all the more be-cause of what was shaping up in his own house.

But there was another possibility she had never considered. "Tim? What if he did it . . . on purpose?"

Halstead understood that the tables had turned. "He wouldn't do that," he said. "I bet he wouldn't."

They held hands across the table and let their tea get cold while dusk filled the house like water. After a while they stood up to-gether, and though he hadn't meant to, Halstead led her into the bedroom. Sitting beside Dorothy on the bed, he told her he was falling in love with her. She didn't believe in his love, but she didn't care. She kissed him. For now, it was her chance to get away.

5

PATCHETT FINALLY HAD the pistons seated right. He fitted the head on carefully and torqued the bolts as well as he could by hand. It wouldn't do to have the whole thing come apart under load.

He had mended his extra sails and stowed them dry. His stays'l and mizzen were reefed and covered. There was coffee, sugar, dried fish, and even a bottle of rum on board. He wished he had some kind of weapon, but all he had was an old gaff. It would have to do, and he bolted a hanger for it next to the wheelhouse hatchway.

Patchy went forward and started the engine, gradually increasing the throttle as she warmed up. The engine sounded so even and strong he was almost amazed. The plugs were clean, the points set, and a hundred minor parts replaced by scavenging with Oman, who had watched the whole enterprise with admiration and disbelief.

Oman had given fuel on credit, as usual, and even let Patchy scrounge some charts, which he had squinted to read and could only make general sense of.

Patchy spent the last two hours of daylight polishing the sparse brightwork on board and scrubbing whatever came under his hand. By sundown the *Hermes* gleamed. Her bilge was dry, her rigging in place, her wheelhouse shipshape.

"Come here, Oman," he said, wiping polish off his hands with a rag. "You are a landlubber till the last judgment, I reckon, but this here is a well-found boat. Take a good look."

Oman sidled over importantly. He gave her a good going over and listened to Patchy rev the engine. Oman folded his arms across his chest and nodded. "Well, it's a pleasure to behold, Patchy," he said. "It's a goddamn pleasure."

6

MARY ROYAL COOKED supper for Keith. He was feeling restless and his hands were in bad shape, the fingers cramped into hollow fists. He had small itching burns on his forearms and shoulders and was uncomfortable sitting around. Besides, he had not heard from Dorothy. The telephone lines had been restored, but she didn't call and, calling, he didn't reach her. He wondered if he had somehow offended her, or because he had gone out in the boat with Malcolm and the crew, if then she thought he would now stay on Hatteras forever.

"How did it feel to go out with them?" Mary asked.

"I don't know. What kind of question is that?"

"Malcolm never talks about it, any of it. So I've never known what it was like." She realized she was jealous—all the storms he had weathered, all the grand things he had done. She was not even welcome inside the station. Yet she was so hopelessly proud of him that she fairly burst with it whenever she heard him talked about in the village.

Keith shook his head. "It was a lot of hard work, mostly."

"Of course. I know that. You're as bad as Malcolm."

Keith watched her. He couldn't help noticing how pretty she was. "I can't tell you what it felt like," he said. He remembered how much it had hurt. He wanted her to know the curious elation that washed over him when at last they landed and fell on the beach at the feet of the crowd, but he couldn't tell her. He said, "It was like nothing I've ever done before."

She waited for him to continue. "That's all?"

"We were saviors, for God's sake. Those men were burning, and we saved them. I was scared to death."

"Of course, you had to be."

"No, that's not what I mean. I mean, it was our choice and we saved them. It scares me to think about it, even now."

The look on her face told him she still did not understand.

"Listen to me: I made up for all my sins last night."

She nodded, her hands steepled on the oilcloth of the table. Keith got up and lit a coal-oil lamp and trimmed the wick carefully, not to have too much glow. With both hands he set the lamp on the table so the flame just caught Mary's eyes. He looked there and seemed to find a message and moved to take her in his arms.

"No, don't," she said. "Not now, not tonight. We just can't." She had not flinched at all, nor moved away. He knew he could have her and she would neither protest nor tell. He was sure about that, had never been more sure of anything in his life. She might not even regret it later, but just then he knew that always he would.

"Where are you going?" she said.

"To see my brothers." And then he was out the door.

7

KEITH SKIRTED Buxton Woods and felt good to be outdoors, walking. The woods was a stunted forest of gnarled scrub oak, pitch pine, and briars stubbornly rooted in sand bog that became treacherous after a heavy rainfall. He followed a path he had walked many times as a boy, and he entered the stationhouse feeling different than he used to, not like a visitor anymore. He had a right to be there, a right to help himself to the teapot and smoke in the company of the men.

Toby Bannister was in the tower. Chief Lord and Joe Trent had the beach patrol tonight. The rest had retired to their quarters, and the Navy men were having a meeting upstairs that included Jack, going over the boat and their duties. The first officer ran the meeting, Keith recognized his voice and wondered where Halstead was. The mechanic had volunteered for sea duty, and the mate had cleared it with Portsmouth on the wireless.

Cy Magillicutty left the common room with a great show of weariness. He had the early-morning tower watch. Jack came downstairs after the meeting to sit with Malcolm and Keith. It was the first time the three of them had been together, alone, since Keith had come back.

Malcolm said, "How do your hands feel?"

"Good enough to pull an oar if I have to." He knew that was what Malcolm wanted to hear, and he wished right away that he hadn't sounded so melodramatic. Jack scowled at him.

"Good boy," Malcolm said.

"How do you like running with that Navy daredevil, Jack?" Keith said.

Jack didn't answer him. Instead he turned away and poured himself a cup of tea. He stirred it for quite a while, though he added no sugar or cream to it. None of them drank it that way, but there was always sugar and fresh cream on the table next to the stove. Jack fiddled and stirred.

"What's got into you?" Keith said.

Jack turned abruptly and spilt hot tea across the fingers of his hand holding the cup, though if he was burned he did not show it. "Go back up north," he said. "You're just a tourist here now, and you know it."

"That's not fair," Malcolm said.

"Don't talk to me about fair. Was it fair for him to go trotting off to college and leave it all to us?"

"I paid my own freight. I had a scholarship."

Jack put down his teacup. "That's not the point."

"You can believe what you like," Keith said.

"I damn well don't need your permission for that—"

"For the love of God, Jack! He's been gone three and a half years, and this is how you treat him."

Jack was nearly shouting now. "He should have stayed away. He had his chance to come home."

"I didn't know," Keith said. "How was I to know?" But there was no forgiveness in Jack's face.

During Keith's first year at Harvard, his mother had taken ill. They had thought it was the cancer, but the doctor couldn't be sure and Mrs. Royal steadfastly refused to go to the hospital in Norfolk. Keith had felt afterward that if he had only been there, he would have hauled her bodily to the hospital, never mind her wishes. But it had happened in December, when he was off on a skiing holiday in the Berkshires. Three days after the funeral he had returned to Cambridge and found a telegram. He had crossed the Charles River to a bar, where he got riotously drunk with no explanations to anybody, including the bartender, who felt sorry for him and hired a cab at his own expense to get Keith back to his room.

"We've been over this," Malcolm said, his voice weary with anger at the edge of it. "I think you blame yourself. That's it, isn't it? You blame yourself."

Jack raised a hand then abruptly lowered it to his uniform pants, slapping at some dirt. He's afraid of Malcolm, Keith thought, and smiled just a little.

"It was not right, what you did." Jack finally said.

"It was out of my hands."

"She asked for you," Jack said.

"What?"

"I can't say it any plainer, boy. Do you understand? She asked for you. She kept asking for you, all night long. She died like that, asking for you."

Jack turned away. Malcolm averted his eyes. Silence settled on them. For Keith, the scene lost its clarity and the faces of his brothers lost definition and familiarity. He went to the window and looked out, thinking of his mother, trying to recall the contours of her face, the gray lights of her eyes. Malcolm laid a hand on his shoulder. Keith continued staring.

"Come over and have some tea," Malcolm said.

"All right."

Jack had gone upstairs, his booted footsteps echoing behind him.

"It wasn't as bad as all that," Malcolm said.

They sat together, and Keith recognized a love that saddened him, because he didn't believe his soul was great enough for it.

"So how is Mary holding up?" Malcolm said.

"Fine. Too much of her own company, maybe."

Malcolm nodded. "She does get lonesome. Sometimes I cannot figure out why I do it, what keeps me here year after year. But it's all I ever wanted to do."

"Why don't you go home tonight? I'll come for you if there's trouble."

"There are rules. You know that."

"It's not the rules, it's tradition. That's all it is. It doesn't make sense anymore, not with the telephone and the wireless. And the others taking turns going home to their families. You're not fooling anybody."

"I don't know—"

"Look, when's the last time you went off station?"

"Maybe you're right. You know that Toby is in the tower?"

"He'll be all right. He wouldn't sleep anyway. He has to have something to do."

Suddenly Malcolm felt profoundly tired. He would be only a shout away in case of trouble at the station. He got up and put on his hat, and then Jack came downstairs. "Going somewhere?" he said.

Malcolm sat back down, relit his pipe, and sat, smoking. Keith wondered again if he should have come back at all.

CHAPTER 8

1

IN THE PURE GOLD LIGHT of dawn, Tim Halstead's refitted rum-runner *Sealion* gleamed with cold, hard lines. She was a dangerous, sleek boat, and he climbed aboard past the night sentry with an easy step, his hat newly cocked a little to one side.

He had something like a smile on his face, and he had none of that nervous look about him anymore. He ran a hand over the rebuilt torpedo sleeve, paced the immaculate, narrow deck to the stern, where two explosive canisters were poised in their Y-guns. Depth bombs.

The warrant officer who had come down in the car promised unlimited supplies and ordnance from the base at Portsmouth. "You shoot them, we'll reload them," he said. Halstead would have been embarrassed with pride a few days ago. Now he realized that behind the warrant officer's generosity lay the discouraging fact that there wasn't a free cutter anywhere on the coast, from the Keys to the Virginia Capes. There was submarine activity off New York and Massachusetts. A wolfpack, it was rumored. Thirteen vessels lost in a single week, five of them fighting ships of the line. There were priorities, and no help for Hatteras but his own cigar boat. Halstead had all the torpedoes, ammunition, and depth charges he wanted, and a truck to deliver them to the slip. They had given his dead engineer a medal. They were big on medals these days. Halstead himself might even get one, but the thought did not cheer him. Their freedom with decorations only meant that things were getting worse. The war was coming home at last.

Jack Royal sauntered aboard like a cocky midshipman, and Halstead, neither angry nor irritable, said, "You're late, Mister Royal. I was getting ready to send a man to fetch you."

"I never miss a fool's errand."

"If you're trying to bait me, save your breath." It was going to be a bright day. He kicked the steel of the torpedo sleeve lightly with the heel of his shoe. He gave his orders, the big engines turned over, and then he took his place in the cockpit, reached for his big Navy glasses, and looked out to sea. He wondered if he would see the German today, and he wondered too about Dorothy's father, whether or not he was still alive. Now as the men cast off and the engines throttled up, it occurred to Halstead that the *Sealion* was built for running away, not for chasing.

2

MALCOLM ROYAL SLEPT later than he had wanted to. He awoke all at once and panicked. Something had jarred him out of dreaming, and he was downstairs in a hurry, buttoning his tunic as he vaulted the stairs.

"Morning," Toby Bannister said. "There's some griddle cakes and hominy, if you're interested."

"Toby."

"It was quiet," Toby said.

Malcolm nodded.

"It's all right," Toby said.

"I know, I know."

"Halstead's gone out."

"Jack with him?"

"Don't worry, now."

"Have you seen Keith?"

"You're a mother hen this morning, Malcolm. He went home a couple of hours ago."

Malcolm went out onto the porch and gradually his heart calmed down. He squinted through the glare toward his house and imagined Mary still asleep in her bed. She always slept stilly and woke fresh and unruffled and all at once, the way Malcolm never did. His sleep was usually a struggle, interrupted by a babble of voices, foreign and familiar, and he would wake relieved, exhausted from his dreams and troubled by the voices. He stretched, imagined Mary slipping out of bed and cooling her face in the basin, combing and pinning her hair, then moving downstairs to heat water for coffee. Whether he slept at home or not, he usually drank coffee with Mary in the kitchen mornings.

Somehow the thought depressed him. His dreams had again been full of words, a confusion of words, soundless and jumbled as bees in a jar.

He stood and listened to it all for a moment: the murmur of men's voices from the mess, the snorting of Homer in his stable, the soft rush of a breeze in his ears, the waves, subdued, sounding a long way off.

He thought he would go home for a while this morning. Maybe he would do that.

3

THE CAPTAIN SURFACED the U-boat early and far out to sea. He had run them very far north and out of the shipping lanes to get his breath. He had been counting torpedoes. He had started this patrol with a dozen, and he had four left. He was learning to fight with his deck cannons, learning to be a surface raider again, and he wanted time to think, time to inspect his boat, time to plan.

He summoned Max Wien to the tower.

"Tell me," the captain said in German. "Why haven't they sent a destroyer after me?"

The first officer busied himself with his glasses, but Max could tell he was listening. Perhaps he was miffed that the captain should be consulting a common seaman on matters of strategy. Two other men were out of earshot, poised in the metal-railed crow's nests along either side of the tower. Bergen and his assistant stood ready at the forward gun. The aftergun was still manteled.

"They don't have one, I suppose," Max said. "Maybe we are doing better than we expected."

The captain nodded and lit a cigar, a rare pleasure. There was, of course, no smoking belowdecks when they ran submerged. Air was too precious. The captain pointed with his cigar. It was not a rude gesture but an elegant one, the kind that comes naturally to gentlemen sipping brandy in a softly lighted library after dinner.

"Yes, I think you are right about that. Unfortunately, we have no way of knowing. *Wir haben Kontackt verloren.*" We have lost our ears.

For the first time Max noticed that the radio mast was gone. There were ragged holes in the wall of the tower, and dents on the hatch cover.

"He was a good shot, Captain."

"You could say that."

"*Glück gehabt*," the mate said, the glasses held to his face like long, doubled fists. Lucky.

The captain ignored him. "I like talking to you, Max. You are a man of sense. You do not overlook the obvious. You would be surprised at how many of us do."

Max said nothing. He had seen men overstep their bounds. He was in a position to get fresh air as often as the officers, and he would do nothing to jeopardize that. He was not surprised it had come to this: that a man should organize his loyalties to insure a little room for breathing.

"Did you ever expect we would go this far?"

Max had to answer a direct question. "There are many who would like to be in our place, Captain."

"Oh, enough of that. We're a long way from the recruiting office now. We can talk as men. We are living on borrowed time in the enemy's home waters without a radio—how long do you think we can keep it up?"

He didn't think the captain really wanted an answer.

"Sometimes, Max, sometimes I think we have come too far."

"*Kapitän*—" The mate turned from his glasses to make his objection.

"It's all right, Kraft. Keep your lookout." He enjoyed his cigar a moment. "You know what we are doing here, Max? Have you thought about it, cowering down below waiting for the depth bombs to come, listening to the bullets piercing our flimsy hull? You men down there all must have thought about it." He poked his finger into one of the holes, and a little blood came off the end of it. He stanched it with his thumb.

"*Ich tue meine Pflicht, Kapitän.* What else can I do?"

"Yes, duty." The captain puffed his cigar slowly, savoring it. The smell was acrid against the salt air, and to Max it was a little nauseating. "You answer well, but you do not sound very enthusiastic." He laughed shortly, then his face took on a stern cast, his eyes set. Now he looks like a U-boat commander again, Max thought.

"We are collecting chips for the bargaining table, Max. When we talk armistice with the English, we must not appear too eager. We cannot afford to be weak. We must do as much damage as we can and make them afraid of what we can do. In other words, we must be as theatrical as possible. And if we do things that—well. It is imperative that we come to terms quickly, before we are found out—"

"*Kapitän!*"

The mate was at his elbow now, his eyes fierce with judgment, as if he had been betrayed.

"It's all right, Kraft. Who will hear us? It is no less a duty because it is unpleasant. That is the noblest duty, don't you agree? We have never been in a position to do more for our country than at this moment—don't you see that?"

Max and the mate both assented mutely.

"We will speak of this again, but only up here and only when I say. These are brave men. There is no reason to rob them of hope. It will not make them fight any better."

Kraft was silent, unsure. He could not tell if his captain was a traitor or a hero.

Max watched Stracken puff smoke against the wind, watched the submarine's bow cut through the green bright water, watched Bergen lean into his deck gun, fooling with the sights. "If I may ask, Captain," Max said, "why did you tell me these things?"

The captain puffed his cigar and threw it overboard before he answered. "You're right, of course, but whom else do I have to tell?"

The starboard watch sang out: a boat on the horizon.

Kraft squinted into his glasses. "It looks like a fisherman, Captain."

Max reluctantly made to leave the tower for his duties below.

"Max, stay up awhile. Let's see who this fisherman is."

Max listened to orders relayed down the hatch and lost in the silence there. Bergen's loader chambered a shell and Bergen wheeled the gun to firing elevation. The engines churned, closing the distance between the two boats.

4

Brian Dant knew they were being watched several minutes

before the long, low shape of the U-boat appeared on the port beam. From the point his father had chosen his course, Brian had been sure this time would come. The pang of recognition unnerved him, but he quickly recovered. He was not after adventure, had not envisioned himself the hero of his own fantasy. He was simply a quiet boy who liked being out on the water. He had no use for heroism. The Malcolm Royals of this world were the heroes. Still, it was just as he had imagined it: the U-boat cruising toward them with all the grace of a log, its hull the color of sharkskin, the crew gaunt and sullen, their faces livid as the faces of corpses.

"Dad—we have company," he said. He picked up the shark rifle with all the reluctance of a ditchdigger taking up his spade after the lunch hour.

"Don't do anything just yet, boy. Let's see what they want."

"I think that's clear."

"Maybe they'll leave us be."

"Maybe. What can we do?"

Alvin didn't answer. Instead, he studied the submarine through binoculars, watched four men inflating a rubber boat on the foredeck under the barrel of the deck cannon, the sun almost directly behind them. Aft, two men were stripping the mantel off another gun. Alvin fingered the grip of his shotgun. He didn't need binoculars now to keep track of the rubber boat of armed men fast making for them, and he didn't have to look again to know that both deck cannons were trained on his flimsy pilothouse. There was nothing he could do.

"What do they want?" Brian said. "Why are they coming over?" And again Alvin said nothing.

"Maybe they want fresh fish," Brian said.

"Then I'm glad I don't have any."

When the rubber boat was a dozen yards off, one of the Germans hailed Alvin in English. "Hallo on the *Pelican*. We will not harm you. We will board you with armed men. Please do not resist."

"Just like them," Alvin said to the boy. "Don't even ask my permission. Well, what are we going to do?" He stepped out of the pilothouse, leaving the shotgun behind, in the locker. He told Brian to stow the rifle, too. Once on deck, he cupped his hands. "Hallo in the dinghy. Come aboard. We are not armed." Not really, he thought. It wasn't the time for explanations.

The Germans handled the dinghy efficiently and soon tied up alongside the *Pelican*. Two men trained rifles on the pilothouse, while a minor officer wearing medical insignia and the interpreter who had hailed Alvin came aboard. Both wore sidearms.

"Good day to you," Max said. He thought they might as well be polite about this. Maybe they'd get further.

"What do you want on my boat?"

"Please, please. How many in your crew, Captain?"

"Just me and my boy. Brian, come out here." Brian's face appeared at the pilothouse window, but he didn't come down. All at once, Alvin knew what was on his mind. He found it hard to speak slowly and clearly.

"Good. Brian—please do as your father says. Come down here."

Brian did not move.

"How old is he?" Max asked.

"Just fourteen."

"I see." But the officer, impatient, was already beckoning one of the boarding party to bring the boy down. Max caught the look in Alvin Dant's eye. Or Alvin swore he did, because the interpreter raised an arm to stop the man. "Wait. His father will bring him down."

Alvin, grateful, nodded, turned, walked slowly to the pilothouse. Inside, Brian had his hands on the rifle.

"Put it down, boy," Alvin whispered in a voice without hope or power.

"Why?"

"It's no good."

"They're just going to kill us—don't you know that? I could get them all."

"No, Brian, it won't work."

"I could, you know."

"Not the ones on the U-boat, boy. Use your head."

Brian stood holding the rifle. Alvin did not really believe he was going to put it down. The boy had got an idea in his head. Had become suddenly and totally independent.

Brian laid the rifle in the rack, where it usually hung.

"Come on."

Now Max was in the pilothouse, too. "What goes on here?"

"Nothing, nothing. My boy is afraid of you, that's all."

Max noticed the rifle. He looked at the fisherman.

"For sharks," he said. "We hardly ever use it."

Max hesitated. Should he confiscate it? He decided he wasn't a thief. "We're not going to hurt you, boy," the interpreter said. Alvin and Brian followed him down.

The Germans were tense. They expected trouble. Alvin smiled but not too broadly. He moved their way directly, but not too fast. "He was frightened of you," he said.

Max had been among warriors for so long that he hardly remembered a time when he too might have been scared out of his wits at sight of foreign uniforms and oil-smelling guns gripped in expert, nervous fingers.

"Who would not be frightened," the officer said. "But we did not come to frighten you." He was growing impatient, Max could tell. Like most mariners, he felt in jeopardy every moment he was off his own vessel. An attack on the U-boat now would strand him and his boarding party in enemy waters in an act of apparent piracy, exposed to capture and worse. He fidgeted and tried to get Max to hurry up.

Max took his time. He liked the feeling of being on this boat, and he did not think beyond the present. Enlisted men have no business with the future.

"We would like to trade with you. We need some things."

"Is that so."

"Yes."

In the end, Alvin gave up half of his coffee and most of his sugar, as well as half a dozen fresh eggs, some oranges, and an ounce of tobacco as a personal gift to the U-boat commander, who Max said used a pipe. Max had done well. They paid in American dollars, and they paid well. They could never spend them anywhere else, and they had plenty.

"Where did you get this?" Alvin asked Max, fingering the bills. They weren't crisp but greasy with use. "It's not queer, is it?"

"Excuse me?"

"You know, queer, phony, bogus—counterfeit."

Max laughed, and the other two sailors relaxed and laughed with him. For the first time, they let their gun barrels lower.

"No it's not 'queer' at all. It's the true McCoy—isn't that how you say it?" Max was doing fine. He was really quite pleased with himself.

"Yes, that's how we say it." Alvin pocketed the wad of bills.

"You're having engine trouble, I take it?"

"Cracked the head. We can't fix it, if that's what you mean."

Max said something in German, and one of the sailors slung his weapon and went aft to look at the engine. He was gone only a few minutes, and reported to the officer, who passed it along unnecessarily to Max.

"He says he can't fix it, either. You need a salvage part."

"That's the way I see it," Alvin agreed.

"Under other circumstances, we would tow you in, but . . ."

"I understand."

Max turned and discussed something with the impatient officer. Then he turned back to Alvin. "He says you can come aboard with us and take your chances. If the opportunity arises, we can come inshore and let you swim for it. That is the best we can offer."

Alvin shook his head. "Thanks, but we don't swim."

Max put out his hand and Alvin took it.

"What's your name?"

"Max Wien."

"MacSween? That's a funny name for a German."

Max didn't bother to correct him.

"Well, good-bye, Mister MacSween. Perhaps we'll not meet again."

Max suddenly felt guilty standing toe to toe with this man. He dropped the other's hand abruptly and clambered into the rubber boat, feeling his cheeks flush hot. What he would have given to have an hour of talk on that sweet deck, breathing fresh air and listening to water slap against wood, not metal. They pushed off and drew quickly away from the *Pelican*.

Alvin watched them go and heard the crack of the rifle before they had covered half the distance. Their officer leaned forward in his seat, shot through the back of the head.

Alvin grabbed the rifle before Brian could throw in the bolt again. He shoved the boy to the far corner of the pilothouse and scrambled to get the glasses. He could see the dead man being hauled aboard by his mates. He could see MacSween waving his fist and glaring. He expected the impact of a shell.

5

BERGEN GOT off one shot before the plane came, a hurried shot that whistled by the *Pelican's* mast and dashed up a geyser some twenty yards beyond her. As he was adjusting the range and his loader chambered another round, the lookout raised the alarm and the order was to limber guns and prepare to dive.

Max Wien helped lower the dead *Marina Artzt*, Ernst, down the hatch. Captain Stracken watched, disbelieving. Ernst, their medical officer, was unrecognizable except for the insignia on his sleeve.

Max had no time for reflection as he hustled down the ladder onto the cramped periscope bridge, the alarm going off all around him, men rushing to the forward part of the boat. But a sense of betrayal choked him. He had left the rifle, had counted on honor, and he should have known better. He thought of Ernst's head bursting, and the sound of the hatch banging shut overhead signaled doom for him. It clamped the lid on whatever hope he may have had, slamming like a cell door at his back. He bit his lip and charged forward with the rest of them, piled in the sweat and filth, remembered the tang of salt in his nostrils, and waited for the depth bombs to come.

When he put his face in his hands, it came away sticky with blood.

6

THE AEROPLANE THE LOOKOUT SAW was a mail plane from Beaufort that had strayed off course. It was not a sub spotter and it carried no bombs.

But in Captain Stracken's experience, an aeroplane often worked in concert with a destroyer, finding the prey, then signaling its position. He wondered if that American speedster was in the area. That one he could outgun. But their luck had been too good for too long, and he fully expected a destroyer to be hunting him before the hour was up.

They would wait. That fisherman had no motor, one of the sailors had said so. She would be there when they came up for air tonight, and they would cut her to pieces to give Bergen target practice.

Captain Stracken had some trouble seeing into the periscope, his eyes were so bright with anger and grief.

7

WHEN THE SHOT WENT over their heads and he saw the gunners covering their guns for sea, Alvin ran out on deck, shrugging off Brian. He spotted the aeroplane immediately and waved to the pilot with both hands over his head. He stripped off his red shirt and waved that, too, but he didn't think the pilot even noticed him.

8

"DID YOU KNOW the emperor Napoleon hired Robert Fulton to build him a submarine? He was tired of the British fleet keeping him all bottled up." Keith was dealing cards. They were playing war, he and Mary. Later she had to go down to the village, and she thought perhaps Keith and Dorothy would want to come along, it was such a lovely day.

"Where do you learn these things? Are you sure it was Napoleon?" She had her hair pinned up, brushed and clean. But Keith had made up his mind to stop noticing her.

"He never had submarines, that's the point." Keith's hands moved, and the cards accumulated almost magically in two piles in front of them. "He challenged Fulton to blow up an old schooner in the harbor at Marseilles by using a submarine." Keith had seen illustrations in a naval history text he had borrowed from Professor Rusonovsky, a retired old Prussian soldier. There was a sketch of Fulton's cronies screwing a gimlet attached to a mine into the ship's hull, all from the safety of their submarine chamber.

They were playing out their cards now, Mary winning. She beat two queens in a row with kings. "Didn't it work?" she asked.

"It worked fine, that was the problem. Blew it sky-high, right under their noses. They threw him out of France."

"I thought you said it worked."

He took two hands with a five and a seven to her three and four. "He scared the daylights out of them. They hadn't realized, you see. No one ever realizes. It would revolutionize warfare, and they weren't ready to take responsibility for it. Not even Napoleon."

Professor Rusonovsky's lectures had turned more and more into diatribes against the war. At first Keith had been in awe of the bewhiskered old warrior strutting back and forth on the dais, punctuating his pronouncements with red fists sunburned on the battlefields of three continents. "The Germans did not want unlimited submarine warfare," he would shout. "They were driven to it by historical necessity. Doesn't that tell you where all this is going to lead?" Keith managed a fair impersonation of the professor for Mary.

"Necessity? God," she said.

In his own voice, Keith said: "Seriously. Their fleet is all sunk or blockaded in harbor by now. What else can they do?" He explained the rest to her: how Fulton went to the British after the Peace of Amiens and how they turned him down flat, reasoning that as soon as one nation had the damned thing every nation would have to have one, and that would spell the end of British maritime dominance. "Fulton had no politics except the politics of progress, so he said."

"So do they all say."

He went on about how Fulton went to the Americans, who discouraged him so much that he gave up and designed a steamboat. But the Germans had already got hold of the idea, and one of their officers, Bauer, built his own boat. By 1914 every major power, even the backward Russians, had a fleet of submarines. Naval battles would never again be fought among only warships.

"That's awful."

"That's what's happening now."

"It can't be turned back?"

"Napoleon's Ministry of Marine tried. It was inevitable, I guess. Things won't be the same after this war, I promise you."

"But merchant ships, innocent fishermen—"

"Our merchant marine is killing Germans in Flanders, from the German point of view. It's all a matter of how far you're willing to go."

"But no one is safe, anywhere."

"No. And wait till we see aerial bombardment." The game was

over. Mary had swept it all in the last dozen hands.

"I've read about the blimps dropping bombs over London," she said.

"That's nothing." Keith collected the cards and tapped the deck on the tabletop. "They'll build aeroplanes big enough to carry tons of bombs, whole fleets of them. It'll come like rain, firestorm from the clouds. Mark my words." He had lifted that line from Rusonovsky, whose students had finally deserted him in the patriotic fervor that swept campus. He was mocked as a seditionist, and even Keith had grown weary of the old man's sermonizing, though now Keith found main truth in the Prussian's words.

"I don't believe it," Mary said.

"Oh, it's true. The old rules don't apply anymore."

She whispered: "But they have to."

9

AFTER KEITH CRANKED, he and Mary climbed into the Winton Flyer and fixed their goggles and settled the skirts of their linen dusters. Keith had one of the few motorcars on the island and was proud of it, even if it had flat springs, unmatched tires, and uneven paint. He had bought it at auction with most of his savings. It was no racer, but on the flat, hard road that lined the island like a spine it could do better than twenty miles an hour, faster on the beach with a following wind.

"Can we bring Rufus?" Dorothy called. She stood on the porch with a man's cotton work shirt tied by its tails around her midriff.

"I don't care," he said. "Whatever you want."

Rufus bounded out of the house all feet and fur and took his position in the backseat, beside Dorothy. Keith offered her a pair of goggles, but she declined. "All set, Captain—take off."

They rode toward the inlet. Dorothy leaned up between them and said, above the noise of the motor, "Nobody has reported any sign of my father's boat."

Keith let it go. Mary looked uncertainly at him, then turned to Dorothy. "Look, I know how you must feel. And I don't want to get your hopes up, but I have a feeling they're coming back. That's all, just a feeling." She had harbored no such hope about her own father Dennis Dant's return.

Keith wondered if Mary were lying to keep Dorothy's spirits up. The island women had taken turns visiting Dorothy until yesterday, when she'd made it clear she didn't want company: It had too much the quality of a wake.

"They were all trying to make me feel good," she said.

"Virginia, Mrs. Patchett, even Mrs. Littlejohn. They were all trying so hard, but I feel bad. Can't I just feel bad?" Dorothy was on the verge of tears again.

Mary reached an arm back to console her. "They'll come back, Dot. They will. They have to."

"Ginny has Jack, and you have Malcolm. But who do I have? Who?"

Mary looked at Keith but did not say his name. She was confused about this. Rufus insinuated his big dark head under Dorothy's arm and she hugged him hard and scratched behind his ears. His big brown eyes rolled with pleasure. Dorothy's eyes were closed.

10

KEITH ROLLED the Winton Flyer down a concrete slab of wharf next to Oman's Dock. Mary wanted to order some fresh fish sent up later. She had in mind a special meal for the crew.

"You could have done that on the telephone," Keith said.

"And done what all the rest of the day? I like to watch the boats come and go."

Dorothy had composed herself. She would remain in limbo until someone would finally arrive with the truth, absolute and unalterable, and when that moment came, she knew, she would be relieved. In the meantime, there was Tim Halstead. After he'd left her early this morning, she had felt utterly abandoned, and she didn't want that feeling ever again. She hadn't felt guilty, but confused and in a kind of jeopardy she recognized but could not name.

"Isn't this Patchy's slip?" Mary said. "I thought he had a boat down here."

"And so he did," Oman said. "He's an odd duck, that one. Worked like a nigger the last couple of days and then slipped his cable before sunup. Beat the other boats out. Damnedest thing."

Mary ordered blues and soft-shelled crabs. When the boats came in this afternoon, Oman would send her a parcel of the best.

"How's the man-mountain keeping in all this excitement, Mary?"

"They're going out so much, you know."

"I've heard. It's time we put a stop to that pirate, if you ask me." Oman turned to Dorothy. "Anything I can do for you today, Dot?"

She shook her head.

"Then I guess you'll have a cup of tea with me, seeing we're not working. I'm keeping pretty shabby company these days. I could use the conversation."

They followed him inside the corrugated tin shed that contained his office and the tables for cleaning fish. Oman's boy Ricky was hosing the place, then sweeping the water out the open side facing the dock. The office was just an old desk and a filing cabinet set back in the far corner of the shed. Oman pulled up some crates for his guests to sit on, and over tea told them that some of the Cape men had been in touch with some of the village men and together they were planning a meeting.

"When?"

"Tomorrow, I think."

"Littlejohn's?" Keith said.

Oman shook his head and scratched it. "Too many folks for that closet. It'll have to be at the church."

There was only one church of any size, the Presbyterian church just south of Buxton at a site the U.S. Post Office inexplicably called Frisco, but which none of the islanders called by any name at all. The place was just the church and a few houses, anyway.

Mary said, "I don't see what we can do."

Dorothy sipped her tea.

Oman fiddled with his yellowed meerschaum. "I don't go in much for politics myself," he explained. "You want politics, talk to Littlejohn. Ask Littlejohn about politics."

"How's that?" Keith asked.

"Never mind. How's your brothers getting along? How's that cranky old man of yours? Haven't seen him around."

"You'll see him coming, all right. He's toting a rifle, waiting for the invasion."

"Ah, the courage of the armed man."

Keith talked about his family while Dorothy sipped her tea. Oman puffed his pipe, and Mary watched the colors change at the windows. Watching the light, she felt she might soon arrange a palette, stretch a canvas, and paint again. She would start tomorrow.

Dorothy said, "Where did Peter Patchett go, Mister Oman?

"Go?" He laughed. "Well, I don't suppose he went anywhere," he said between leisurely puffs. "That is to say, he didn't tell me. But he's always trafficked on the Sound, he never goes out onto the big water."

Dorothy nodded. She was on the verge of a thought, but it slipped away like an eel in dark water.

11

ALL ALONE WAS Patch Patchett.

Ahead was a vision of open water, and he headed for it, skipper of a well-found boat. He'd studied the charts, but how they translated into a green sea he didn't know. Still he would try.

He knew the rest of it all had somehow gone too far. Men were forgetting themselves, as he had the first day on the beach when all that mattered was getting out of the way of exploding sand dunes. Now he had collected himself, despite a wife who did her best to confound him and two kids who defied his best parenting, which he knew had never been any too good.

But men all around him were getting caught up. The U-boat was their problem. Alvin Dant and Brian would be his problem. Patchy smiled. The others would be surprised. "Patchy?" they would say—"not Patchy!"

His father had pulled an oar with the Chicamacomico crew up north. There had been a storm and a wreck on the shoals and Patchy's father, though bony and loose-limbed, was Captain Dailey's No. 1 just as Jack Royal was Malcolm's No. 1 and should have been with his crew. But there he had stood by his wife's deathbed, dripping water off his sou'wester onto the floor. His wife, Patchy's mother, had said, "What are you doing here?" And there had been no answer, only a look of shame in his father's eyes. So Patchy's father had never gone back to the station but got a job first at a shipyard in Norfolk and then dragged four-year-old Patchy north with him from port to port to grow up on the sawdusted floors of rough taverns and learn variety in swearing and fornication by the time he was fourteen.

In the course of time, Patchy retreated to the island and married old Fetterman's granddaughter, who was neither pretty nor especially kind, but who owned a house near the sea. No one was pleased by the union but no one remarked it, either, for old Fetterman commanded enough respect that they would keep their objections to themselves so long as he sat carving on that throne at Littlejohn's.

Patchy had few clear memories of his mother, only that she was very blonde and used to take him to the seashore almost every day in fair weather. She had helped him gather seashells and held his arms when he waded in the breakers. Afterward, her hands had toweled him gently dry. He could not save any more than that of her. As far as Patchy was concerned, his father had done the right thing.

12

IN THE LATE AFTERNOON, Ricky Oman stood in a bloody apron at the cleaning counter, whipping the heads off channel bass and carving fillets with a dexterity that would have made old Fetterman proud.

CHAPTER 9

1

MALCOLM ROYAL DIDN'T breakfast with his men. Instead, he sat outside, watching the weather come in over the ocean. It would be a minor squall, probably. The sky changed in a matter of minutes, as it often did, from clear and blue to roiling dirty clouds scudding up from the south.

Malcolm decided to go home for a while.

He was in good spirits now. There had been no incidents in the night, Toby Bannister had carried out his long night's watch, and now Keith had taken his first great step toward becoming a surfman. When Malcolm got home he'd ask Mary for a good strong cup of coffee. He had drunk enough tea. Maybe he would take her walking on the beach.

It seemed a long time since he had done anything special with Mary. When she used to paint, set up on the dunes in sight of the station, he would take beach patrol just to walk by the place where she sat, to wave a clumsy hand at her. He admired that she could do something fine. His own dexterity was limited, his fingers just too big for most delicate things. He had watched her brush paint onto the canvas in light, graceful strokes. There was magic in it.

Malcolm hurried his steps home now. It was only a little farther, and he had things he wanted to tell Mary. But he had always been a little thick of speech. Once, tentatively, he had tried to explain about a rescue he'd made in which one of his men had almost drowned. But there weren't words for it, and whenever he tried to tell a story like that she would be gloomy for days afterward, brooding.

So they did not talk much and Mary did not paint anymore. Often she walked the beach alone, or now sometimes with Keith. They were drawn to one another, Malcolm knew, but Keith had always been a good boy, and now that he was back everything would come around. The three brothers would work together, just as Malcolm had always imagined. Jack could be a sonofabitch, but all it would take to straighten him out was for him to get a station of his own. There had been talk that at the end of the war the Coast Guard would add a station on the bight, where Halstead's boat slip was. It was a good location. If Malcolm could have Keith, he would surrender Jack, let him run his own show, pick his own men.

At the house Malcolm realized Keith's motorcar was gone. Probably down at Littlejohn's, or down at the village. Keith was certainly proud of that damned thing. Malcolm opened the door to his home like a suitor, but Mary was not there.

2

Ham Fetterman shifted in his seat. These days his bones tended to stick out in awkward places. He accepted discomfort as the price he paid for seeing all he'd seen these many years. In younger days, his bones had been padded with healthy muscle and fat earned in ports all over the world—Singapore, Djakarta, Istanbul, Sydney, Calais, Hong Kong. He had sailed on most of the ships he now modeled, or their cousins.

But not this new, gray thing. He turned it in his hands. The shape was still not right, not sharp enough. And the tower—he could not get the tower detailed exactly. He was used to being exact.

"Are you coming to the meeting?" Littlejohn wanted to know. He was limping very perceptively now, with the weather.

"Your pin acting up again? So's mine. Couple of gimps."

"It's all this excitement. When I get anxious, you know, it comes back."

"See that you don't strain it too much."

"I know to take care of myself."

"That'll be the day," Mrs. Littlejohn said from the back room.

Fetterman absently turned the model in his hand. He was looking out the window. There were clues he had missed.

Littlejohn limped from behind the counter and sat in an old rattan chair next to Fetterman, whose hands immediately quieted and laid the model aside.

"How's the missus keeping?" Fetterman asked just loud enough for his voice to carry into the back.

"Better than she deserves. Do you know how old that woman's getting?"

Mrs. Littlejohn emerged then and said: "Never mind that. In a previous life, I lived to be a hundred and four." And disappeared stiffly, like a figure on a Swiss clock.

Littlejohn said, "I got to ask you, Ham. Is there any hope for Al Dant? Is there any way that salty rascal can find his way home again?"

"Shh," Fetterman said, resuming his work. "Don't be speaking ill of the dead."

3

JACK ROYAL FELT the full spray in his face and at his elbow that puffed-up martinet Halstead, a man fool enough to think a couple of ash cans on the stern and searchlights in the cockpit had transformed the boat into a deadly subchaser. The kid reminded Jack of stories his Scottish relatives told of submarine patrols on the channel coast at the very start of the war: Picket boats of men armed with hammers and burlap sacks plied the coast, and the strategy was to spot a periscope sticking out of the water, sneak up on it from behind, bag it with the burlap sack, then knock out the periscope glass with the hammer. Like killing a chicken.

Nobody knew what he was doing these days, Jack reflected, not even Malcolm. He was pretty sure Malcolm was responsible for getting him assigned to this nonesuch. What did Malcolm have against him?

Cross said: "The German's been seen north of the Light. This morning. It came over the wireless—a mail plane spotted him making for the open sea."

"That's dandy," Jack said. Maybe now there would be an end to any more crazy heroics. Let the real Navy fight that guy. Jack was as brave as the next man, but he had no wish to give up his life for his country. For Virginia, yes; for his father, his family, for his island. But not his country. "Maybe we're rid of the bugger, then."

"I doubt it," Cross said.

"I think," Halstead said, "that he's just hiding from the plane— I mean, wouldn't you? He's a little far from home, gentlemen." Halstead thought the "gentlemen" sounded effective. It was what they said at the Academy. He would remember it and use it again.

Jack studied the clouds rolling in behind them.

4

THE SQUALL BLEW down on them in one driving gust. Rain lashed them and the seas churned lead-gray and held deep troughs. "Face her to the wind," Halstead commanded. *Sealion* was riding too heavily. Her new hardware kept her stern low and reduced her freeboard to almost nothing in this kind of sea.

"Weather, Mister Halstead," Jack Royal said.

"It'll blow over," Halstead said. But he was amazed that such weather had come up so fast. They had watched it a-building, so far off it was, and now they were smack in it with nothing to do but try to ride it out.

"We're shipping water!" the new engineer called. "The engines are swamping—"

Halstead threw in the throttle. They had one chance—to plane at speed. He took her up to twenty knots and held her there, riding each wave recklessly, gripping the wheel in bloodless hands.

Jack Royal had his cork vest well fastened. He had no illusions about rescue so far out in such a heavy sea. Even Malcolm would concede defeat on this one, he thought, but it did not cheer him.

The boat nosedived into each new wave but, because of the sealed superstructure—proof against the prying eyes of revenue cutter boarding parties—the boat stayed afloat. Halstead drove *Sealion* like a spear into the teeth of the gale as he ran for the bight.

They might make it at that, Jack Royal thought, they just might. And then he thought: Let this goddamned boat go down, let this nonsense end. But let's get closer in first.

5

KEITH, Dorothy, and Mary braved the rain and wind in the open car and headed back to Buxton. The backseat was stuffed with groceries, and Rufus was hanging his shaggy head over the side and nosing into the wind. Keith felt sheepish for getting the ladies drenched, but there was something undeniably pleasant in feeling the wind and rain.

As a boy of ten, he had salvaged a catboat on the Sound side of the island and refurbished her for sea. He used to hell around the Sound after school, and half a dozen times Malcolm had hauled out somebody's powerboat to track him down, becalmed or, more likely, barely holding his own in a squall. He never ventured too far out, and the danger wasn't all that great, but Malcolm would come for him just the same, grave and determined.

"Don't tell the old man about this," Keith would say, and of course Malcolm never did. It got to be a game almost, though Keith knew now that Malcolm had never seen the lighter side of it.

The motorcar's windscreen wasn't much help. The squall was blowing directly off the ocean and coming at them broadside. Keith was smiling at memory, Mary was content, and only Dorothy seemed to mind the weather. Keith suddenly surrendered his smile: Of course—her father was still out there.

In this weather, he thought, the U-boat was safely hiding under the waves. This was not good hunting weather.

Keith thought briefly about Halstead's patrol boat, about Jack, an islander, serving on her. It was bad luck for one of the islanders to drown—it portended a sudden, violent end for someone on shore.

When Mary's father had died, though, it had been the reverse of tradition: Dennis Dant disappeared soon after Dorothy's mother passed away in childbirth.

All at once Keith Royal knew something. It was something you'd have to go away and then come back to see. What if the coincidence of Dennis Dant's death so soon after Dorothy's mother's was no coincidence at all? What if Dennis, not Alvin, was Brian Dant's father?

It was apparent now that the storm was not just a minor squall. The sky was dark as evening and the wind kept forcing the light car sideways off the road. Twice the wheels spun in deep sand and Keith maneuvered it carefully back onto the road.

"How about if I drop Mary and come back for awhile?" Keith asked when they reached Dorothy's house. "It won't take me very long." He half wished she would say no, but he felt obligated to stay with her at least some of the time.

"You're sure?" she said. "I wouldn't want to keep you from anything."

"No, it's all right."

"Of course," Mary said to her. "He'll be back. Now run along and get in out of the wet."

Dorothy stood poised on the top step of her porch for a long second, then turned quickly and slammed the screen door behind her.

Mary gathered her wrap around her shoulders and huddled against the storm while Keith drove on, his headlights barely any help at all in finding the way.

6

WHEN MARY ROYAL OPENED the door to her house, her heart leapt. She had a sudden, overwhelming sense of Malcolm's presence, and she welcomed it. His vacuum bottle was on the kitchen counter. "Malcolm!" she called. But of course he wasn't there. He had left her a note, and he hardly ever wrote notes. She felt as though she had done something terribly wrong.

7

"PUT YOUR ARMS AROUND ME," Dorothy said. "I want to feel you being strong."

Keith was trying to account for her radical shift in mood, and couldn't.

She had toweled and brushed her hair, and it shone dark gold. She looked more a woman than he remembered. She had more weight, more substance to her now. Her eyes went deeper. He kissed her mouth and from time to time her damp hair.

"I've decided," she said abruptly. Her head was tucked into his shoulder the way he liked it.

"Decided what?"

"I buried them today. I made up my mind before we left Oman's. I made it up, Keith Royal, and you're not going to change it."

"I'm not trying to change it." Very matter of factly he unbuttoned her shirt. She did not help him at first. He knelt in front of her and burrowed his face into her lap, felt her hands finally touch his ears and temples, as if she were sculpting him.

Later, they lay on the floor listening to the rain pelt the roof like handfuls of gravel, and she said, "I'm leaving. If you won't take me away, I'll find someone who will." She twisted a strand of hair between her fingers.

"I get it," Keith said. "But why do you need someone at all. Can't you do that little thing by yourself?"

"That's not the way it works."

Keith got up to go out on the porch.

8

ALVIN DANT HELD the wheel. His boy stared out the window, waiting.

"You should have let me get them all," he said.

"Don't you understand, boy?" Alvin shouted. They had been having this conversation off and on ever since the U-boat retreated and the weather moved in. Alvin had a sustained urge to beat Brian. He held the wheel instead. "Don't you realize? Don't you get it?" Brian had always been a good boy, the kind you take for granted and rely on around the house.

"They are the enemy," Brian said.

"Have you no sense of honor? They trusted us!"

"They are the enemy. They would as soon killed us as not."

"And I won't blame them when they do. They came as gentlemen, and you shot one of them."

"Do gentlemen lie up underwater all day, then sink merchant ships without warning?"

Alvin shook his head. The boy was stubborn, but it was a good thing that the boy had some backbone. It had not bothered him to blow off the back of a man's head after talking civilly to him only minutes before, and fully expecting to be killed in reward. Alvin was proud of the boy in spite of himself. When had he grown up? He opened a bottle of brandy—no sense wasting it, if the Hun came back. May as well meet the Maker with a smile and a hail-fellow-well-met.

"Have a full glass, boy. Apparently you're old enough."

They drank while the boat quaked in the weather. Alvin thought it funny, and the more he drank the funnier it got. Brian didn't smile, but Alvin could see he understood the humor of it. They had beat the Hun at his own game, and now they were hiding from him. The wind and the currents were pushing them all over the place, Alvin knew, and for once he didn't care.

They toasted Alvin's brother Dennis, whom Brian resembled more than ever with the glass in his hand, and Alvin was sure he could die happy if only he could save the boy. He was a good boy.

He asked him: "What went through your mind when you pulled the trigger on that Heinie?"

Brian looked puzzled.

"Did you hesitate? Were you afraid? You were afraid, weren't you."

"Yes," Brian finally answered. "I was afraid. The boat kept moving, and I was afraid I would miss."

Alvin stared at the boy. "You're not a fisherman. I don't know what you are, but you're not a fisherman."

The light left the sky. The rain was so thick and incessant Alvin fancied it was saltwater. They were pushed a little south and a little west, right into the shipping lane. They were both drunk by now and didn't care about anything. They were toasting Brian, shouting at each other to be heard above the wind, hanging on to the wheel while the deck pitched under them.

The first they saw of the tanker *Proteus* was a black wall reaching from sky to sea on the starboard side, close enough to prod with a gaff. Their bottle shattered on the deck as they were thrown off their feet. The *Pelican* pitched violently, and the noise of the tanker's engines was like pneumatic hammers. Alvin looked up to see a propeller as tall as his own pilothouse churning through the black water.

9

UNDERWATER it was calm. Captain Stracken tried the periscope twice, but the weather was too bad and there were no lights to take a bearing by. With his radio mast gone he could not pick up the signals of other vessels even on the surface. He summoned Max to the periscope bridge just to sit there and stare at the charts over a cup of coffee.

Max Wien had not had real coffee in over a month. Still, it tasted sour. He finished it only for the captain's pleasure.

Captain Stracken stabbed a finger at the chart.

"Where is the *gemeine Hund?* Where? You find him. I don't care if the whole American fleet is upstairs. We will blow that fisherman out of the water and hang his head on our jackstaff."

Max thought: I know where he got that, he's showing off his history. Robert Maynard had impaled Blackbeard's head on the bowsprit of his sloop *Ranger*. A pirate's fate.

Max pondered the charts, Kraft standing by. He looked at the horn of the island, marked the arrows that showed the Labrador and the Gulf Stream, and took in the pattern of the vessels they had sunk—the names, the tonnage, the whereabouts.

"There," he said, pressing a finger to a spot where no ships were tallied for tonnage. *"Dort ist er, dein Fischer."*

The captain studied the chart, nodded. "We'll see, Max. That's the first order of business. If you're right, you will have the honor of boarding."

CHAPTER 10

1

HALSTEAD CURSED his luck all way into the bight. "Ain't that the way," he said to Jack Royal. "We try to go for the bastard, and the weather turns rotten. Dammit to hell."

Jack said: "Be thanking the Lord for what you've got—don't be raising hell for what He might have given you."

"Shut up, Mister Royal."

"Aye, aye, sir." And so it went.

The new engineer had proved a reliable, plucky boy. Twice the engines quit and he restarted them. He was a skinny red-head who already had a bad sunburn, and he had lain prone over the engine bay with his arms down inside like he was trying to extract live young. When the engines caught, Halstead listened to their roar the way sailors of another day would listen to their sails snapping with wind after a calm, the sound of men resuming command over their destinies.

Pulling into berth, *Sealion* was sluggish, her belly heavy with seawater.

2

PATCHY HAD NOT expected rough weather, but he was prepared for it. He would go through the storm, and somewhere on the other side of it was Alvin Dant.

Patchy wore his father's sou'wester. He had gone north up to Wilmington, Delaware, to claim it after the letter came. His father had been working a rivet gun six stories up on the hull of an oversize tanker when a crane swung a load of ventilators against him, brushing him off the scaffolding like a bug.

His buddies all said he was a good Joe, a hard worker who never complained, didn't drink much, and pulled all sorts of overtime. Nobody knew what happened to all the money he must have accumulated in all those years of muscle work, since he didn't believe in banks, didn't gamble, and had never remarried.

It was a genuine mystery, they said, and Patchy had no reason to doubt it. He never saw a penny of that money. He used to lie awake and concoct stories about his father's fortune, what shadowy investments the old man had made, what great acts of philanthropy had been done in the Patchett name. He still harbored cautious fantasies.

Patchy became frightened as the weather worsened. He wasn't up to this kind of seamanship, yet it had been left up to him. Truth to tell, his stomach gave him trouble on boats—that's why he kept to the land so faithfully.

He thought that there must be only two kinds of men, after all:

those meant to be on the water, and those meant to be on the land.

Then what was he doing out here? Well, sometimes there were special circumstances, he told himself. The word was default. He felt scared in an important way, knowing that things larger than himself depended on his actions, and he decided every man had a right to feel that way just once. The Rough Riders must have felt that way struggling up San Juan Hill. The Wright brothers must have felt it as they launched themselves by turns to a giddying height over the Kill Devil Hills at Kitty Hawk, daring nature and held aloft by faith and a science they were only guessing at. Patrick Etheridge must have felt it the night he went out in place of Patchy's father.

Patchy had hoarded a few bottles of beer, and he figured now was a good time to start in on them. No sense in going down with a full virgin cache, if down he must go. He snapped off the cap with one hand and held the wheel with the other, then sipped the warm foam from the mouth of the bottle. He almost smiled there, all alone.

In between gulps he sang bawdy songs to keep his courage up. He had sense enough to know he was not a brave man.

Hermes plowed ahead at a good clip, showing no lights yet. He would give that Hun no target. Speed was his friend in this weather and on this trip. He felt it pulling at him, drawing him toward an inevitable rendezvous on the treacherous water, in the heart of an unnatural twilight.

He hadn't planned on meeting the tanker, cutting out of the curtain of rain like a ghost ship. He veered hard right to run parallel and in the opposite direction. There was no life on her high decks, no lights on her mast, no movement on her bridge as she cut across Patchy's sky. He read the name, *Proteus*, and crossed himself quickly.

It was the last ship his father had built.

3

THE CAPTAIN did not need a listening device to hear the ungodly churning of those big propellers overhead. It was quarry, and he had nearly missed the main chance by hiding out from weather.

Cursing, he raised the periscope in its hydraulic sleeve until it locked. He reversed his cap and put his eye to the spyhole and saw black. The metal shaft stunned him, and he reeled to the deck, his eye socket crushed and his feet kicking the air. He heard the wrench of metal on metal, the gunshot sounds of rivets popping, the sudden rush of saltwater as voices answered in alarm. Men clamored about him, stifling him, and he interfered with their legs.

Kraft was yelling for him to stay calm while they plugged the leaks. Someone pressed a towel over his eyes. Max, he thought, and heartbroken knew all at once the ship had steamed right over the periscope. His luck had turned.

4

FETTERMAN WATCHED the rain and turned the hull of the model in his hand. It puzzled him, the way his granddaughter Patricia puzzled him. It had an odd shape to it, as her life had an odd shape if you looked at it from the beginning. Why of all men had she taken Peter Patchett to her bed?

It wasn't a matter of forgiveness—Fetterman felt sure he could forgive anyone anything, or damn near. And he knew of no one else who could make that claim. He supposed it was a function of age, of perspective. And anyway he didn't hold with that sins of the father stuff. That was all right in the Bible, where you were trying to make a point, but it broke down in real life, where you had to get along on approximations. The people in the Bible were just characters to Fetterman, not real people. He just didn't believe you could be so hard on one another and still hold it all together.

Patchy wasn't a mean man, as far as he could tell. He just wasn't anything. He was stillborn, neutral of life, a parody of a man. He wondered if there was love in the man, deep love like a man has for a woman, responsible strong love, like a man has for his children, sacred love, like a man has for his God and his people.

Peter Patchett's emotions seemed to Fetterman the unformed emotions of a child, changing by the moment, fickle and obnoxious, and that kind of love was just a caprice of mood and digestion.

He lit his pipe. The meerschaum was yellow and browned in spots, like his own hands. He could not remember how old it was, or that it had ever been new. It was his favorite of forty or so pipes he had collected and not broken or given away in his lifetime. Littlejohn had asked him once why he didn't carve his own pipes, if he was such a master carver.

"You could make a fine pipe," Littlejohn had said, "a work of art."

"But they're not ships," he had answered. "Pipes are not ships." A pronouncement that summed it all up, as far as Fetterman was concerned.

Littlejohn had never asked him again.

Now Littlejohn lingered at Fetterman's elbow. "You'll be going to the meeting, then."

"Aye," Fetterman said. "I dearly hate going to church in midweek, but if we must, we must."

"Oman's bringing men from the village. Malcolm's even coming from the station. I expect men from all the stations will be coming."

"Good. It's their business, after all."

"So it is."

The match flared brightly in the bowl of the pipe. The bowl held the flame even after Fetterman discarded the spent match.

5

BECAUSE THE medical officer was dead, it was left up to Max Wien to work on the captain. Max, his fingers trembling, cleaned away the blood and mucous mess that had been a bright human eye.

"Our luck went bad when we spotted that damned fisherman," Kraft said.

"Shut up," said the captain, who was coming awake with an effort of stoic will. They'd lost their ears when the radio mast was shot off, and now they were blinded as well, but he didn't intend that such minor damage should undo a fighting ship.

"Hold still," Max said with an authority that surprised even him. Stracken grimaced.

"I'm not foolish enough to think you can save the eye, but can you save me?"

Max had little hope but said, "Yes, we can do that, Captain."

The bone of the socket had splintered and caved in, and Max gingerly put it right. The captain fainted. Max worked more surely now, and mopped the attendant blood with a succession of gauze patches that kept arriving from other hands. He stuffed the empty socket with sterile cotton and over it pressed a thick, soft patch that quickly darkened with fresh blood. He pondered whether to have the captain sit up or remain on his back, and ultimately decided to have him propped up on his bunk, his head thoroughly protected by pillows. If there was a depth bomb attack he didn't want that fragile head banging against the bulkhead. The captain had already sustained one severe concussion. A man was assigned to wake the captain at intervals. Max would relieve him by turns.

"He's had it, hasn't he," Kraft said, when they had gone to the other end of the boat.

"I don't know that," Max said, washing his hands.

"Do you know what this means?"

Max dried his hands thoroughly. "No, and I don't think you do, either."

"You're awfully insolent for an enlisted man."

"Hah. And I thought I was the doctor."

"You're a doctor for exactly as long as you have a patient."

"The way this is turning out, I may be a doctor from now on."

"And you may be under arrest if you keep taking liberties."

"You're in charge now. We can make for South America to be refitted."

Kraft shook his head. "No, I don't think so."

Later, when the captain was awake, Max asked him what was going to happen now.

"We have to come up, that's all. We'll simply fill with water and sink to the bottom if we don't surface soon. Can't you feel how we move?"

"I guess Kraft will have to decide—"

"That man is in command of nothing," he said. "You hear? Nothing."

When they surfaced the seas were calmer but the weather was still thick. There was no sign of the tanker, no sign of the fisherman, no sun or light, just seas and a crippled submarine lying heavy in the water, looking no more dangerous than a big fish played to exhaustion and ready for the gaff.

The captain insisted on going to the tower. Max accompanied him, pulling the captain by his arms through the hatchway.

"My God," Max said. The lookout tower, the stalk of the periscope, a good piece of the railing around the conning bridge were sheared clean away.

"Not the time to be calling on that One," Captain Stracken said. He leaned on Max Wien and his one eye was like a telescope, with no perception of context or depth. Max's face was strange to look at. Bergen was on the bridge. Apparently discipline was breaking down now. The tower was torn and flattened, and Captain Stracken knew how close they had come to being sent to the bottom. That would have been ironic, he thought, because when a submarine sank like that there was hardly ever a trace, and their enemy would never have the satisfaction of knowing their fate.

Bergen scrambled onto the deck to inspect his precious gun. It looked serviceable, but the aft gun had been uprooted like a tree stump, leaving a ragged star in the metal deck.

"So that's where all the water was coming from," the captain said. They could hear the pumps humming below. He wondered if his batteries would recharge with them working like that. He was using a lot of power just to stay afloat.

"We have holes to plug, Max." Max was imagining the boat rocking like a toy under the weight of the big ship. The bow must have dunked from the blow to the tower, levering up the stern to get chopped by the big slow screws.

"I wonder what kind of damage we did to her," Kraft said.

"Damage?" the captain said. "Damage? You must be joking."

The welding teams had come to the bridge, serious, pale young men scared to death to be exposed on the flat seas in broad daylight. Let there be no aeroplanes, Max thought. The captain looked at him as if he had understood, and nodded his head.

6

MARY ROYAL POURED herself a healthy slug of brandy and sat drinking and listening to the storm.

I have the wrong brother, she thought.

She had never expected any more of her marriage than what she had, but lately she felt opportunity passing like some ship plying the coast to the big cities up north. Not one great ship, perhaps, but a fleet of opportunity, sliding by one at a time on no particular schedule, concealed in weather and at the mercy of war, the tides, and the ingenuity of the men who steered them.

She knew Malcolm no better than the day he had first approached and showed her the brass coin that each beachman carried to trade with his opposite number on the adjoining station's patrol. It proved they had met, the beach covered thoroughly, no part left unguarded. Their lovemaking was like that—meeting face to face at regular intervals, trading proof, then turning and retreating to their own private shores.

Mary hardly ever drank and never alone, but now she sipped one glass of brandy and then three more, her eyes fixed on the stars of rain against the window. She thought of Malcolm and Keith, and as she drank, the stars ran down the window.

7

KEITH KNEW that if he asked Dorothy to go away with him, now, anywhere, she would go. It might not even require marriage. He tried to imagine Dorothy in five, ten, twenty years, no longer fresh, no longer on the beach, Rufus a fond memory, Malcolm, Jack, Mary, and Virginia just names signed to infrequent letters two weeks old before they reached him. Fetterman a ghost, Littlejohn a marker in the wind-scoured graveyard, old Seamus invincible, though, living out his glory in the house on the only hill in Buxton. Keith's future separate, bound only with Dorothy's, Hatteras Island no more than a quaint subject for conversation at cocktail parties where knowledgeable men and women with refined voices engineered history, morality, destiny.

"Just why did you come back?" Dorothy asked. He couldn't tell if she was angry or just out of patience. There was some small sympathy in her voice, some slight challenge as well.

"For you," he said and felt tricked.

"Did you? Did you really?" She turned away, and he reached for his coat, befuddled. He would have left her then, holding himself to a sense of honor.

"No," she said, "you're not going anywhere. I've waited this long, and I know my chance when I see it."

They loved again. Dorothy wanted this thing settled.

8

THE STORE WAS empty except for Littlejohn and Fetterman. There was the scrape of the carving knife, the drumming of the rain, Fetterman's slow, heavy breathing. Littlejohn monitored the wireless, thinking about the meeting tonight, about action.

Littlejohn had once shipped aboard a schooner trading woolens from Ireland and Indonesian rubber, with plenty of coastal trading in between. The *John Shay*. The captain was a Brit named Baker, a real bastard—haughty and irascible, a man who required of his crew not service but servitude. For him the British Empire was the whole world. The trouble was, except for a few swarthy deckhands picked up in the Africas, most of the crew was Irish. There had been a mutiny led by a man named Moran. Littlejohn had listened to Moran and the others, to all the arguments that added up to the same thing: men dissatisfied with themselves who thought taking over a ship would better their lot. Even then he had seen the folly of it. The logic, not the justice, was faulty.

He could picture now, twenty-two years later, Moran's plump Irish face peering over the rifle he had pilfered from the captain's locker, and Captain Baker, in his vainglorious stupidity, trying to meet force with bluff.

In the end the *John Shay* was cast onto the Wimble Shoals and broke up quickly during the night. If there were any other survivors, Littlejohn never heard of them. When his lifeboat had capsized, he had grabbed onto a piece of flotsam and come ashore somewhat more prosaically than Ishmael, a half-filled cask of malt under his arm. With that cache of bootleg he had managed to insinuate himself into the economy of the island.

Littlejohn mused about tonight's meeting, distrusting all the talk of action. Action had a way of making things worse.

The radio crackled and through the static the captain of the tanker *Proteus* broke to report running afoul of wreckage fifteen miles off the Light. Littlejohn copied down the latitude and longitude.

"I guess I had better tell Dorothy."

"I guess somebody better," Fetterman said.

"At least we know."

But Fetterman wasn't listening. His knife had slipped, gouging the fragile top of his model.

9

THE CHURCH FILLED UP FAST and there was not even the pretext of a prayer before they got down to business. All the life-saving crews were represented. Malcolm and Chief Lord had left the station in Toby Bannister's charge. And Jack had come with his boy Kevin, who was on hand as a runner in case the telephone line between the vestry and the station was interrupted.

Jack and Malcolm sat on either side of Chief Lord, their combined shoulders a wall almost ten feet long. Their wives were at the back with the other wives, including Mrs. Patchett, with an urchin on each arm, unaccountably silent.

Keith Royal sat with Dorothy, and Halstead insinuated himself behind them so he could talk to Dorothy when the opportunity arose. Littlejohn, his wife, and Fetterman sat in the front pew with Seamus Royal, who propped his rifle on the rail in front, its oiled barrel reminding them all why they had come.

Reverend Simmons quoted from Job: " 'He divideth the sea with His power, and by His understanding he smiteth through the proud.' " Then presided for the half a minute it took to introduce Oman, Littlejohn, and Malcolm, civic leaders that they were.

Oman, as mayor of the Village of Hatteras, went first. His duties thus far had not included disarming a submarine menace. In fact, except for dealing with telephone service and flood relief once in a while, he had few real duties at all. The island had never needed a constable—the families settled things between them, and crime as it was known on the mainland was unheard of—and most of its prominent citizens worked for the Government.

Oman explained all this and watched them nod their heads. "You know why we're here," Oman said. "We have trouble. We're here to decide what to do about that Heinie pirate prowling around offshore."

The crowd was waking up, shifting to get comfortable, getting ready to listen.

"This has never happened before," Oman went on. "Our beaches are sticky with black oil, we're pulling drowned men out of the surf, and our fishermen can't even go to the banks for fear of their lives and their boats."

Above the general murmur, Tim Halstead's tenor rose crisp and official. "Excuse me, may I address this meeting?"

Oman waved his hand in an exaggerated gesture of invitation, and Halstead, now sunburned and with his rough edges rubbed off a little, came to the lectern.

He cleared his throat like a valedictorian. "I'm an outsider. I was not born on this island, and I know that makes what I say suspect." There was a more vigorous murmur of assent than he would have liked, but he kept on. "The Navy is quite busy at the moment. There are submarines attacking all over the coast—Narragansett Bay, Long Island Sound, Delaware Bay, Hampton Roads—"

"We aren't needing a geography lesson, Horatio!" a man in the back called out, drawing a nervous laugh out of the crowd.

"I'm just trying to tell you why the Navy hasn't sent a cutter."

"They've got bigger fish to fry."

"No," Halstead said, "they're just swamped—"

There was a titter from some of the men, Jack Royal included. Halstead hadn't intended the pun.

"The Navy sent me here to handle the situation, and I intend to do just that."

"The way you handled the *Abilene City*, son? The way you handled the lumber ship? The lightship?" Different voices naming each ship.

Malcolm Royal stood up slowly. He spoke quietly and no one

interrupted. "Ladies and gentlemen, please. This man has already put himself in harm's way on our behalf. Which of you can say as much? The least we can do is listen politely—or is that no longer our custom here?" He looked around, his great shoulders half turned like a turret, then resumed his seat with a gentle settling of breath.

Chastened, the company attended.

"Thank you." Halstead spoke more evenly now. "I have one of your best men, Jack Royal, navigating for me" A round of scattered cheers and applause: "Good for you, Jack," and "Jack's true blue."

"—and you have to admit, this U-boat hasn't been very bold lately. It's my guess he's getting a little timid."

"You mean, he's afraid of you?" a voice called out, thick with incredulity. Laughter followed.

"That's not what I said. But he is being more cautious. I ask your patience. We'll go out again in the morning, and we'll keep going out every morning until we get him." He paused, hands on the rails of the lectern. "Let the Navy handle this. That's all I have to say."

He stepped from the lectern, his shoes clicking sharply on the lacquered wood floor of the church. He had a sense that somehow he had failed. His own men sat at something like attention, and he was bucked up by sight of them. They, at least, would follow him anywhere, he was sure. He had their respect now. That's all that really mattered. He had got them in today, hadn't he? He had got off a shot at the U-boat that other time, hadn't he? All they had to do was worry that submarine until a cutter could be dispatched to blow him out of the water.

He could do that. *Sealion* could.

"Anyone else like to venture an opinion?" Oman asked.

Seamus Royal caned himself to the front with his rifle, commanding their attention like an old general. "You're damned right, I would. Now I been on this sandbar a lot of years, and ain't nothing like this ever come up before. I think . . . I think we have got to expect an invasion."

There were shouts of disbelief, groans, and general disorder.

"You're way out of line, Seamus!"

Seamus raised his rifle like an Arab, pumping it up and down in his fist while the crowd broke out at him, calling:

"You're seeing bogeymen on the beach, old man!"

"Why would they invade us?"

"You're all wet, Seamus Royal."

"You can't be serious."

"Been at the jug again?"

"The *Huns?*" .

"Don't be getting carried away with yourself, Seamus Royal." The last voice was Littlejohn's. "Don't be starting at shadows."

"Nevertheless, we have to be prepared," Seamus countered.

"We have nothing they want."

"We had nothing the Yankees wanted, either! Yet they came and took it just the same. Are you forgetting how they crawled over this island like crabs, picking it clean—"

"The Huns are not the Yankees."

"I don't know about that!" Seamus was pincering his hand and drew general laughter. "They may be worse."

"What would they want here? All we have is sand—"

"And room!" Seamus's big finger poked at Littlejohn across the rail. "They can assemble their troops here for a general assault on the mainland, don't you see? That's what I'm saying. And we've got to be ready. We can't depend on the Government. The Government sends us a posturing nonesuch and a toy speedboat! We need a militia! We'll be defending our homes, man!"

"Back up a little, Seamus," Oman said. .

But as outlandish as his argument sounded, it had the ring of possibility about it. The Yankees had taken the island by surprise, and Norfolk, Portsmouth, Beaufort, and all the capes of Virginia and the Carolinas would be easy game for an army that got this far. Hatteras and Ocracoke islands had harbored whole fleets of pirates in the old days.

"The question remains: what do we do about the U-boat?"

Oman held the floor. Already the men itched, craving a smoke. Reverend Simmons intervened in a timely manner and granted permission for smoking, just this once, due to the circumstances, and the pipes came out like flasks at a funeral. Oman waited for the filling and tamping and lighting to get over with, then went on, "What can fishermen, storekeepers, surfmen, and their families do about a submarine warship killing and plundering within sight of our homes and threatening our lives and livelihoods with each day more that it hides in the Diamond Shoals?"

It was a good question, and not many had ready answers. Even Seamus's militia project was of no immediate value in neutralizing the U-boat. If and when the Huns tramped ashore, "like red ants from a rotten tree," as he put it, that would be the time to keep the powder dry and dig in on the beaches.

There was a general clamor as the islanders talked it over, shouted about it, argued, laughed, cajoled, or gave up.

Fetterman rose from his seat like an artificial creature being erected one stage at a time. Littlejohn sat with his head in his hands. Fetterman leaned on the rail of his pew and turned around, not bothering to approach the lectern.

"I have something to say."

"Another country heard from," Oman said graciously. "Go ahead, Ham. And the rest of you cork your holes and listen to the gentleman."

"I have lived longer than ever I hoped or wanted," Fetterman said. "I have seen Yankees and pirates and bootleggers and a good deal worse. And now I've seen this, too. And I tell you: this is different.

"This murderous lurking Teutonic bastard is hunting by the Light—*our* Light! He navigates by it, he ambushes by it, he kills by it. He knows exactly where the shipping will pass—he can estimate by tonnage just how close in they'll dare. For him, it's shooting fish in a barrel. With that Light, he is damn near invincible."

"We can raise a false light," someone said. "The way they used to do at Nags Head." To the north, Nags Head, according to legend, was named for the practice of tying a lantern to the neck of a horse and leading it along the beach to lure disoriented vessels onto the shoals, where they would run aground for easy looting.

"There's only one thing we can do," Fetterman said. "We can turn out the Light."

Then there was silence. Only twice had the Light ever gone out: once when the original wood tower burned down from lightning, and again for two years during the Civil War when the lens was dismantled by vandals who wore either butternut or blue, depending on who told the story. But on neither occasion had the islanders themselves been a party to it.

"You can't be serious." It was Keith Royal. "Civilization going to pieces, and all you can think to do is make it worse."

Malcolm stood up. "You don't know what you're saying, Ham. It would be a disgrace. To even contemplate it is a disgrace—"

"Wake up, can't you!" Dorothy Dant shouted from beside Keith. "Can't you see he's right? This island is not all there is! Turn out your precious Light and run him onto the shoals! Then he won't be so damned clever."

But even as she said it she had a vision of her father and Brian, struggling through a heavy sea looking landward for help, for the Light, and seeing only unrelieved black sky. But they were dead, she knew. Littlejohn had told her. It must be a mistaken vision.

Malcolm spoke just once more, and then the meeting disintegrated into groups of men and women arguing hotly or solemnly about a matter which rendered consensus impossible and frightening.

He said: "Not while I'm Keeper."

CHAPTER 11

1

SEAMUS ROYAL LEFT the meeting feeling so many things at once that he could not rightly get it all straight in his mind.

First and foremost, he was proud of Malcolm and Jack.

Everybody knew Jack was the only thing that had kept that posturing fool Halstead alive this long. God willing, Jack could bring that ridiculous cigar-shaped boat home every time. Jack was the lucky one. Nobody would ever drown shipping with Jack. Jack had a temper, true enough, but he was a family man, the salt of the earth, a father and a husband, a progenitor of tradition, the kind of man who would turn up again and again in stories, same as Malcolm. Maybe more. Jack was smarter by half, and he was a courageous man who knew how to cut the risks and do the job without any fanfare.

Malcolm thought him a hothead, Seamus knew, but Malcolm was so steady even the Light itself seemed by comparison capricious and unreliable.

Malcolm was damn near a legend already on the island, the way Seamus himself had been once. The old-timers—salts like Oman, Littlejohn, and Fetterman—knew all about Seamus, and he had served notice tonight. He had done that.

But it troubled Seamus that some had not taken him seriously. Maybe he should have left the Krag at home—maybe that was just a tad too melodramatic. People frowned on overstatement.

But he was angry about the Dant men—that godless Hun had destroyed a harmless fishing boat. There was no mystery about it in Seamus's mind: The German didn't need a reason to destroy— that was the error here. These people, his people, were treating this emergency far too rationally.

How could you be rational about a German submarine? It was piracy, and worse: it was spiteful.

Now there would be action, Seamus knew. Fetterman's speech about turning out the Light would provoke something, and Seamus would need to sort this all out over a bottle of bond before he could throw the weight of his reputation and experience behind any scheme.

"Mister Royal—can I talk to you?" Dorothy Dant was walking beside him. He hooked an arm around her and felt her squeeze into him. He unclamped his pipe so as not to trouble her with the smoke.

"You can have all my time you want, Dot. It isn't in such great demand."

They went together through the balmy evening. The weather had calmed down. Tomorrow would be a wonderful day, he knew. He could tell. He had read the sky often enough all these years.

"Where's Keith?" Seamus said.

"I was wondering about my father."

"Yes. The wireless report, wasn't it. I can't tell you anything, girl. Your dad was a fine man, we all respected him. We'll look after you now, every one of us. You have all the family you'll ever need."

"You know the currents around here better than anybody." She paused, having a hard time with what she wanted to ask. But Seamus had not been Keeper of the Hatteras Light for all those years by being thick to what was on people's minds.

"Dottie, I can't say for sure. But it seems to me—and I can only go by the wireless report—it would have to be around Kinnakeet. Maybe even a little farther north."

"I see."

"But Dottie . . ."

"I'm listening."

"The thing is, if the Labrador got them? They may never come ashore at all."

She stared up at him, and a shadow of fear passed over her face. He had seen that look before. That was the one thing she had not wanted to hear from him.

"Then he's joined Uncle Dennis," she said, mostly to herself.

"There's no use fretting, girl. The worst is over. We can hope a little, can't we?"

She drifted away without answering, and he felt like a very old man to be talking of death so glibly.

2

THERE WAS A WIRELESS MESSAGE waiting for Malcolm when he returned. Toby had taken it down himself. In two days' time a cadre of staff officers would arrive to present Malcolm with the Gold Medal for Life-Saving.

The men all shook his hand. Jack waited till the rest of the crew and the Navy people had their turns and then offered his right hand to his brother. Their eyes fixed on one another's, and

Chief Lord watched the two brothers square off in a handshake.

"This is no good," Malcolm said at last, withdrawing his hand, and Chief saw that Malcolm was embarrassed by all the fuss.

"No," Jack said, "but it's what we have."

3

THEY WOULD RIDE the surface all night long, drifting. They had no other choice.

Captain Stracken lay fevered in his bunk, his head bloated with concussion and infection. Max stood over the man and felt the blood swell and pulse against his own temples. He breathed deep and exhaled. He listened to the frantic rasp of metal files, the hammer of rivet guns, the hush of welding torches, till he couldn't stand it any longer. He climbed aloft into the terrible moonlight and watched his shipmates labor on the flat deck on a quiet sea. Their arms and legs, their shoulders and heads shone with a nimbus of moonlight, though he could not make out their faces. They started and froze at every alien sound, like deer. He remembered deer in the snow under a moon like this one.

"What are you doing up here?" It was Kraft. "Never mind. I can see it's no use anymore. You do what you please. I wash my hands."

"Will they finish by morning?"

The mate shrugged. Max thought he looked different than a few hours ago but could not locate the difference in the map of the man's face.

"Who knows." He lit a cigarette, one of a precious few he had left. He offered one to Max, who declined. Kraft nodded, and Max knew he had redeemed himself a little. "I don't think we can dive no matter when we finish. I don't think we are much of a shark anymore."

Max nodded. He felt sorry for the men working so feverishly, glancing over their shoulders in dread of being taken by surprise.

"Look at them." Kraft dragged on his cigarette, held it out inspecting it between puffs. Max thought all he lacked was a blindfold.

"Our captain," Kraft said, "is used to things the old way. He doesn't understand what we've been doing, not even now."

"He's a natural submariner. You can't deny that."

"Is he? I don't know. He is born to command, but I think submarines are not his line."

Max considered that, surprised to hear Kraft say it. Max had always pictured Stracken at the bridge of a grander ship, a battleship or a cruiser, but still he would have looked thin and worried there. He would have looked his best on the quarterdeck of a sailing ship, a clipper or a schooner, the masts raked for speed and the bridge open to weather, the sails a brave target a dozen miles off. "He doesn't see much honor in skulking around, you mean."

"Yes, that's it. I think you've hit on what I was trying to say."

"And you?"

Kraft laughed a quiet, pleasant laugh. Max couldn't recall ever having heard him laugh before. "That's the thing, boy. It is easy to start liking it, if you're the right sort of man. Honor is not what applies here, that's your mistake. I would not leave the U-boat service if you gave me my own dreadnought."

Max understood now why Kraft was so relaxed: It was over for him. He had no faith in Stracken's or finally even his own ability to get them home, or to a rendezvous. He knew he would never have his own command. What did ship's discipline matter to doomed men?

Kraft checked his chronometer. "Three more hours of darkness," he said. "After that, we are in the hands of God, and I for one am not counting on His sympathy."

He smoked and stood watch over the laboring sailors the rest of the night, Max going below by turns to check on his captain and returning to stand beside a man who offered nothing to admire and every reason to be afraid.

Max strained his eyes toward the island. Twice ships passed to the west and the work was halted while the men held their breath and lay flat on the deck, not to offer a silhouette.

The captain continued in his fever and then, with dawn at his back, Max saw the low profile of land. It hugged the horizon the way he imagined U-55 did. Above the land, he thought he saw a tower, and at the top of the tower a glinting flash, the Light searching for them.

4

AFTER THE VILLAGE MEETING, at their father's request, the three sons joined Seamus at his house, their old home. Malcolm stayed only a little while, and this he did reluctantly, as he had wanted to spend a few minutes with Mary on the way back to the station.

The sons arrived more or less separately and met at the door. Malcolm had not had his good news yet, and Keith was still brooding about Dorothy. They mumbled greetings before going inside.

"Don't just stand around like a bunch of hens, come on in," Seamus said. He had already cracked a good bottle and poured out four generous helpings.

"Boys, we have not had a conference in so long I don't know." His rifle leaned against the wall behind the table. Keith was at first overwhelmed by the odors of his childhood: the greasy burn of the kerosene lamp, the salt smell of old wood, the sour odor of lacquer, the heady aroma of his father's pipe—all of them gone a little stale now. The house smelled like the house of an old man, like the man himself was steaming away into essence.

"I agree with you," Jack said, scraping a spool chair away from the table and taking a seat. "Let's get that straight right off the bat."

"With me or with Ham Fetterman?" Seamus asked.

"Both," Jack said, and scratched a match. He held it into the bowl of his pipe.

"And you, Malcolm?"

Malcolm and Keith pulled out chairs. Seamus crossed his hands on the table.

"How can you even ask? It goes against everything. And you, of all people."

Seamus looked at Keith. "And you?"

"I'm not sure I have a right to an opinion anymore."

"I will hear you out. So will they."

"I just don't know. You can't be sure it will work, and if it doesn't, then you will have disgraced yourselves for nothing—"

"Ourselves, you mean," Malcolm chided. "You're here now."

"If you want it that way."

"There's a time for thinking and a time for action," Jack said. "I'm tired of all this thinking."

"It never was your strong suit." Keith was immediately sorry he'd said it.

"That's enough of that," Seamus said.

"You haven't told us how you stand," Keith said.

Seamus didn't have it all worked out yet, but he had a strong inkling Fetterman was right. "I am fairly sure it will kill that Heinie bastard if we pick the right weather. He strikes after sundown, most times, or just at dusk. If the weather was treacherous and he had the Light long enough to take the bait, he would get all turned around on those shoals and come to grief by morning. It would depend on where he was and what kind of weather we got."

"The worse, the better," Jack said.

"That's about it."

"Listen to you," Malcolm said. "Do you forget what business we're in?"

"He can just dive and avoid the weather," Keith said. "That's nothing to him. We have to catch him on the surface in shallow water."

Jack said, "That makes sense. Go on, surprise me some more."

"There are a lot of risks," Keith said. "Suppose our own ships get caught out there on a night like that? Without the Light to steer by?"

"They wouldn't have any stars," Malcolm agreed.

"We can keep track of shipping, that's all," Jack said.

"There are other risks. It's not ours to turn off, you know. It belongs to the Government. That makes all this the Navy's decision. And that means Halstead."

"That one! He's in charge of enough things he can't handle as it is," Jack said. He poured more drinks all around. "He has no authority over the Light. None. It's ours."

"He is our superior officer," Malcolm reminded him. "We can all be shot for disobeying orders in wartime—have you thought of that?"

"Sabotage is sabotage," Keith said.

Jack sipped his drink. "They would never do it," he said.

"You don't know," Keith said. "They've done it before in other places."

"If it turned out all right," Seamus said, "I think then they'd be forced to grant us our due."

"That's too easy," Malcolm said.

"We must act together," Seamus said. "We will worry this thing to a conclusion."

"Not me," Malcolm said, rising. "I have to go on station, and so does Jack. We've bent the rules about enough for one day, I reckon."

"I'll be along," Jack said.

"No," Malcolm said, suddenly afraid of conspiracy. "Now."

Jack rose and knocked back his drink before following Malcolm out.

Keith was alone with his father for the first time in years. There was an awkward moment in which Keith watched the old man across the table. He had never understood his father at all and understood him now less than ever. Yet, he liked the old man. They drank the whiskey and just smiled at each other. He was aware of the pull of his father's personality, the draw of a current as persistent as gravity. He did not fight it; he did not want to. "I should have been back when she died," Keith said. "I know that."

"Shh. Don't," the old man said. "It's all right."

"But—"

"No, don't," the old man said. "I think I know how it was up there, and how it is now. I have corresponded with your dean. I felt it was my duty."

Keith had had no idea. How much did his father know? Had he known about Dorothy's visits as well? Who could figure the old man?

5

A KNOCK AT SEAMUS'S DOOR had brought Littlejohn and Fetterman in out of a night almost brighter than the lamplit kitchen where the four of them sat now, starting the talk all over again.

Littlejohn said, "I am not awfully fond of this scheme." In the last minutes of the *John Shay*, the masts had shuddered in their steps as the hull rammed the sandbar, crushed by its own weight while the sea hammered at her beams. All because a man of inferior seamanship who believed himself right had taken the helm in a crisis. "It feels all wrong."

"*It is not wrong* to protect your own and your country against the enemy," Seamus said.

"It is when you've got to do it this way."

"You're both missing the point," Fetterman said.

Seamus poured another round from the second bottle. Keith drummed his fingers on the tabletop. These were the men who had peopled his childhood, yet he did not know them beyond their shapes, the spaces they occupied in the community. Littlejohn had a territory, so did Fetterman, and his father owned all the territory of his youth. Now the men, and Keith too, drank and smoked, working up to the final question, a thing Keith damned over and over. This was what he had fled from up north: decision.

"Who will do it?" Fetterman asked. "Someone will have to take charge."

Littlejohn showed a wry smile. "Nothing good ever comes from this kind of talk."

Seamus got up to stretch his legs. He arced his back and sighed deep from in his chest. He coughed. There was congestion in his lungs these days, and he could only suppose it came from all those nights in the open, a hazard of accumulated weather. He drew a handkerchief and coughed into it. "And what do you think of all this, boy? You've been to school. You know history. Advise the old men who don't know anything."

"Yes, lend us the benefit of your store-bought wisdom," Fetterman said, then quickly added: "I don't mean nothing by it, Keith."

"What are you after, Seamus—a friend in the history books?" Littlejohn asked. "Something to justify what you would have us do?"

"Not that," Seamus said. "I just want—I want—what's that lawyer's word?"

"Yes," Keith said. "Exactly. A precedent. But I'm afraid I don't know of any. I don't think there is one."

Fetterman snorted. "I could have told you that."

"Then we're right back where we started," Seamus said.

"Yes," said Fetterman. "So who? Which one of us? Seamus? Littlejohn? You, Keith?"

"I don't know," Littlejohn said. "You can count on opposition."

"Malcolm," Keith said.

"Halstead," Littlejohn said. "And his crew, every man armed."

"By God," Seamus said, "I'll do it if no one else will."

"We'll see," Fetterman said. "In the meantime, it's enough to know we're all in."

"I have to give it to you, Ham," Seamus told him. "You saw right to the heart of it."

"All my genius is not in my hands, Seamus."

They laughed, but not much. Keith didn't feel very good. He was in a conspiracy—was that too strong a word?—to sabotage Hatteras Light, probably the most important navigational aid on the Atlantic seaboard. He watched the men's faces, their brown hands, his ears full of white noise.

Fetterman had an urge to carve. He was too drunk for that, he knew, but his hands fidgeted with his knife anyway, opening and closing the blade.

Littlejohn spoke to no one on the way out, and walked back to his house alone, head down. The *John Shay*. The British captain. The look on that silver-whiskered gentleman's face when the blunt Irishman raised the rifle and insisted on humility, the one attitude the captain was incapable of. An impossible moment. The crewmen become thugs, abetting their leader, binding the captain hand and foot so that at the grounding he had no more chance than if he'd been trussed in a weighted sack. And the African hands, who had witnessed the mutiny with more apprehension than comprehension, were no swimmers, either. That's why they made such good sailors: they had faith only in the ship.

How long had it taken to run aground—a minute? An hour? Time stalled the instant the Irishman took on the ship's master. But the moment of the grounding was unforgettable: There is no sound like the sundering of massive timbers deep in the heart of a great ship, or the ungodly shriek that precedes the splintering of a cedar mast and sounds like it issues from your own spine. A sound a man might stand to hear only once in his lifetime.

Littlejohn's survival had been highly accidental and vaguely just, since he'd refused to be a party to mutiny. It all had something to do with the Irish problem, with which he was not intimate, and he stood by dumb as the Africans, watching. Justice had been selective rather than fair.

He walked by his store and saw it quiet, lightless. In the moonlight it seemed to glow at its edges, which were straight and elegant as a ship's lines. The beams he had fashioned from salvaged ship's timbers. For all his prosperity, he was just another castaway. He reached up and ran a hand along the lintel, wishing it was new lumber.

There were pirates in Littlejohn's family. His forebears had poached the gray seal, privateered against the British, smuggled *personae non grata* during the opium wars, pillaged the Barbary Coast and the Côte d'Or. He was one of them. He had not acted to prevent mutiny. He limped behind the store to his house, the leg suddenly paining him badly. His wife would be waiting, she who knew little about him and didn't ask, who studied palms and worried over dreams and kept a hemlock switch over the doorway as proof against witches.

By way of greeting, she said to him, "Mrs. Patchett told me a robin got in her house today. She had the devil's own time getting it out again."

"If that's all she has to worry, about."

"Mister Littlejohn, you are a peculiar man. Why, that's the worst omen there is for a man who's gone on a journey."

"And who's going anywhere."

She smiled knowingly. "You're not as dense as you let on. Now come on. I've got biscuits making."

6

WHEN KEITH GOT BACK to Malcolm's house, Mary was sitting on the porch in the moonlight, painting.

"I had intended to paint by the dawn," she said, "but I almost prefer this."

"What is it?" There were only a few tentative lines on the canvas, but they troubled him already.

"Can't you tell?"

"You've never used browns and grays before."

"It's something I just came up with."

"What is your subject?"

She lifted the paintbrush like a wand. In the eerie nightshadow he half expected magic from it, electric and sparkling.

"Not what—who."

"A portrait?"

She nodded, applying a faint brush stroke. "When you recognize it, let me know."

Keith watched her paint for a while, smoking from nervousness now. Watching her, he relaxed, and the conspiracy and Dorothy too slipped from his mind. He went to the stove and made a pot of tea. When she had finished painting, and for a time they had quietly sipped tea, she said to him, "Would you like to see the sunrise?" And hand in hand they walked over the dunes and found a hollow to sit in. There was the Light off to the left and down the other way Halstead's unlit mooring. Keith wondered if he was on board now, sleeping.

"You don't mind putting an arm around me, do you? It makes me feel safe."

"No, I don't mind." They sat together, looking out to sea.

As a youngster, Keith had tagged along behind Malcolm patrolling this beach. Whenever Malcolm would get too far ahead, without looking back he would stop and wait for Keith. Sometimes, Malcolm would let him carry the brass coin, but never the signal rocket.

"Will you marry Dorothy and take her away?" she said. There was an edge of challenge and sadness in her voice.

He dug idly in the sand, feeling the cool flow of it between his fingers, cleansing them by abrasion. "That seems to be the question of the hour."

"You once loved each other very much."

"Yes, I remember that time." But he didn't. There had been weekends in hotels when he was at college. Dorothy seemed to enjoy those meetings, but they troubled Keith. There was so much space in between, and Dorothy was different each time she came. Things were happening in those spaces that were not common ground, and the mystery and the wondering sickened his stomach. There was no certainty between them, no fidelity, or if there was fidelity it was an accident. In all the time before he had gone away from the island they were just kids, and kids loved one another in a reckless, generous way that did not endure. You could never live up to your childhood romance.

"I love Malcolm," Mary said.

After a long silence Keith said, "There will be some history going on here. Maybe that's what brought me back."

"You don't believe in destiny."

"No, not like that."

He stretched, loosened his arm on her back, turned to watch the Light's beacon circling toward them and away again. "But it may be a mess, all the same. Folks are going to be butting heads."

"That's what I'm afraid of. Once people take sides, they may never get back together, never really trust one another again. Sometimes I think we should let the Light decide itself—on or off? It's guarded us all these years like the Cyclops in the Ulysses story. Is it really up to any of us?"

"The Cyclops was a monster."

"Only to Ulysses, who was a foreigner. On the island he was a tower of strength. He was a shepherd."

"You mean Ulysses was the impostor." He stared at the Light awhile.

"What are you thinking?"

He rubbed his hands clean of sand. "The Dark Ages. I'm wondering if they're coming back."

"What do you mean?"

"When the Roman Empire started collapsing at the end of the fifth century, the Vandals swarmed all over Western Europe. They held the coastlines and used the lighthouses to lure ships close enough to attack them. To put a stop to it, the Roman keepers destroyed their own towers, and the lights went out all over the coast. Funny, I just now thought of it." Here, then, was Seamus' precedent.

The Light turned round and round, sweeping the silvered sky, while all around its beam the darkness deepened. There were thunderheads far off and high, moving fast and throwing shadows across the moon. Keith didn't think there would be any weather. He expected a clear, mild dawn.

They sat together in the sandy hollow. Mary rested in his arms, and far across the beach, down by the waterline, they spotted the beachman moving ghostlike on his rounds, his footsteps silent on the wet sand, his head bent as in sorrow.

7

LONG AFTER THE BEACHMAN HAD PASSED, they filled the hollow together.

8

KEITH HAD BEEN RIGHT about the weather: The high clouds scoured the moon and then kept right on going, and the dawn was cloudless and untroubled. The combers broke gently against the shore, and the tidal pools were busy with pipers and gulls.

"Look!" Mary said.

Keith sat up now. "I don't see anything."

"North a little, directly off the Light."

The profile was so low in the water it almost seemed shimmed into place between sky and sea. At first only the hump of the tower had made him notice it at all.

"Good Lord—come on!" Keith yanked Mary to her feet and led her running through the break in the dunes.

9

ON THE CATWALK of the lighthouse, Malcolm spied the U-boat through his glass. He drew back from the eyepiece and caught movement out of the corner of his eye. He turned to watch two lovers on the beach trying to outrun daylight. He followed them with half an eye, saw only their backs, envied them their freedom. Then he bellowed a warning to the men on station and clambered down the wrought-iron spiral staircase inside the tower, his footsteps ringing like bells.

Here, at least, was the main chance.

CHAPTER 12

1

TIM HALSTEAD HAD CALLED on Dorothy Dant with little satisfaction late on the night of the meeting, as much to consult her on politics as to court her. If there was going to be trouble at the lighthouse, he would be smack in the middle of it.

"The island has no politics of its own. They're imported," she said, putting him off immediately. She had an orneriness about her tonight, a kind of bitchiness. She kept her distance, and he wondered about the ease of their lovemaking two nights ago. It angered him to have given in to his passions so readily—did he have no will of his own? It caused him to wonder if, indeed, he were truly a gentleman.

"You come here from the outside, you bring the politics with you."

"Yes. Of course." He had answered deferentially, the way he might have answered an upperclassman at the Academy. What had got into her?

"If you can't get that damned Hun, then they'll get him for you, that's all." Now she was insulting his professional abilities. He stood that, too, meekly, hoping for a better opening.

"I'm sorry it worked out this way, Dot."

"Yes, I guess you are."

She let him hold her awhile, and they fell off to sleep with no further words between them. That, too, took him off guard. He was pleased that he'd recovered from a bad beginning: Here was a chance to prove his intentions honorable. He would guard her, awake or slumbering, all night long.

In the dead time just before sun-up, the quiet awoke him. He rose from the couch, lowering her head to the pillow with what gentleness he could manage. Quickly he smoothed out his trousers, bloused his shirt, and left across the beach without even a note.

Let her just wonder, he thought.

As he crested the dunes he spied two running figures off to his left, between himself and the Light. One of them looked like Keith Royal, but what was his business this early? He quickened his stride toward *Sealion's* dock, then halted all at once.

It must be an illusion, was his first thought. It sat on the glassy sea like a duck. He sprinted toward *Sealion*—her deck already a stage of action. Good boys, he thought. Cross waved him on wildly.

Halstead leapt aboard as the engines turned over and before he had a chance to feel the fear knot his stomach Jack Royal shoved a cork life-vest into his chest. "Put this on, Horatio," he said. "We're going to get wet today."

2

SEAMUS ROYAL PASSED the night at the kitchen table, his shaggy head cradled on his fists. In his dreams he wore the gold medal and handled the steering oar, making for a dismasted schooner. His hands burned from blisters and salt. There was a woman he had to save, that much he knew. His crewmen all wore black hoods instead of yellow sou'westers, and their faces were hidden under the cowls. They leaned into their oars and drew them back again in rhythm. Seamus spied the woman, waving, high on the deck. They'd never get to her in time. He just knew it.

3

WHAT WOULD YOU THINK OF US—a submarine that cannot submerge, a warship without a captain, a raiding boat with only one gun, a crew without hope or discipline, a spy without a radio? A shark with no fin, condemned to ride the surface slowly, to defend with sheer courage rather than attack with stealth, cunning, skill? Would you pity us, would you laugh, would you gloat, would you kill?

Max Wien was in a philosophical mood. He had been up all night and was so punchy he felt drunk. It was a good feeling. He had not got drunk in so many months he'd almost forgotten what it felt like, and he promised himself that if he ever made shore, any shore, he would swill good stout beer until his belly swelled and he collapsed like a sail being doused.

The work parties were almost finished. Kraft held the section of undamaged rail in both hands, his back turned to the rising sun. Max stood by him, and together they spotted the wake of the American speedboat.

"*Ist der Kapitän klar im Kopf?*" Kraft asked, raising the glasses to his eyes. The work parties were gathering their tools and hurrying off the deck.

"Is he lucid? I would not use that word, exactly." The captain was as delirious as an opium eater. "I think you must assume command, sir."

Max's tone roused Kraft. He ordered Bergen and his man to their places by the gun. "Get off two rounds before they close and then we're going under," Kraft said, "with or without you." Bergen grinned.

The American bore down on them straight on, not even zigzagging in what had already become the classic antisubmarine maneuver. Max wondered: What's wrong with him?

Bergen embraced his gun and fired. After the first sharp report there was a three-second silence, then a splash by the American's bows. She kept coming, firing on her own now.

The second shot caught the American in the stern, spinning her to a violent stop, and a black cloud of metal, wood, and fuel erupted and then settled on the water.

Kraft ordered all hands below and U-55 dove leisurely. We're still in the game, Max thought. He went to Captain Stracken's cot and held his hand. Only then did he realize his own hand was bloody. A bullet had grazed his right arm. Now the pain came, and Max sat down beside his captain and kept his eyes open so he would not spin. He listened for the sound of leaking water drowning them all.

4

"WE'VE GOT THE BASTARD NOW!" Halstead shouted. *Sealion* scored a long wake on the gray water. Halstead leaned into the wind. He gave Cross the helm and clutched the cockpit armor for balance. The wind of their own velocity whipped his face.

Jack said, "You're out of your stupid mind."

Halstead ignored him.

"You can't do it this way, straight on! Goddamnit, listen—"

But *Sealion's* forward machine gun was already hammering at the enemy. Jack shook Halstead's shoulder. He hollered at Cross to zigzag, but Cross was caught up in it, too.

The U-boat was lying low in the water, obviously damaged, her silhouette marred by missing parts. But the German was firing, his first shot narrowly missing *Sealion's* bows. Jack wrested the helm from Cross, elbowing him out of the way. Cross stumbled and fell behind the armor, and that saved him from injury. Later he would remember that Jack Royal had been his savior, and credit intention on Royal's part.

So when the second shell burst on the crowded afterdeck just back of the cockpit, Halstead, Jack, Cross, and the forward gunner were spared. The men aft of them were obliterated in a single flash. The steering went but not the power, and all of them watched the sky spin round and round above them, a placid blue square turned vortical with the sound of unstopped engines running all out.

That didn't last long.

Halstead was the first on his feet. The coaming of the cockpit burned his hand to the quick, and he could hardly keep his legs. Jack Royal was bloody, but the blood was mostly not his own. His life-vest had been stripped off and his ears rang. The forward gunner had broken his leg on the deck, and Halstead had caught shrapnel in his cheek. Only Cross was unscathed.

The engines finally quit and their racket gave way to a howling silence. The boat turned more slowly, finally ceased turning altogether, and listed heavily to port, throwing Halstead off his feet.

The cork raft stowed on the outside cockpit wall was gone. *Sealion* was sinking fast. Halstead watched the submarine disappear: Confused, he was sure the enemy was sinking, too. One of his own torpedoes was missing, and he imagined he had fired it and he congratulated himself.

Jack Royal, man of action, got to his feet, grabbed Halstead and Cross and, nestled between them like a float, flung them bodily into the cold water. He called to the forward gunner who was sprawled on the inclined deck. "She's burning! Get off—get off while you can!"

The man slid rather than jumped into the water and sluggishly made his way toward them, howling about his broken leg. *Sealion* burned briefly but sank before she could explode. There was no sign of the rest of the crew.

Jack worked his feet to tread water. He held to his companions and shivered. The gunner got close and flailed his way over to them, and the four held onto one another.

On the beach a boat was being launched. Malcolm's boat, Jack knew, and pedalled his legs.

5

IT WAS A GRIM RESCUE. Malcolm's men pulled through easy water with even strokes; soon they were close enough to take on survivors. When Malcolm saw his brother in the lifeboat, he wanted to say something soothing. Jack's face was bloody, and his lips and fingernails were blue. Malcolm wondered if they would be burying him this time. He wanted to say something kind out loud, but Jack was still in shock.

Beyond them, on land, the Light had not been extinguished with the dawn. Malcolm watched it grow larger with every stroke of the oars, its spiraled black stripe narrowing at the top, above that the black iron crown of catwalk, and from the glass turret the weak pulse of the lamp in daylight.

6

TO REMEMBER PAPENBURG at all Max had to reconstruct it. Was there a wooded hill mounting to a house? Had his father been a doctor taken ill in the course of caring for his patients? Had his mother succumbed, her shape under the bedclothes smaller each morning, her faint breath expiring in a fever, like steam boiling off a pot?

Had his little brother Thomas been smothered too by the mysterious fever that swept the countryside like brushfire in those last months before the war, annihilating families wholesale, defying cure, and sparing only a few, at random, like Max?

Sound was extinct in his world. The collective stink of the men huddled close around him sealed his senses like mucus.

7

AFTER THE SURVIVORS of the *Sealion* had been landed and their wounds treated, and Malcolm had completed his chores in the carousel room, it was time to get ready.

"This is not the time to be giving away jewelry," Malcolm muttered to Chief Lord as he pulled on a pair of dry uniform trousers, stiff as Sunday clothes. He combed his thick beard and brushed the sleeves of his double-breasted tunic, secured with ten gold buttons in a double row, then went downstairs to the common room of the station. The ceremony was to be held on the porch.

Halstead sat in a rattan chair in the shade of the porch, his cheek scarred with stitches, his face drained of color, staring out to sea.

The Life-Saving men stood at attention at the foot of the porch. Jack, rested and his face washed, stood shoulder to shoulder with his fellows. Seamus Royal stood beside the last man in the row, Cy Magillicutty, who had crewed with him and was old enough to remember a similar ceremony when Seamus had received his own medal.

Halstead's forward gunner relaxed in a wooden wheelchair, waiting for a ride to Portsmouth after the presentation. This would be the first and probably last chance he would ever get to ride in a car with staff officers. He grinned carelessly and tapped a finger against the long cast on his leg.

Keith watched it all from behind the assembled spectators. Mary,

Virginia, and Dorothy huddled in a group, excluding him. Fifty yards away, up in the tower, Toby Bannister had the watch. He looked out to sea and wondered about his brother. He didn't care much about medals. Everybody had medals anymore.

On the porch, a full commander from the admiral's staff gave a short speech about sacrifice and duty and hung the ribbon over Malcolm's shaggy bowed head, the medal dangling from the end like a spoon lure.

Malcolm shook his hand, they saluted one another, and that was that.

8

HALSTEAD, groggy from morphine, shook Malcolm's hand in turn and traded compliments with the staff officers before they collected their party and headed north again, taking with them the remainder of his crew: Cross and the gunner. There was a chance, they said, that they could free a cutter now under repair at Philadelphia and send it down to finish the Hun.

Halstead requested and got permission to recuperate on Hatteras Island while waiting to be reassigned. When told he might not get another command, Halstead said nothing. He had no reason to think he deserved one.

9

AS THE MEN resumed their duties and the spectators went home, Halstead approached Jack Royal. "I've put you up for the Coast Guard Medal, Mister Royal."

"What would that fix?" His father's medal gathered dust on a shelf. And so, too, would Malcolm's.

10

MALCOLM HURRIED OFF the porch to catch Mary before she left. They strolled in front of the lighthouse and stood close in its shadow so that not even Toby Bannister, pacing the iron catwalk high above, could see them alone.

"I'm not a hero. That's not what this is about. That's not what this is about," he repeated. He looked first to one side, then to the other. Mary took his face in her hands, pulled it down, and kissed him. She didn't mind the stiffness of his uniform then as he drew her to him and enclosed her with his arms.

11

FOR THE FIRST TIME since receiving his commission, Timothy Halstead, Lieutenant Junior Grade, wanted the company of a bottle.

He had taken his part in the greatest war in history; he had met the enemy in open battle and had lost his first command. His boat was sunk, his crew dead, mutilated, or scattered, his mission failed, his career ruined, his name disgraced. In all likelihood, he would face a court-martial. Men were dead because of his bravado and bad judgment, and nothing he could ever do could change that. Nothing. He could not stand it that Cross did not hold it against him, just as he could not stand it that Jack Royal did. Even now he didn't know what he'd have done differently. He had gambled on speed at the expense of maneuver, and he had lost. Simple.

He had reports to file, letters to write, accounts to square. Tomorrow, he thought.

Halstead could not go to Dorothy tonight, even if she'd have him. The one person who could actually help him, his lost honor made unavailable to him. What could he offer her now? Ignominy? Shame? He had tried and failed.

From Littlejohn he cajoled a bottle of bootleg rum and trekked out across the dunes, careful to find a place off the route of the beach patrol. He settled down in a hollow and drank.

In front of him, somewhere off in the darkness, the sea snapped like flames.

12

DOROTHY, Mary, and Keith had supper at Jack and Virginia's house. After a silent, uncomfortable meal, the two men went outside on the porch. Jack filled his pipe and Keith lit a cigar.

"What's going on?" Keith said.

Jack fooled with his match a little, having trouble with it in the wind. It was a lovely, balmy night with a freshening breeze.

"Malcolm is wrong this time, Keith."

"So you say."

They smoked awhile.

"I want you with us. Dad does, too."

"I don't know."

"You don't get it, do you. You're either with us or against us. There's no middle in this thing."

"I just haven't made up my mind."

"Now that's the story of your life, ain't it. Well, make up your mind. You can't just keep dabbling at things, do you understand?"

"Malcolm is dead set against it, you know that."

"We're not talking about Malcolm, college boy. We're talking about you. It's time you started making your own way." Jack tightened his fist, then relaxed it.

"You wanted to hit me, didn't you? Like the other day. But you were scared to death of Malcolm."

"Is that what you think? Then you're even dumber than I thought." Jack unclamped his pipe and regarded Keith through the silver threads of smoke, his eyes suddenly reminding Keith of his mother's eyes, years ago. What was it? From inside the house came the murmur of women's voices, rife with tension.

"Maybe. Then why don't you hit me now?"

Jack smiled and put a hand on his shoulder. "Maybe you get it after all." He laid his pipe carefully on the porch railing, and then he drove a fist into Keith's eye. He brushed his palms together, retrieved his pipe, and went into the house.

Keith lay on his back in the cool sand, watching the muddy sky go round and round.

13

AT PRECISELY TWELVE MIDNIGHT Malcolm seated himself before the logbook and began the familiar ordeal of inventing a dozen or so words to describe tonight's quiet and the ceremony of decoration. He would be embarrassed to include that, but it was necessary. Staff officers' visits to the station had to be duly noted, according to regulations. Still.

He opened the big book, facing the slab of paper, blank as an uninscribed tombstone. He wrung his hands, shifted in his chair, scraped a shoe back and forth on the floorboards.

Outside, the quiet was like water. He listened to it seep in, felt it fill in around his shoes and knees and waist and chest and ears. He listened to the slow beat of his own heart. He fingered the medal, now in a plain wooden casket no bigger than a snuffbox. Seamus had one. He hefted it like a coin, like currency.

Malcolm was reluctant to begin. He had the right words, he was sure, but they whirled around in his brain, disorganized, elusive, random as electrons, and he could not conjur them to order.

When he had composed himself, he wrote: *Just after first light brought in four survivors of U.S.S.* Sealion, *sunk by Gmn, U-boat. At 1430 Cmdr. Yost & Staff Officers on station, awarded Gold Medal to Keeper on behalf of Crew.*

CHAPTER 13

1

CHIEF LORD HAD the tower watch. He had taken it knowing full well something would happen tonight. He did not always know in advance, but ominous feelings had been building inside him ever since the first sheaf of lumber had grounded like a landing barge from the vanished *Hauppage*.

The omens had accreted like sediment on the mainland side of the island. The odd weather pattern, the fishermen lost in the stream, Keith Royal's return, the loss of Mary's baby midterm, Halstead's defeat, Fetterman's ugly model, the lightship sunk, Patchett's disappearance, the U-boat prowling offshore like some minion of Neptune, waiting to pull them down severally into the netherworld,

Mrs. Littlejohn's hoverings and mutterings. Chief Lord had seen magic before, local magic worked for revenge or fertility or profit, but this was bigger. This had the power of the weather in it, the depth of oceans, the breadth of continents, the wrath of gods.

The sun and the moon shall be darkened, he thought, and the stars withdraw their shining. Things were accelerating, as they always did in wartime. He smoked his pipe to build his own magic and scoured the sea with eyes that seemed locked into the workings of the Light itself.

He paced the catwalk as the silence prickled his spine.

For a long minute he couldn't even hear the ocean. He dug a finger into his ear and sound resumed sluggishly, like a Victrola starting up. He had been dreaming things the past few nights, and the dreams had accumulated a power and will of their own. Four nights running he had dreamed of the island. Each time the island was smaller, eroding at the edges; each time the horizons were closer. Last night Chief Lord had dreamed of running from the station toward the sea where Malcolm and the old horse had dragged the boat without him, something that had never happened in all the years he had been on station. He found himself knee-deep in salt water, spilling into his boots, anchoring him, pulling him down. He had called out to Malcolm, but Malcolm was gone, he and his oarsmen ferrying people away from the island. Chief stood there, feeling the cold water rise about his waist, his armpits, his shoulders, his oilskins clammy and heavy.

At last, the water was in his eyes.

Tonight he welcomed the night watch, a reprieve from dreams. He paced and smoked and saw into the transatlantic darkness with clarity and suspicion.

When he spied the lights of the freighter steaming north, hard by the shoals, he didn't hesitate: He raised the alarm with a great blast of breath. Then he watched four flashes, like matches striking, felt four concussions in his own chest, regular as heartbeats.

2

THE *D'Arcy McGee* was a coal burner of Canadian registry bound for Newark with a cargo of rubber from the Far East. She took four direct hits that swamped the engine room and left her listing badly in the shoals. Her final momentum and the action of the waves and a mild breeze were driving her hard toward the Bight of Hatteras and a shallow grave.

"She's too close in," Malcolm said. "If she comes in any closer, we can't use the boat." In the choppy breakers, a rescue by boat would be foolhardy. "Let her stay in deep water."

But she drove toward them even faster now, the wind freshening. Chief Lord and two men were already fetching the Lyle gun and the breeches buoy on a boxcart. Chief led Homer to the waterline and waited. They could do nothing until the *D'Arcy McGee* came to rest.

Jack and Keith Royal came on the run, summoned by Cy Magillicutty on the telephone.

"Good Lord! She's almost on the beach!" Keith said. "What was she trying to do, anyway?"

"Hug the shoreline, save some fuel," Jack said. "Outsmart the Hun."

Malcolm didn't say anything.

"At least she's not burning yet."

Malcolm shook his head. "She's burning inside her belly."

Keith could smell her now. Soon the flames waved like pennants above the deck, backlighting the low squared silhouette of the ship.

"There's nothing to stop him now," Jack said. Suddenly he wished Halstead's boat were back in action. It was a silly defense, but at least it was a defense.

Malcolm stood between Keith and Jack, powerless. If he could, he would swim that surf and drag the survivors back two at a time under his arms, but all he could do was wait. The crew had been making progress along the shoreline, stalking her as she drifted south in the shallows, and now the *D'Arcy McGee* was almost directly abeam of the slip where Halstead's boat had been docked. Then the black ship grounded with a prolonged shudder that echoed in her great iron belly and escaped her holds like a death rattle.

"Now," Malcolm said, assuming command. "Go to it!"

Joe Trent and Toby Bannister dug a cross-shaped pit and buried the sand anchor, while Ian MacSween and Will Fetterman unlimbered the block and tackle and raised the high wooden crotch that would support the shore-end of the lifeline. And then Malcolm, shrugging aside Chief Lord and Cy Magillicutty, hefted the two-hundred-pound Lyle gun out of the boxcart himself. His chest swelled with purposeful strength. The brass barrel was warm to his touch.

The other men meanwhile laid out the breeches buoy—a cork ringbuoy with canvas trouser legs sewn underneath. Through his megaphone, Malcolm hailed the *D'Arcy McGee*.

She lay no more than a hundred yards out, her bow pointing south. On the inclined deck, several dark figures moved about drunkenly.

"Try the signal lamp," Malcolm ordered.

Toby Bannister manipulated the blinds of the signal lamp and in a few seconds another light blinked on deck.

"They're ready for a line," he told Malcolm.

The Lyle gun was loaded, the thin white messenger line coiled perfectly in the faking box beside the barrel. Hal MacRae elevated the muzzle and aimed it amidships, since the fire was so far confined to the stern.

He tugged the lanyard and a sharp report stung the air. The line uncoiled in a long arc, swallowed by the sky, bending in the wind, lifted. And missed.

"Windage, Mister MacRae—windage!" Malcolm bellowed. Cyrus and Will Fetterman hauled in the line hand over hand and McRae coiled it as perfectly as before.

The second try sent the line waggling like spittle over the

water in a higher arc. It caught on a boom, and they could see men scurrying to retrieve it. When the signal came, Chief Lord attached the stout hawser to the light flying line and Toby sent another signal. The men on the ship hauled in the light line until they had the hawser, which they ran through a block on the boom. The other end was run through the pulley on shore, completing the circuit.

Malcolm and Chief Lord rigged the breeches buoy under the hawser, and on Malcolm's signal they hauled it out to the *D'Arcy McGee*, the men lined in the surf as the breeches buoy sailed over their heads like a miniature tramcar.

Jack Royal took his place on the crew, but his ordeal aboard the *Sealion* had taken more out of him than he knew. Giddy after only a few minutes' exertion, he faltered to his knees in the surf and felt a strong hand on his shoulder lifting him by the scruff of his jacket.

"Malcolm—" he started to say.

But it was Keith. He pulled Jack to his feet as roughly as he could and put his own hands on the hawser, hauling in concert with the others as the first man rode the breeches buoy in above the inky seas.

3

HALSTEAD HAD MANAGED to finish most of the bottle before curling up with his knees under his chin and the corked bottle wedged tight in his crotch. He heard a clamor of voices and the crack of cannon fire. The wind carried ammonia, salt, and cordite, and ventilated his dreams with that confusion of smells. He woke up and grunted. Something was going on.

4

THE FIRST FIVE MEN to ride ashore in the breeches buoy were badly injured and had to be lifted out of the lifesaving seat. Three were burned and two were all cut up from shrapnel. In the two and a half hours it took for those five to make it ashore, the weather worsened. The seas turned to chop and the fresh wind seemed to come from all directions at once. The man in the buoy seat bobbed like a monkey on a stick.

"It's the outside edge of a hurricane," Chief Lord said. "I can feel it."

"It's all wrong for the season," MacSween said.

"Ain't they always," Chief Lord said.

They were working to a crowd now. Littlejohn and his wife were passing out cups of coffee and Mrs. Patchett's children took turns playing with Homer. Virginia, Mary, and Dorothy congregated around Seamus, who stood like a statue in a town square, his rifle shouldered like a minuteman's, his head cocked to the wind, taking it all in. Jack reclined on the beach alone. Mary watched Keith labor in the surf. She noticed that her father-in-law wasn't the only armed man on the beach. Rifles poked out here and there, and a few pockets bulged with the weight of pistols. Mary wondered how it would all turn out.

The men on the crew didn't talk much, conserving all their wind for the strenuous job of retrieving the breeches buoy again and again.

The sixth man to come ashore was lucid enough to tell them there were scores of men on line behind him.

"What are you talking about?" Malcolm seized him by the collar. A freighter that size, he knew, shouldn't carry above two dozen hands and probably carried fewer, with the wartime shortage of manpower.

"Marines," he said. "Australian marines. Came ashore at the Falklands for transport to England."

"Lord of Hosts," said Chief Lord. "At the rate she's burning, we'll never get them off in time."

Malcolm said, "We might."

"Who are you kidding?" Chief Lord said.

The crew continued hauling in sooted sailors and marines, one by one, the process an agony of failing hope. There were so many still to get off, and now the conflagration on deck was general, lighting the whole beach like an early sunrise. Soon the deck would be untenable, and the men huddled there with such remarkable discipline would be forced to hurl themselves into a sea where currents crossed like cyclone winds.

The stink of rubber burned the breeze.

The hawser stretched out to the vessel like a high-tension line, black and precise against the orange glow behind it. A dark cloud accumulated above the *D'Arcy McGee* and crawled steadily shoreward.

"There's just one more thing," Malcolm said, and took a coiled line out of the boxcart. He slipped Homer out of harness, then he led the horse to the water.

5

CAPTAIN STRACKEN WAS still out of his head, reciting Tennyson in English and hearing the bells of Bach ringing off the bulkheads.

"Max. *Kommen Sie hierher!*" he called.

But Max was topside, where First Officer Kraft was having the devil's own time maneuvering the balky submarine in the chop. Submerged, she had shipped entirely too much water, and now he wanted to run on the surface, pump out the bilge, recharge batteries, and satisfy his own curiosity about what was going on. The attack had been a surface affair, a bold thrust under a waning moon.

"Can you smell it, Max?"

"Rubber. Of course I can smell it."

"No, not rubber—death. The death of armies. Tires, boots,

gaskets, balloons. Tires, most of all. An army without transport going nowhere, dying on its own ground. Can you smell it?"

Kraft made an exaggerated sniffing sound and drew the acrid
scent deep into his lungs.

"How can you do that?"

"Penance." He laughed. "My God, she burns bright."

"Bergen's work."

"Have you ever thought what they would do if they captured
us?"

"I know what I would do."

"For killing the innocents? Let me tell you, boy, they are none
of them so innocent."

"That's not it."

"For firing on merchantmen on the high seas?"

Max shook his head and lit a cigarette he had pilfered from the
captain. "For mocking honor."

"You want heroes in this war? There are no heroes in the
Schlachthof."

"No, only *der Techniker*, like our Bergen."

"He's due for promotion, don't you think? And so are you. You
have held up admirably."

Max smoked and kept his own counsel for a few minutes. He
did not want a promotion. Above all things, he didn't want that.
His only hope lay in his common station, his only dignity in the
fact that he wasn't in charge, not of anything, and never would be.
He smoked until Kraft lost interest in him and began bothering
the crew about navigation, casting orders about like a man fend-
ing off blows. The rudder damaged, they were drifting in dangerously close. She wasn't responding to the helm as neatly as Kraft
would have liked. They couldn't send a diver over, not at night in
these waters, so they would make do. Sluggishly, U-55 came about
and steamed south, close off the Bight of Hatteras.

Max noticed movement and lights on the beach. He raised the
glasses for a closer look. He saw the breeches buoy, slung out over
the water, crawling toward shore, saw the line of broad-backed

men leaning into their task, some of them waist-deep in water, now the spume breaking over their shoulders. Then he saw something else.

He started to call Kraft but thought better of it. What he saw, burnished in the glow of flames, taking each breaker head-on so that foam splashed and curled about it, was the figure of a man on horseback struggling toward the doomed ship.

6

MALCOLM ROYAL HAD no illusions about his own safety, but he worried about drowning a good horse. On he drove, his mouth clamped shut to keep the little courage he still felt from spilling out. Homer balked under him, pincered by his powerful legs. He compelled the horse forward by main force of will. He was scared enough to be grateful for solitude. No one required calming words, no one required assurance, no one required commanding. The beast was simply mastered, as Malcolm was, the pair of them in full career in a direction neither wished to go.

Halfway there, Homer was foundering. Stupidly, Malcolm felt for stirrups to raise himself.

Homer staggered in a riptide, then found a sandbar and gathered his legs onto it and they moved forward once more, Malcolm now carressing Homer's neck and soothing him with nonsensical murmurings that were meant as much for himself as for the horse.

The men aboard the *D'Arcy McGee* realized at once what was going on. When he was close enough, Malcolm raised a hand and indicated they should jump. He watched them hurtle into the surf like bundles of rags. He cast the line toward them in a singing arc, and someone tugged at the end of it. Malcolm fastened the bitter end around his waist and stiffened to keep his seat as weight accumulated on the other end, then all along the length of the line. They had the idea. "Good boys," Malcolm said, "good boys."

He pivoted slowly, timing the waves just right. Homer was swimming now, blowing spray out of his nostrils, and took a couple of minutes finding something solid under his hooves. Malcolm held on to Homer's mane. Homer leaned out like a thoroughbred running toward the cheers. Behind them a line of men bobbed along the rope and tried not to drown.

7

JACK ROYAL, the wind whipping tears out of his eyes, his face clenched like a fist, observed Malcolm's progress.

8

"DEAR GOD," Mary Royal said. "Have you ever seen anything like it?" Virginia held her arm.

"He's a showboater, that one. I always said so."

Dorothy, standing behind the sisters, said: "They're all crazy."

"Don't start," Virginia warned.

"Would you look at him!" Mary said. "Just look at him!" Her heart was flung high in the overwhelming adventure of the moment, then plummeted, and she was instantly miserable.

9

HALSTEAD HAD COME OUT to the beach, sobered, and volunteered. He was amazed. He watched Malcolm Royal coax the horse out of the breakers onto the beach while the rest of the crew, the breeches buoy temporarily stranded on the crotch, waded in to pull out the survivors trailing Malcolm. Chief Lord and Cy Magillicutty hauled in the line, and the others heaved the survivors bodily from the foam and onto dry land.

Malcolm stood heaving, head pressed into the horse's neck.

"Good boy," he said, stroking Homer's neck. "Good boy." Homer staggered to his knees and Malcolm with him. Mary stood over her husband, kneeling in the surf.

10

OLD FETTERMAN LEANED close at Littlejohn's ear, pointing with his cane, and said, in between coughs: "Look what Malcolm caught."

11

THEY HAD GOT every man who was coming off the *D'Arcy McGee*. No one could really believe what had just occurred, least of all the men who had been saved. Malcolm worked among them, organizing, reassuring, congratulating. The women lent a hand dressing wounds. It was time to get out from under the storm before it delivered its cargo of rain. They watched the *D'Arcy McGee* burn.

In the glow of the flames, the U-boat was suddenly visible behind the freighter.

"It's the Hun!" Seamus cried. "They're landing!" He raised his rifle without hesitating and let go the magazine in quick unaimed shots.

"Stop it!" Malcolm yelled, running toward his father and then ducking at the last second to avoid having his head taken off.

Seamus fired out the magazine and fetched another from his pocket. Now others were moving close to the water or picking out perches in the dunes and firing on the German, their muzzle flashes illuminating their faces.

Some of the women screamed, others fled. A few clapped their hands over their ears and flung themselves on the beach, ready to die. Someone behind Mary Royal hammered at the sky with a cap-and-ball pistol. Fetterman shook his cane over his head like a sword. "Bastard," he said, "bastard."

The melee lasted about a minute and a half. Then the rain came, and they broke and ran for cover, as the German U-boat floated off into the storm, and the air, tasting of rubber, smothered their lungs.

12

MALCOLM LABORED.

He held the pen upright between his index and middle fingers, his swollen thumb against the point to keep it in place as he wrote in a careful but ragged script: *Freighter* D'Arcy McGee, *Canadian registry, grounded shortly after midnight south of the Light after U-boat attack. With breeches buoy & Homer, our horse, removed sixty-two men, incl. Australian marines.*

There, it was finished. His hand throbbed from the effort. He wanted to say something about the confusion he was feeling. He felt no better than a mooncusser or a wrecker, luring ships to disaster with the assurance of a light. It was all turned around now, and each lost ship somehow counted as a betrayal, although he could seriously entertain no alternative to his duty.

Malcolm wished the wind would dash the windows and extinguish the Light, that lightning would intervene, or accident. But it was a Fresnel lens of the first order, the glass of the bonnet was reinforced and had never buckled in all the forty-seven years since it had been installed, and he, not God, was its Keeper.

He rubbed his hands on the soft indigo flannel sleeves of his fatigue uniform and his hands stung with the new circulation. With the knuckles of his thumbs, he cleared salt water from his eyes before it could fall on the page and blot his words.

CHAPTER 14

1

ALVIN DANT HAD LABORED most of his life under threat of breaking even. When the fishing was bad, it was worse for him. Somehow the others always managed a catch. When it was good, it broke his nets with a bounty of table fish he could not collect. With his profits he was always paying off past debts, cancelling what was owed, so that his future was always slightly in mortgage and he was forever trying to catch up.

He worked with determination, drank only occasionally, and was a conscientious if imperfect father. And luck was a thing he had heard about, all right—other men sometimes had it. But Alvin

Dant never gambled at cards, avoided borrowing money for luxuries, and trusted his boat and his seamanship and not the gods.

Brian was working the bilge pump by hand, as his father had done until just a few minutes ago. "One more hour," the boy chanted as the pump handle stroked up and down, "one more hour." That was the modest goal Alvin had set for them.

The main force of the storm had not yet reached them. The turbulence now was just the preliminaries. For the time being they were safe enough. For the hour.

"Brian—come up here."

The boy complied. He is so easy to command, Alvin thought.

"How's she doing, boy?"

"Holding all right, I guess. It was all the water we shipped in the hatches last night did it."

"I know that."

Brian was bearing up well, except that his eyes had assumed a sunken cadaverous quality, as if he were watching from deep inside himself. It was a way of looking that reminded Alvin of Malcolm Royal.

Brian wrung his hands to get the stiffness out of them. Alvin took the boy's hands into his own and inspected them, turning them over. It broke his heart to see them so raw and blistered. For all the hard labor Brian had done the past few years, he had never developed calluses. Alvin had them thick as bark on the undersides of his hands. When he would stroke Dorothy's cheek in a moment of forgetfulness, he would leave a scuff of rash, as if he had scratched her. The hairline marks would swell pink and sometimes remain visible for days afterward—her skin was every bit as delicate as Brian's. But Dorothy never minded, or if she did never said so. Alvin Dant wondered if other men made marks on their children by loving them.

Without a word he salved the hands and wrapped bandages around them, binding them so they resembled boxing gloves.

Brian threw mock punches.

"You haven't lost your spunk."

"And you have?"

"I guess we know each other pretty well."

Brian laughed quietly.

"You're in an awfully good mood, boy, considering."

"How many times have I gone out with you, Dad? For an afternoon? For a three-day catch? For a week's?"

Alvin was blank. His mind had lost its edge. He was listening, but it was hard to figure things. Everything was moving, mixing, muddied.

"How many? Fifty? A hundred? A thousand? And how many words did you ever say to me?"

Alvin thought about that. The boy sounded glad. "I—I didn't ever know what to say."

Brian held his father's arm in his bandaged hands as the deck swayed under them with the motion of the sea. "Neither did I," he whispered. "You see? Neither did I."

2

PATCHY WAS feeling tired. It wasn't easy being heroic, but if his muscles ached and his eyes burned, his determination did not flag. He had no choice anyway. To go back now, to quit, would just make him the object of more ridicule. He would drown out here alone before he would go home to that.

The *Proteus* had scared hell out of him. But it had also confirmed him in his mission. Littlejohn's wife could have interpreted it more exactly, he figured, but for the time being it was enough to recognize it as a sign. For once in his life, Patchy was in exactly the right place doing exactly the right thing.

Maybe if he succeeded, his father's memory would at last be admitted to the history of the island. They would know once and for all it was not duty but choice that mattered to a man. As long as there was choice there was hope. They had never granted his father the choice. There had been precious few choices for anybody, up to now. That was why they were all so scared: In this crisis there was no clear tradition to follow, and they must make up their own minds.

For the past day he had zigzagged east. He knew he was heading north as well because the Big River had him. He could feel it under his keel, bearing him along at six knots above his own speed. So far, *Hermes* had held up well under the strain of the sea. He congratulated himself on that. But he felt the weight of water in the bilges, and he knew he had barely enough fuel to get back to Hatteras Island, assuming he could break loose from the grip of the Gulf Stream.

He drank a grog of his own concoction—rum and orange juice. His eyes were hard slits and his head was accumulating fever like a boil.

As the wind freshened across his beams he hallucinated walls of dark steam that resembled rock, and when he had steered safely between these phantom cliffs he encountered more. On either side of him spun waterspouts, shrieking and hissing.

He had entered a realm he had only heard about in the tall tales of fishermen, tales he had mostly discounted as the brag of the profession. Now he wasn't so sure. Banks of colors sliced across the seascape like razors. Waterspouts died and then resurrected in his wake. Vaporous walls shifted and settled like glaciers. The noise was incredible and varied: rushing, hissing, shrilling, crackling, an unsettling cacophony. He drank steadily. There was no telling where his course might lead. He skinned his eyes, half expecting a giant nautilus or a plumed sea serpent to breach on his bows. He handled the helm, watching, hanging on. Dant was out there. He would cross this infernal place and find him, or he wouldn't come back. One way or the other, Peter Patchett would become a legend.

3

CAPTAIN STRACKEN REVIVED for a few minutes in the afternoon. "Where are we?" he demanded.

"Don't worry," Max told him. Kraft stood next to him with arms crossed, lips pursed.

"We have come too far," Stracken said. Then: "We must get the fisherman."

"Yes, my Captain," Max said without conviction.

4

PATCHY COULD NOT REMEMBER when he had ever been alone for so long. That part of it he liked. He had a feeling that important things were always accomplished by men working alone.

For the time being he had shed his wife and family, his personal history as a shiftless ne'er-do-well. He was forging a new identity for himself, and he liked that part, too.

Truthfully, he was amazed that the boat had held. He had launched himself prepared to founder, drown, fail, do no one any good, and here it was all working out according to his hazy plan. Incredible.

Patchy wished his children, Penny and Parvis, could see him now, being a good father. His own father, serious and reliable, had been a better family man. Still, where was his father's treasure? The company had buried him, and all the man's worldly possessions had fit into a cardboard box small enough even for a child to carry.

Among the waterspouts now he glimpsed a new mirage, the dark bulk of something less vaporous.

He sounded his fog bell and was unnerved to hear a reply.

Or was it only echo? The timbre, the pitch, were the same. He tried again, and when two bells answered this time he said, "Praise the Lord."

ALVIN HEARD THE BELL the same time Brian did. Startled, they looked at one another. They had been adrift so long they had really given up rescue as a real possibility.

"You don't think it's the Huns?" Brian said.

"I doubt it, boy. I think their greeting would be a little different. That's a fisherman's bell."

Alvin answered with one bell, then two. Once the idea of rescue had sunk in, Brian appeared nonchalant. "Boy," Alvin said, "there's something in you that takes a little getting used to." Brian said nothing. "Ready the towline in case this is our day for a miracle."

The seas were slate gray and choppy. It would be tricky setting up a tow. Alvin squinted at the approaching boat. He didn't recognize her until he saw the disheveled figure leaning out of the wheelhouse.

"My Lord, it's Patchy!"

"Ahoy on the *Pelican!*"

"Ahoy yourself, Patchy. Come in closer."

"Do you want a tow, or shall I take you off?"

"We could use a tow, all right, Mister Patchett. Brian has a line."

It took all three men working two and a half hours to manage a line between the stern of Patchy's *Hermes* and the *Pelican's* bow.

Patchy would have liked to confer with Dant about tides and direction and chart coordinates, but he did not dare risk drowning the man by hauling him across between the boats. They had no bosun's chair, and the sea was just too rough.

"If you start to founder, sound your bell," Patchy shouted over the wind until Alvin got it. He nodded vigorously and then retired to the pilothouse to take the helm from Brian.

"I hope to God he knows where he's going."

"He knows," Brian said with so much conviction his father turned and stared at him, then dug his fists into the sockets of his eyes to clear them.

"I never would have expected that one," Alvin said. "I wonder why he came."

"It doesn't really matter, does it. It only matters how bad this storm gets before nightfall."

There was no arguing with that. Now that safety was at hand, Alvin was terrified. Here was hope, a damnable thing.

"When we get back, it won't be the same," Brian said. The bandages on his hands made him seem helpless.

"What do you mean? What won't be the same?"

But Brian didn't answer. Instead, he braced himself at the wheel beside his father and watched Patchy's boat flog the sea.

6

PATCH PATCHETT HEADED HOME with the weight of his future trailing him on a two-inch hawser. He had never had anything so firmly in tow. He was slightly giddy with lack of sleep and too much grog, a little unsteady on his legs, but never mind. He had the wheel for balance, and by the time they neared Hatteras Island it would be dark. All he would have to do would be to steer straight on for the Light, then veer south by southwest until the harbor opened to receive them on the other side of Hatteras Inlet.

Hermes was pitching in the storm now, and there was so much spray between the two boats that he would lose sight of the Dant boat for minutes at a time. He had laid a fire ax handy to part the line if it came to trouble. If it came to trouble, they could swim for it and he'd pluck them out of the drink with his gaff.

He thought about his father as he rode the sea home. He couldn't understand how a man who had tasted this could settle for a riveter's job in some shipyard. Maybe it was God's mercy that peeled him off that scaffold, Patchy thought. Maybe his father had waited and prayed for that day ever since he left the island and the Life-Saving Service.

Patchy had not waited or prayed for this moment, but now that it was here he felt more like himself than he had ever felt; a strange thing, he reflected, since this new man who had taken control of him bore no resemblance to the Patch Patchett he had played all his life.

"Steady as she goes," he said to no one.

Under him, he could feel the powerful current of the Gulf Stream fighting the wheel. He knew his direction unerringly because it was the hardest course to steer. As long as the Big River resisted, he was homing.

The waterspouts were starting up again, and walls of spume like the bluffs of icebergs closed in on either side. The Stream, the wind, the waves, the forward thrust of the engine, made the *Hermes* shudder with tension that threatened to pull her apart with each trough gained.

Patchy swigged at his grog and plowed a course for Hatteras Light.

7

A WIRELESS MESSAGE came into Littlejohn's store from Portsmouth. A transport, unescorted, was heading south from Jersey to reinforce the garrison at the Panama Canal. It would pass off the Hatteras Light sometime after midnight. The captain had been instructed to stay well clear of the shoals, especially with the weather turning and the submarine menace unchecked. The transport would be running without lights, but all life-saving crews were being alerted just the same. On board were more than fifteen hundred men.

"Well, that's the one," Littlejohn said. "I knew it wouldn't take long."

"I wonder if the Hun has a wireless."

"No doubt, but he'd have to be on the surface to pick it up, and he won't be, not on a night like this."

Fetterman was finally getting to the detailing of his model. It was curiously unlovely, not at all like the schooners on the back shelf, but held a fascination all its own.

"What's that lump there?" Littlejohn asked.

"That? Oh, that's the conning tower."

"I think you're losing your touch, that's what I think."

"Think what you like. I'm an old man and I don't have to answer to anyone, least of all a storekeeper. I'll do my answering soon enough."

"You may have company."

Fetterman fiddled with the model. The work of the knife was done. Now it was a matter of smoothing, fitting, arranging, then painting. That would be easy, but he would do it in the light.

"Do you think they'll go through with it?"

"They'll need Malcolm," Fetterman said. "He's the only one that can work the whole apparatus."

"That's not so. The Chief can do it, so can Jack and Toby. Or Seamus, for the matter."

"No telling what the Chief will do. I can't read him at all."

"No," Fetterman agreed. "He's a cagey one, but I can guess."

"Toby will go along. He lost a brother in all this and he's got a right, I guess. As much as anyone has."

"They'll need Malcolm," Fetterman repeated.

Littlejohn pondered that.

Seamus Royal came in, the barrel of his Krag sweated with rain. "Seems like we've got a show tonight, boys," he said.

"Mind if I warm myself at your stove?"

Littlejohn nodded.

"You've heard about the troopship, eh, Seamus?"

"Bad news travels fast."

"He might miss him altogether in this storm," Littlejohn offered.

"Might. Might not."

"What makes you think the Hun will be close enough in for it to matter?"

"Nobody can know a thing like that."

"Exactly."

"But he always goes to the shallows after a kill. Like he has to digest it." Seamus loosened the leather sling and stood his rifle against the counter. He drew his pipe and filled it and didn't say anything until he had it going good and steady.

"We have our storm, Ham."

"We sure as hell have that."

"Are you with us?"

"What about Malcolm?"

"Malcolm will do the right thing when the time comes."

Littlejohn said: "Seems to me you're gambling on it a lot."

"Even if we do nothing, it's a gamble."

"So you say."

"I'm not alone in this."

Jack Royal came in and flapped the water off his sou'wester.

"It's blowing up a gale out there. Going to be a bad one."

"The weather's all cockeyed," Fetterman said.

"It's because of those big railroad guns they're shooting off in France. They're breaking down the stratosphere, mark my words."

"Aw, Seamus."

Fetterman limped over to the counter and sat on two stacked crates of tinned meat. "You reckon it's time?"

Seamus looked at Littlejohn. "It would be better if we all went along, together. That would keep the Government from asking a lot of questions."

"I haven't seen any of you tonight. I haven't heard any of this." Littlejohn disappeared through the door to the back room and scraped out the back way to his house, where Mrs. Littlejohn said, "It's an evil night, Littlejohn."

Despite himself, Littlejohn felt a chill. "And who says?" he demanded.

She said: "This morning, the moon was drowned in blood."

CHAPTER 15

1

LOOKING FOR KEITH, Jack went to the Keeper's house, where he found Keith and Mary sitting a little too intimately around a dice game. Jack snorted to clear his sinuses. "Come on, little gambler," he said. "We've got work to do."

Mary was quiet as Keith put on his sou'wester and stepped into his boots. She watched him with her arms folded across her chest the way she always watched Malcolm when he left her. Whatever she might have said, she wouldn't say in front of Jack.

"Are you all right, Mary?" Jack said, putting a hand on her cheek. "You look too pale."

She blushed under his hand. "I'm all right. It's considerate of you to ask."

Jack lingered a moment, frankly appraising her and Keith. She did not look away from him. Keith shuffled his feet. Jack nodded disdainfully and went out.

"Tell me the truth, boy," he said over the rain. "Are you warming her nights?"

"Knock it off, Jack. Just stop it now."

"Then it is true. It's not such a secret anymore. By God, one of these fine days even that squarehead Malcolm will figure it out."

Keith clubbed Jack on the temple with a fist, but Jack didn't go down. He rocked unsteadily for a second, then shrugged off Keith's grasping hand.

2

VIRGINIA ROYAL WAS WORRIED about Dorothy. That was the excuse she gave herself for braving the storm to her house with the fixings for supper in her covered basket. She knocked on the salt-bleached door and then out of habit turned at the handle and pushed. The door rebuffed her arm. It was locked, an unheard-of thing.

"Dorothy?" she called, more out of curiosity than alarm. In these islands, even when a body wasn't home she left her door unlocked in case her neighbors needed baking powder or milk or shelter from the weather. Keys were often misplaced in old drawers, lost for good, though the doors were always hung with locks. "Dottie? You home? It's Ginny."

She leaned close to the rain-streaked pane of the door glass and scanned the kitchen for movement. She saw none, but heard human shuffling indoors and knew Dorothy was at home. Virginia Royal did not go away. She knocked again, patiently, knowing Dorothy would eventually answer.

"What do you want?"

"Let me in, Dottie. It's blowing awful out here."

"I'm not feeling well. Please go away."

"Then you need me. Please open the door. I want to chat with you. I brought fixings."

A few minutes passed. Virginia heard muffled noises at the back of the house, then the creak of a window opening, sliding against wet wood, and thudding closed. She heard movement outside, and what she had suspected all along was suddenly so visible she did not immediately believe it: Lieutenant Tim Halstead was retreating over the sand, his collar turned up against the rain, his back hunched to lower his profile in the wind.

Dorothy shot back the bolt and Virginia greeted her with a face rosy from embarrassment.

"Are you after something special, or just nosing around in general?"

Virginia stepped deliberately into the kitchen. "That's no way to be, Dot. I just came to make sure you were all right."

"I'm just dandy."

"And to talk a little, you know."

"The only talk anybody's had for me lately is bad news. You got good news?"

"Not like that."

She unwrapped her shawl and laid it over the back of a spool chair. "Do you have any hot tea?" she said, arranging herself in a second chair. The basket she laid on the table.

"We always have damned tea. Kinnakeeters, yeopon eaters."

"We're not really Kinnaketters." Over the years her family had drifted north from the inlet and accumulated around the lighthouse in the company of Royals, Fettermans, and Littlejohns. "Anyway we'll get English tea again when the war is over."

"Do you think so? Do you think it will ever be over?"

"Soon."

"That's just for children, when they get impatient. Don't do that with me, Virginia. I like you too much."

Dorothy busied herself making tea from the bitter yeopon leaves and added a dollop of cream to cut the acid.

"I guess your secret is out," Virginia admitted.

"Oh? What secret is that."

"Oh, come on. I saw him shucking for parts unknown in a brave hurry."

"You don't know."

"You've got the wrong man, Dot. Can I tell you this? You always had the wrong man." Dorothy had flirted at one time with the Trent boy, now gone away to fly aeroplanes, and a succession of Ocracoke boys with tenuous futures in the fishing fleet. "You don't want to break Keith's heart, honey."

"It may not be as fragile as you think."

"He's a good boy."

"He's an ass, all right."

"Dorothy."

"Look, I don't mean to be rude, but what do you want? This hasn't been a good day."

"The good days are behind us for a while, I'm afraid."

Dorothy sat down. "It's none of your damned business and you know it."

"He's an outsider. It's everybody's business, don't you know that by now?"

"That's no way to judge a man."

"Maybe not, but it's the only way around here. He won't stay. He'll break your heart like you've never had it broke."

"You're the queen of the heartbreak tale today."

"Be snappish if you want to. But you and I both know he's going away when the war goes away, and you'll still be here with us. You have a lifetime to consider."

Dorothy stood and went to the door. "You think you have Jack. But no woman on this island really has a man."

Virginia rose and busied herself at the stove, setting the potatoes to boiling and preparing cabbage and pork for the two of them. When she had it all working, she sat back down and poured herself more tea.

"I won't eat that," Dorothy said. "You can make it, probably you should do that, but I can't eat it."

"All right." Virginia thought of her husband in the company of other men at the life-saving station. They would be smoking out the night and lying to one another with great gusto, some of them carving or doing scrimshaw, others reading old papers and handling cards. "Better ask your young man," Virginia said, "why he showed me his back if he's so proud to be courting you."

"That's enough."

"I take care of my man." She gave Dorothy her back and when she was gone, Dorothy delivered the pork, cabbage, and potatoes to the steel trash can out back where Rufus and the cats would get it, and scraped the pot clean with a knife.

3

AT THE LIFE-SAVING STATION the men were nervous. They rubbed their eyes with the horny heels of their hands and fussed distractedly with pipes, smoking them hard and fuming pungent burley clouds that sank to the floor and hovered there like ground fog, while they grew restless and irritable and moved too much, talked too earnestly, laughed too readily and too loud.

"I wish it would just happen." Cy Magillicutty said.

"What are you talking about?" Toby Bannister asked.

"Whatever it is that's waiting."

"And what's that?"

"Nothing," Malcolm broke in. "Nothing's going to happen tonight that hasn't already happened."

Chief Lord came in. "That Homer is awful spooky tonight. Chasing the wind like it was made of ghosts. I wonder what's got into him."

"You've all got too much imagination, even the damned horse," Malcolm said. He alone was not smoking, and the others could tell it was deliberate.

"Maybe so, Malcolm," Toby said, "but don't hide out upstairs. Have a cup of coffee with us. We have a little bit left."

"The hell with it," Malcolm said, almost in a whisper, and went upstairs.

4

Tim Halstead's collar flapped in the wind. He bent his head and stalked through the storm, unsure where to go. He had just been hustled out of bed and off into the night like a fugitive. These were not his people. This was not his place.

He watched the lighthouse beacon make a full revolution and thought about going into the stationhouse for warmth and company, but a hundred yards off he turned toward Littlejohn's, where there was sure to be a bottle of bootleg rum, even for an outsider, at the right price.

5

Upstairs, Malcolm considered: Somewhere, bearing down the coast, was a troopship running without lights. All those men. He lit his pipe and watched the flame of the wooden match disappear into the rough black bowl.

6

When Halstead bought his rum, things were queer. The store was full of men in weather gear, and a new box of tool handles had been prised open. The blond wood was new and bright. Conversation went off like a light when he entered, and the men stared at him with blank, humorless eyes he could not read.

"Awful blow, eh?" he ventured, and nobody answered. Littlejohn got him a fat bottle and smiled with his lips, handing it across the counter. Halstead took a long swallow and offered it around. Nobody took him up on it. The fire in the stove was loud and unsettling.

"Good night, gentlemen," he said and turned his back on them, not knowing what might happen. He was so rattled that he crossed the road and sat out of the rain under an old rowboat and poured rum into himself like fuel. He felt better. Across the road, the shadows of men moved in front of the window of Littlejohn's, blocking out the light.

He corked the bottle, got up slowly, and went to his billet to fetch his sidearm.

7

JACK ROYAL ACHED all over. But he was feeling strong, and he enjoyed the pain: it made him focus. The men followed him single file down the dark road. Seamus with his Krag, Oman with a fish billy, Joe Trent, Ian MacSween, Hal MacRae, Will Fetterman, and a dozen others from the village wielding ax handles, these were his army. They made for the Light.

8

HALSTEAD, a .45 automatic strapped to his belt, descended the staircase and approached Malcolm.

"Malcolm," he said. "I've got to talk to you."

"You think I don't already know what you have to say? I've been counting hands myself."

"What will you do when they come?"

He shrugged and took out his pipe but did not light it, only scraped half-heartedly at the bowl. "What do you expect me to do, Lieutenant? Just how many choices are there?"

Halstead lit one of his few remaining maduro cigarettes. "You've got a point there."

Chief Lord stood with them against the sideboard. "How long, Malcolm?"

"Soon, Chief."

"Shouldn't we tell the men?"

"If they don't know by now, there's no use telling them."

"In the British Navy, they would be hanged to a man."

"Well, Chief, that's a thought."

Halstead smoked nervously, trying to slow down, calm himself. "I never thought anything like this would happen," he said.

Chief Lord was feeling the magic working, but not here, out there on the water somewhere. This magic had the flavor of life. He knew there were things nobody could see. "Wait and see how it all turns out," he said. "You may be surprised some more yet."

"I don't know about that," Halstead answered. "I have a lot to consider as it is."

"How are you feeling now?" Malcolm asked.

"I can fight."

"That's not what I meant, boy. We don't need you to fight. You've done your fighting. If it comes to that, fighting won't help." Chief Lord nodded and played with a string cradle, whipping it back and forth, weaving shapes out of the air. "I just wanted to know how you are, that's all."

"Better. No real harm except—" Halstead was thinking of dead men and lost ships, courage for naught and loyalty where loyalty was a mistake in judgment. "I am an outsider," he finally said.

"We are all of us outsiders," Malcolm said. "That's what nobody remembers. Who are we Hatterasmen? Fugitives, castaways, pirates, deserters, people who ran out of places. Huh. We have no call to be such snobs."

Chief Lord smiled broadly and nodded. "Refugees," he pronounced.

"This submarine will go away," Malcolm said. "That's what no-body understands here. This submarine is not the point."

Halstead went upstairs as Chief Lord recited, "And I beheld as it were a sea of glass mingled with fire, and them that had gotten victory over the beast."

Before anybody had a chance to make sense of that statement, Cy Magillicutty put a hand on Malcolm's arm and said, as softly as he could, "They've come, Malcolm."

9

MARY ROYAL WAS FINISHING the painting when Keith burst in. He didn't even look at the portrait, though the lines were definite now and the figure had taken on identity.

She didn't turn when he entered, but sat with brush in hand, poised on the brink of color.

"It's happening, Mary. Now. Come on."

She dropped her brush on the floor, grabbed her coat, took hold of his hand, and went with him out the door and into the storm.

10

ABOARD U-55 the quiet was so complete and unnatural that Captain Stracken thought upon waking that he had died and gone to hell, since he imagined that kind of quiet would drive a living man mad. Max Wien imagined instead that they had sunk to some unheard-of, unplumbed depth, that the gauges were in error, that very shortly they would bottom out on some deep ocean shelf where they would breathe up their allotted air and lie entombed under the tides.

The quiet was only the pressure on their ears and the dullness of senses that had been too long awake.

But the propeller noise was suddenly insistent and growing closer, and Kraft ordered them up.

"There she is," he announced, once U-55 had breached and settled and Max had clambered with him onto the conning bridge. "Do you know how many men are about to be drowned?"

Max stared at him. He understood it was a troopship; no one could mistake the high prow and square superstructure, the broad, ungainly bulk of her. Inside, every square inch would be packed to capacity with men, confined six deep in claustrophobic hammocks, allowed to go on deck by turns only once a day or so, otherwise breathing air so foul most of them wouldn't be fit for duty for a week after landing. When the torpedoes struck, they would be trapped down there in darkness, with no way out. The companionway hatches would already be barred from the outside by Naval marines, against the possibility of mutiny or riot, and in the confusion no one would act to unbar them in time.

Max trembled in advance of the slaughter, and the troopship steamed on, lining itself up nicely for them, showing no lights.

When she was as yet a thousand yards off, Kraft said, "Ready torpedoes. Ready the goddamned things." Max watched, hand on the rail, unable to let go. Kraft intended to steam up to point-blank range and take her on the surface, where they could watch the whole thing. Max heard all the machinery go into motion belowdecks.

11

RUNNING FOR HOME, Patchy was afraid. Now there was a chance. Now he was responsible. Now the history was working itself out in a way that no one would have dared predict a few days ago. He imagined the faces of the crowd on Oman's Dock as his low-bellied *Hermes* plowed into the pale of canehung yellow lamps, towing in the lost boat.

His vision was going. He rubbed his eyes with grimy, benumbed hands, tried to stare into the blankness at the end of his wake, but caught only the vaguest outlines of the Dant boat and the dim light of her paraffin lamps. He felt the struggle of his own balky engine to pull such a heavy load.

He talked to himself. He sang bawdy songs. He hit the grog.

He gripped the wheel with both hands and closed his eyes to clear them and make sense of the jumble of information in his head about direction, current, bearings, wind, and landfall. He had the sense that his boat knew the way home.

He was in tune with the labor of the engine, the churn of water off his bows, the creak of rigging, and the moaning of the old timbers as they settled to their work. And then a sound stopped his heart: the bilge pump had quit.

Hermes plowed heavily ahead, the roughening seas breaking down inside her now, seawater leaking in through a hundred rotholes, wormholes, and splayed boards, until at the end of an hour her bow was riding so low that each new sea broke over her gunwales and left the foredeck awash in black water. The towing hawser held the stern from seesawing hard on the trough, so the bow had no spring to point her head high on the crests, and *Hermes* was now submarining into the waves, not surfing over them. It was only a couple of miles more, Patchy figured. He kept the ax handy and gave her all the throttle he dared.

And when he closed his eyes to clear them again, his mind's eye held a picture of a man falling, tumbling soundlessly from a high place, releasing his treasure as he landed.

12

ALVIN DANT HELD THE WHEEL, trying to be of some use to Patchett by lining up in his wake as best he could. They were moving more slowly now, he reckoned, measuring his headway against the foamy wake that was eerily luminescent on the black water. His eyes were fastened on the hawser, anticipating the moment when it would snap like a whip, curling through the air with the sudden dramatic release of tension, and leave Patchett's boat invisible in the sea ahead of them.

"It will hold," Brian said.

"You seem to know something I don't, boy." He couldn't deny

that Brian's confidence was infectious. Suddenly he had plans, visions of a future that good judgment told him he had no right to have. But they were getting closer all the time.

"He's riding lower," Brian said.

"I can feel it." The hawser was no longer strung above the seas but cut through them, with the *Hermes* invisible on the other side. The gimballed paraffin lamps flickered in the *Pelican's* pilothouse. Patchy's lamp was lit, too. It twinkled uncertainly ahead like Polaris on a cloudy night.

"You didn't expect it to be him, did you?" Brian's hands were now on the wheel, overlapping his father's.

"I've given up expecting anything. You take what comes."

"You don't believe that any more than I do. We missed Dottie's birthday party, you know."

Alvin Dant laughed. "If that's all you've got to worry about."

"Can you imagine what this has been doing to her?"

"What? I haven't had time, boy."

"We can't lose her."

"What? What are you talking about?"

"You heard me," Brian insisted. "We just can't lose her."

"We're not losing anybody. Nobody, you hear?"

But Alvin kept seeing the German officer slump forward in the dinghy, Brian's stubborn hands around the old rifle. Alvin felt the lump of dollar bills in his shirt pocket. "Carry on, Patchy boy," he said to no one. "Keep her moving."

He skinned his eyes for Hatteras Light. Any minute they would see it, he was sure. They should have seen it by now. Inside the Light they'd be in range of Malcolm and his boys. There was all kinds of hope tonight.

13

THE TROOPSHIP WAS DARING THE SHOALS, running close in and fast. Kraft kept the glasses on her as she closed with the U-boat, noting the sharp outlines of miscellaneous guns on her superstructure.

"What's that?" the lookout whispered in alarm. He pointed due east at two puny lights that seemed to blink on and off.

"Is that our destroyer?" Max asked.

"*Nein, ich glaube nicht,*" Kraft announced after a moment of study. "If it's anybody, it's a fisherman. He's making slow progress."

Max wondered if it was their fisherman.

"No," Kraft said, apparently reading his mind. "That would be too much luck even for this patrol."

The lights grew closer as the big ship bore down on them from the other direction.

"Bergen. Fire on those lights as soon as they are in range."

"What about the troopship, sir? Won't that give us away?"

"It will be too late for them."

Max took the glasses and studied the lights and wondered if whoever it was would understand what was going on, the necessity, the inevitability of it. Of course not.

"Steady," Kraft said. "Steady, we're going to have quite a night."

Max had no energy to curse him. Instead he pinned his eyes on Hatteras Light, and wondered what chance a man in the water would have of getting there, if he had something to float him. For the first time on any patrol he laced on a life preserver.

"Don't be dramatic," Kraft said. "We're in the catbird seat, my friend." Down below, Max heard the murmuring of the crew, and from the main hatch issued a steady draft of foul, dead air.

14

AT LONG LAST, Patchett spied the Light. He had been looking for it so long and fearing he would miss it so hard that he gasped. His legs went watery under him, and he was forced to steady himself against the wheel. His vision cleared, and the numbness left his hands. He felt the ache of his bones, the tightness in his joints, the uncomfortable swell of his bladder, the pang of each individual organ jostling for position around his stomach, his ribs sore from the hard labor of his lungs all night long, his tired eyes, his swollen feet, his brain burning inside his thick bucket of a skull.

He pictured the sun rising behind him as he made the final mile to the Inlet, casting him in heroic silhouette. He thought of old Fetterman's approval and his wife Pat's joy: Now she could hold her head up with all the Royals of this world. She would be easier on him from now on, he was sure.

He envisioned long rainy nights around Littlejohn's stove with a bottle of good stout beer in his hand, telling his story in all its delicious detail with scarcely an exaggeration. They could gibe him all they wanted about fibbing. They would know the truth when they heard it, whether they said so or not.

Life was good. Anything was possible—he had proved it. He steered for the Light, to make landfall a little south of it. He hoped his bilges were deep enough to last that far.

15

ALVIN AND BRIAN SPOTTED the Light just after Patchy did and hugged one another. The hawser held. They rode the Labrador south now, and it pushed them in so close they knew that whatever happened they were within reach of Malcolm's boat. Alvin kept his lamps burning bright.

16

JACK ROYAL STRODE into the station and assumed some kind of command. "I'm sorry, Malcolm," he said. "It's time for action." Seamus stood at his elbow, and Malcolm thought his old rifle looked more foolish than ever. Jack had called Toby Bannister down from the catwalk, and now he herded him against the wall with Malcolm's crew.

"You don't know what you're doing," Malcolm said to them.

Chief Lord crossed his arms. "Whatever you decide, Malcolm," he said, and the rest of the crew lined up with him.

"Not like this," Malcolm said. "Not like this."

Keith elbowed his way into the station. "What in the hell do you think you're doing?" Mary waited behind him on the porch.

"Shut up, boy," Jack said. "You're coming with me." He turned to his men. "Keep them all in here. I'll be right back."

Roughly, Jack ushered Keith past Mary, through the rain, and into the lighthouse and pushed him up the spiral staircase. "What do you need me for?" Keith said. "I'm not going to help you."

Jack had a handful of Keith's sou'wester. "You don't know what you're going to do till I tell you."

At the catwalk deck Jack paused to get his wind back. Then he bullied Keith up the last stairs, opened the door to the carousel room, and shoved him inside. "You're the one to do it," Jack said. "I'll show you how."

17

DOWN BELOW in the stationhouse, Malcolm started for the door. Four men grabbed him, steered him to a chair, and held him there. Old Fetterman stood aloof, listening to the storm.

Seamus Royal paced. "Malcolm," he said. "Malcolm!"

Halstead came softly downstairs and lingered on the landing, trying to decide whom to shoot. He fired his pistol twice into the ceiling, and everybody but Fetterman dived for cover. Then the men were on their feet and throwing punches. Halstead dropped his weapon and joined the fray, and in the commotion Malcolm broke free. He shouldered his way out the door, ran inside the tower, and threw the bolt behind him. Mary stood in the rain.

18

ALMOST THE SAME instant that Alvin recognized the silhouette of a big ship, two things happened: The Hatteras Light went out, and Patchy's boat exploded and disappeared.

19

IN THE LAST MOMENTS Patchy's bilges were so heavy that the foredeck was awash constantly now. He headed gamely for the Light. The next he knew, the pilothouse was carried away in a flash of lightning and he was left on his knees with a broken wheel in his hands, the water rushing around his feet. He was deafened by the explosion, and suddenly the Light was not where it had been. He must be blind as well. Hope expired in him, and he made no move to save himself. What was the use? He felt the water around his shins and then the *Hermes* submarined into the next sea, with Patchy still at the helm.

20

THE HAWSER WAS pulling them under. Alvin scrambled onto the foredeck with ax in hand but took a header on the slippery deck and lost the ax over the side. There was no time to lose. He lifted the single cork life ring off its hook, rescued the last bottle of brandy, took Brian's hand, and catapulted them both into the water as far away from the boat as he could.

21

WHEN HE HAD GAINED the top of the staircase, Malcolm stood giddily surveying the gloom. There were lights on the staircase all the way up, and his eyes had to adjust to the sudden absence of light outside the iron door. He pushed it open, stooping by habit to fit through it easily, tentatively emerging into the carousel room.

"Jack?"

A shadow loomed on the other side of the glass reflector, against the window. Malcolm had never been in this room when it was not full of light. "Jack?"

"Get out, Malcolm."

"Stop this, Jack."

"It's done."

Malcolm began his routine of relighting the lamp, a routine he knew by heart and in the dark, until Jack grabbed his arm. "Let go!" Malcolm said, and shook him off so hard Jack stumbled against the window. He got to his feet and jabbed a fist into Malcolm's eye. Then Jack grabbed Malcolm around the waist and tackled him in the doorway. He knelt across Malcolm's windpipe until Malcolm started to black out, then dragged him down the short stairway to the catwalk deck. Then, as Jack broke loose to go back upstairs, Malcolm recovered and hauled him down by his ankles.

Keith watched from the doorway to the carousel room.

Jack struck Malcolm again and escaped onto the catwalk, Malcolm following. On the waffled iron deck of the catwalk, Malcolm knelt over Jack, gripping him by the throat, and hit him in the face again and again.

"That's enough, Malcolm!" Keith said, tugging at Malcolm's hunched shoulders. Malcolm kept on hitting Jack. Keith tugged harder. "Malcolm!" he said, "I did it. *I* did it!"

Malcolm turned his head, his fists hanging loose on the ends of his arms. Then he stood up, heaving for breath. Without a word, he went inside to light the lamp. Outside on the catwalk, in the wind and rain, Keith sat with Jack and waited for Malcolm to return.

CHAPTER 16

1

KRAFT WATCHED the lights go out to the east and congratulated Bergen. Down below, Captain Stracken heard the report and sat up in his berth, glassy-eyed. He had dreamed of men burning, on fire with a flame that not even the sea could quench. Max was at his side, saying good-bye. Stracken misunderstood and thought he was dying. He clutched Max's hand and then released it for the sake of dignity. Then Max left him.

2

KRAFT WOULD BE cold-blooded and sure. He had a moment of

panic when the Light went out, but, as the troopship was only 300 meters off, he ordered the torpedomen to fire two at once. He counted off the seconds from his order. When he got to three, the front end of U-55 ignited with a great gush of water and white flame, vaporizing the forward crew.

The sea door being jammed, the torpedo had detonated inside the tube.

Max did not recall diving off the conning bridge, but from the water he watched successive small explosions rip out the back of U-55 like chain geysers. The light was intense and short-lived, illuminating the troopship that bore down on him now, her bows a plowshare with giant blades. Pieces of the forward gun rained down nearby. An arm landed on the water next to him and sank. When the conning bridge blew, a long flame shot straight up out of the hull, like the flame of a welding torch, and he imagined it was all that bad air igniting in one blow.

U-55 was gone. Max Wien drifted on the oily black sea while the troopship passed a dozen yards off, then disappeared.

On shore the Light burned again.

3

MALCOLM, Jack, and Keith watched the explosion together. Malcolm carried Jack downstairs fireman-fashion behind Keith. Jack was in no shape to go out, so Keith would take his place.

Chief already had Homer in harness, and they were away in good order, the brawl forgotten, the crew wearing bruised lips, black eyes, and skinned knuckles, pulling toward the last light they had marked.

"There's the troopship!" Malcolm shouted. "I don't understand—" The great shadowy bulk was already disappearing.

"Pull," Chief Lord said, "there's somebody else out here."

It was only the sheerest accident that they found Max Wien. He hailed them in German when they were nearby, and using a paraffin lamp they spied his glossy blond head bobbing among the flotsam. They hauled him into the boat roughly and dumped him at their feet.

"It's a goddamn Heinie!" Cy Magillicutty said, elated and troubled. It meant that the U-boat was sunk.

"Please," Max said, "there's another vessel." He made Malcolm understand that they had spied lights to the east, and the crew made for the spot as best Max could direct them. Amid the chop of the sea and the dying wind, Malcolm heard it. He ordered the men to ship oars and listen. A dozen strokes away, Dant and his boy were clinging to a ring buoy, drunk as lords, singing bawdy songs. Alvin sank the empty brandy bottle in sight of Malcolm's crew.

"It's a miracle," Chief Lord said.

"Where you been?" Malcolm asked.

"What do you do with a drunken sailor—" Alvin sang. His boy said: "Patchy Patchett brought us in."

Malcolm was all for searching for the *Hermes*, but Brian finally convinced him it was no use: "I seen him go down, Mister Royal. All of him."

They pulled for shore and watched the Light sweep the sky ahead of them, the sun still hours from rising.

4

EVEN IN SUNLIGHT, to Keith, Mary's portrait looked like no one. It was the figure of a man, standing, looking out to sea—his back to the artist, his head lifted to the wind like the muzzle of a dog, his hands raised as if to embrace someone who wasn't there.

When Keith stood over her, appraising it, the blacks and grays took on a funereal potency. "This is what you see?"

"I can't help it."

He looked at the painting harder, feeling a knot behind his tongue. He was so close to Mary he could smell her. "Then it's finished?" Hands on her lap, shoulders narrowed like the folded wings of a bird, Mary wept.

5

AT NOON KEITH took the tower watch, and no one objected. He circled round and round on the catwalk and watched the island spread out far below, the ocean side limned by surf. It reminded him of one of old Rusonovsky's geopolitical maps--the boundaries were just as clear. The wind whistled through the iron railing and beat across the dunes to the southwest. North, the road ran through Kinnakeet. Salvo, Chicamacomico, then off the map, all the way to Cambridge, and beyond.

6

FETTERMAN THOUGHT he might as well die this year, although he was pretty sure he wasn't going to get off that easy. He felt he had about a decade left in him, give or take a few months, and that depressed him. He was unhorsed, as he had not been since Littlejohn came to the island buoyed up by strong spirits. Just when he had thought he'd seen the whole performance, there was a change in the program. He wondered if he had the energy for it.

He held the finished model in his hand. Patchy had conferred upon him great honor. His son-in-law, who probably hadn't realized even at the end exactly what he was doing out there. Nevertheless, his legacy would do Patricia more good than the man himself ever did her alive. Fetterman knew this.

And some of the glow would inevitably reflect back on him, warming him in his senility, if he ever got it. He felt a real fondness for Patchy now. God bless him. He had stuff. But who could have known?

No one else was at Littlejohn's. They were still out on the beach, where Fetterman imagined Patchy would wash up tomorrow morning or so, hardly looking dead, a common beachrat resting on his beach at last. He would. Ah, Patchy . . .

No sentimentalizing, he warned himself, taking a long pull at a fresh beer. He was what he was.

He settled into his chair, enjoying the solitude. He had no more use for this model. He balanced it across his good knee like a seesaw board and jostled it to get it rocking. How had he known? He couldn't say even now. One afternoon like other afternoons he had just had a vision of war, what war would really be like next time it came to the island, and this ugly vessel was what he got. He carefully laid a hand on bow and stern and, knee levered underneath, pressed until he snapped her spine and let the pieces fall to the floor.

Just then Littlejohn walked in. He had a confession to make, and Fetterman would hear it whether he wanted to or not. "I'm ashamed of myself, Ham," he said. "I watched. Again, I stood by and watched."

"That's nothing." Fetterman said. "So did I. Were we supposed to do something else?"

"That's the trouble, all right."

Littlejohn fussed behind the counter and came up with his meerschaum. The two men smoked awhile. Fetterman said, "I think I'm going to do the *Gloriana* next. She was a racing sloop, you know. I saw her pass the Lizard Light under a full suit of sails, gorgeous lady. A spoon bow and overhanging stern counter, enormous flat cotton sails, a bowsprit that could pierce your heart."

"Now you're talking," Littlejohn said, noticing for the first time the mess on the floor. "Do her right."

Mrs. Littlejohn entered at that moment. "I dreamed I lay in the shadow of the gallows last night," she said.

Littlejohn said: "Goddamn it, woman, the only thing hanging is your tongue. Now go and find some useful work."

She laughed. "Go ahead, die young. See if I care."

"She's a comfort," Fetterman said, after she had left.

"She surely is that." They hoisted their beers together.

7

HALSTEAD ROAMED the beach. He jettisoned the empty holster—he couldn't recall where he'd left the gun. Must have been at the stationhouse after the ruckus. He wasn't an officer anymore, that much he knew, and that comforted him. He was still in the Navy, but he was sure they'd let him out quietly when the war wound down. Maybe they'd ask him to resign right away, once they took a hard look at the way he'd handled his first command. How could he know they would promote him?

In the future he would try something more in his line. He flung away his hat and ran his fingers through his mussed hair, feeling the fresh air on his scalp.

He walked hatless down the beach, shedding the various parts of his uniform as he went. Maybe he could get hold of a sailing scow and get lost on the Sound for a few weeks. Maybe he could get detached down here until the war was over and they forgot about him in the places where it mattered. He would see Dorothy, take care of her, marry her eventually. But not right away. Give it time, take it easy, let all the pieces settle back to earth into some kind of order. Let the fever of ambition subside. Let humility fill him up. How had he ever had the arrogance to command? How had he ever supposed he had the stuff of history in his sinew, the blessing of destiny? He bent and unlaced his shoes, slowing a little to shuck one, then the other, and lob them onto the sand like dead fish. He hopped on one foot at a time and peeled off his socks, wadded them, and discarded them in the same offhand way. Good Navy socks, virgin wool and hardly worn. He took off his shirt and tied it by the sleeves around his waist, rolled his trouser legs to the calf, and approached the water.

He bent and splashed the cool spume on his face and neck, rubbing it on like ointment. He closed his eyes, feeling the sun strong on the outside of his eyelids, hearing the gulls complain. When he opened his eye, he watched pipers wade into the surf, flirting with the waves. He felt weary, overcome. He felt like going on a long drunk. He felt like sleeping in the shade and letting his beard grow. He stroked a hand along his chin and was rewarded with a prickle of stubble there. He smiled. A beard would be the thing.

Out on the water he could see no boats or ships, no threat or emergency. He could hear no call to duty.

He continued south along the beach, from time to time wading in and out of the breakers. Once he waded in as deep as his chest and felt the gritty salt foam stirring under his trousers, not an unpleasant feeling. He discovered a bright pied rag washing in the surf, wrung it out, and wrapped it around his temples Indian-style. He rather liked it. It rather appealed to him. He decided there was a host of things to discover on a beach like this one. He smacked his salty lips in anticipation.

He would stay on the beach all way to the inlet and the village. He sank his bare toes into the wet sand and curled them luxuriously, padded on with a light step. He would do that. Walking, it might take days.

8

WHEN ALVIN and Brian Dant marched up to the house leaning on one another for support, Dorothy could not believe her eyes. She hugged them and cried, brought them dry clothes and hot food, and sat with them while they sobered up and told their tale.

"Who would have thought?" Alvin said over and over, and Brian agreed.

"You should have seen it, Dot," Brian said. "You should have seen what went on out there." She had never heard him sound so cocky.

"I bet you gave up on your old man," Alvin said, and fished out a bottle to share with Brian. "Didn't you? Well, happy birthday, Dot. Have a snort."

"No, thanks," she said.

"You're a good girl. I've got myself a good girl."

But she wasn't listening. They were saved, but it was not possible. She had already imagined her future.

Soon both Alvin and Brian were dull from drink and exhaustion, and she helped them to their beds, where they lay on their backs fully clothed as she tucked the blankets around them. Rufus settled down at Brian's feet.

Then, as she hung up their wet clothes on a wooden dryer in the kitchen, she found a soggy roll of bills. She counted it out— two hundred dollars—and put it in her sewing basket. Dorothy doused the lamp and sat in the parlor in the dark, listening to them snore. In a few hours, she would make breakfast and listen to her father talk about getting another boat. Brian would take Rufus out to the beach to comb for wreckage. And one day soon she would haul a single slim bag out to the road and hitch a ride with the mail truck, north.

9

As THEY HAD pulled for the Light, Malcolm's crew had argued about what to do with the Heinie. At long last, face-to-face, here was the enemy.

"It's hard to believe you're evil incarnate," Malcolm said. Max didn't answer—his English was limited.

Malcolm sighed long and hard, the air catching in his throat like dust, dreading the moment of landing when all of this would have to be sorted out. He would have to go to Mary sooner or later. And the logbook would be lying in wait like a trap. How would he ever capture all that had happened in words? He despaired of it. Wasn't it enough just to do it? Difficulty with the Light, that would have to go in. That would be truth. How many minutes, seconds? He would have to count them, add them up like the seconds of a dream of death upon waking. He had slipped, faltered, misjudged. The Light had blinked. An eternal lapse, he felt.

To Keith he said: "You sure have a way of getting into things."

"I know what I've got coming."

"Don't always be so damned quick, boy. Keep your mouth shut and your eyes open and learn something for a change."

Keith rowed steadily.

"That's better," Malcolm said. "Now I don't want to hit you so bad."

"You've got a right. Fair is fair—"

"There you go again! What do you know about fair? I've got a secret for you. It doesn't all match up so neat in the end. That's what this business is all about, or haven't you noticed?" He waited for Keith to interrupt, but Keith kept rowing without a word. "We take each other's places. It's what we do."

"Then you want to just forget?" Keith said.

Malcolm shook his head. "Nothing is forgotten." Now Keith was part of it all, he knew. Now Keith could go anywhere he pleased.

Malcolm steered the boat with weary assurance. Working the boat was the easy part. He wished they were miles out with a full day's pull in front of them, to postpone the reckoning, clarify what was now possible.

Nobody any longer felt antagonism towards Max Wien, shriveled in the thwarts amidships. He cowered there like a man caught in a machine, afraid to move. The sea was settling down.

Alvin Dant and his boy sat wrapped in blankets in the bow. Nobody said anything for a while. Alvin kept looking at the German like he had something to say.

Then Chief Lord said, "This old world goes round and round."

Nobody responded, so, encouraged, he continued: "There are chances, and there are chances. Believe me."

To the German, Malcom said, "What's your name?"

"Max Wien."

"Ah, MacSween, my long-lost cousin," MacSween said, and drew a tentative laugh. Chief Lord kept smiling. He lifted Max Wien gently to a sitting position. "A strong boy, good teeth." He peeled back his lips and showed off his gums, soft from lack of vitamins and colorless as squid. "A little wiry, but tough. MacSween. I like that." The others nodded and handled their oars carefully and rhythmically. None of them had anything against the German, not even the Dant men, though Malcolm could not fathom why. He was past looking for motive in men's behavior. Let them do the kind thing. Let them keep him and put him to work. Let him marry somebody or open a store or build a fishing boat or keep goats. Where was the harm?

Chief Lord sang: "Our boots and clothes are all in pawn, go down, you blood red roses, go down." He applied the low, sustained tones like salve, and they listened to their spirits mend. "And it's mighty draughty round Cape Horn, go down, you blood red roses, go down."

Max Wien smacked his lips. There must be beer on the island, and by God he would have him some. He watched the breakers lick the broad slab of beach at the foot of the lighthouse. He felt like a Jonah—rebirthed from the leviathan womb of that metal fish, his destiny in the hands of Providence. When the beamy lifeboat finally skidded home on the sandy shallows, he leaped out at once, overjoyed, quaking on his sea legs, the surf resounding in his ears like applause, thinking: at last, there is the island.

Gramley Library
Salem Academy and College
Winston-Salem, N.C. 27108